THE CRESCENT

Life in Old Dundee

By

Ian Campbell

Copyright © Ian Campbell 2021
This book is sold subject to the condition that it shall not, by way of trade or otherwise, be lent, resold, hired out, or otherwise circulated without the publisher's prior consent in any form of binding or cover other than that in which it is published and without a similar condition including this condition being imposed on the subsequent publisher.
The moral right of Ian Campbell has been asserted.
ISBN-13: 9798505417270

I dedicate this book to my Granny and Granda Grace and Johnny McKee, and their son John, who lies with our son Steven.

CONTENTS

ACKNOWLEDGEMENTS i
CHAPTER 1 *The Bridge* 1
CHAPTER 2 *The Murphy Brothers* 8
CHAPTER 3 *The Parish* 12
CHAPTER 4 *Tam Pepper and the High Cheekers* 19
CHAPTER 5 *The Recruiting Sergeants* 25
CHAPTER 6 *A Pound a Round* 31
CHAPTER 7 *The Smell of the Crescent* 40
CHAPTER 8 *Marriage* 43
CHAPTER 9 *Growth of the Empire* 53
CHAPTER 10 *John Garland's Job* 56
CHAPTER 11 *Teething* 68
CHAPTER 12 *Wee Grace in the Jute Mill* 80
CHAPTER 13 *The Jute Barons* 91
CHAPTER 14 *The Beer Tent* 94
CHAPTER 15 *The Boer War* 96
CHAPTER 16 *The Highland Division* 104
CHAPTER 17 *Waiting for News in the Crescent* 112
CHAPTER 18 *Magersfontein* 114
CHAPTER 19 *The Courier* 122
CHAPTER 20 *Prisoners of War in South Africa* 129
CHAPTER 21 *Churchill in South Africa* 138
CHAPTER 22 *A Stabbing Affray* 140
CHAPTER 23 *The Dundee Arms* 147
CHAPTER 24 *Grace and Johnny* 154
CHAPTER 25 *Blackness Road* 160
CHAPTER 26 *An Annoyance to the Land* 164
CHAPTER 27 *Garland Fraser* 172
CHAPTER 28 *Rolled Down the Stair* 184
CHAPTER 29 *A New Hat* 187
CHAPTER 30 *Another Home Birth* 195
CHAPTER 31 *Suffragettes* 197
CHAPTER 32 *The Scouringburn* 207
CHAPTER 33 *The Black Watch* 212

CHAPTER 34 *Larch Street*	221
CHAPTER 35 *Back to the Beer Tent*	232
CHAPTER 36 *Last Night on the Hilltown*	241
CHAPTER 37 *Australia*	246
CHAPTER 38 *The Coalman*	248
CHAPTER 39 *Churchill's War*	253
CHAPTER 40 *Dundee's Own, The Black Watch*	255
CHAPTER 41 *Adelaide*	263
CHAPTER 42 *The Royal Victoria Hospital, Belfast*	275
CHAPTER 43 *Mesopotamia*	279
CHAPTER 44 *The Crescent*	285
EPILOGUE	289
ABOUT THE AUTHOR	292

ACKNOWLEDGEMENTS

My family history was the basis of this book and was collated mostly by my wife Liz, who, when researching our ancestry, was constantly adding fruitful relevant instalments daily to the life of Mary-Anne, my granny's sister, who seemed to have her own account with the courts in Dundee and the daily newspapers that relayed her every appearance before the magistrates for one reason or another. I am also grateful to A. Conan Doyle who was inspirational in writing *The Great Boer War, 1899-1900* which was a Sandhurst stock version published two years before the Boer War ended.

I also thank my daughter Vicky Sullivan for her time and effort in proof reading and editing the first pass of this book so well. She has demonstrated her professionalism in the literary field as well as her depth of historic knowledge of global locations she has lived in.

My thanks also to Eulaine Kruger in Durban, South Africa who has reviewed and guided my story in those South African elements of the book so well that I could not have completed it without her. Additionally, Eulaine has critically viewed the whole story and has enhanced it from an "outlanders" point of view.

Finally my thanks go to Lisa Pope in Queensland Australia, who has provided vital information for the story by way of compelling evidence from the Australian military database that completes the mystery.

Further, I would like to acknowledge the Black Watch Museum, Perth, Scotland web sites which were an inspirational source of information and verification of action described herein. Also, the Australian War Memorial Website.

CHAPTER 1

The Bridge

When the wind blew from the River Tay, a whiff of methane permeated the air outside and inside constantly. The culprit was the gasometer or *'Gassy'* located between the foot of the Blackscroft and the river. It stood in Dock Street and was filling up from the gas barge berthed alongside the gas tank quay, bringing fuel for lighting the dark and grimy streets of Dundee.

Upriver, the new rail bridge over the Tay was illuminated against the lights of the HMS *Mars*, the old sailing ship now a training vessel for the bad boys sent away for reforming, as was common in Victorian times. The *Mars* was permanently moored four hundred yards from the new railway bridge, in the middle of the river and now, lit up like a Christmas tree. It was after all, Christmas Eve, 1879.

The bridge stood proud in the river carrying another train full of homecomers for the Christmas festivities. Dundee station was the first real sign of home for the travellers who gladly alighted after a fearful journey.

Across the town in the area of the Scouringburn called 'The Crescent' the Murphy family occupied a two-bedroomed flat at 8 Littlejohn Street. Simply called 'the Crescent', it was known throughout Dundee due to its proximity to the busy Dudhope Crescent Road. Mary-Anne Murphy was four years old and looking for Santa Claus in the sky. The cold dark nights and the streets lit only by ghostly gaslight made it hard to feel warm and fuzzy that night but electric light was coming to Dundee soon, they said, and just needed to be paid for and turned on by the Provost. Until then the smell of gas putrefied the air.

Her father John was an Irish hawker who plied his trade in Lochee, an area at the west end of Dundee that was home to fourteen thousand Irish Dundonians. These were the weavers and spinners, shifters, packers and porters now working in the myriad of jute mills that industrialised and polluted the town that Dundee had become. They had moved to Dundee in search of work following the Irish potato famine and settled in the Lochee area where accommodation was cheap and they could make a living at a trade they knew well.

Mary-Anne wanted her dad home now because when he was home the family was safe again. She would eat her tea and be warm and happy then her mum would tell them a Christmas story at the fire. She might fall asleep there and then and miss Santa but that would be OK because she would wake again after he had been.

The storm grew stronger that night. The wind blew and the cold skies grew lighter with snow clouds until silence fell across the town. Snow descended in waves on Dundee that Christmas and not a sound was to be heard but the smell of methane returned when the wind dropped.

Santa had been and gone. Mary-Anne knew that because two new dollies sat on her bed where the cat should be and a sheet of ten scraps, small paper prints of five duplicates of angels and cherubs with rosy cheeks full of air, blowing the clouds on which they lay.

As soon as she showed them to her mum, Annie cut them out with a pair of weaver's scissors. Mary-Anne positioned them in different pages in their pairs within a blue hard-backed book on baking by Mrs. Beaton, which Mary-Anne couldn't yet read. Mum then carried on cleaning a rabbit that Dad had skinned earlier at the *jaw-box* over the kitchen sink. Her big brother, Tommy, had a new wooden gun and little brother Joe found his new spinning top, and both of them stuffed their faces with sweet tablet, all of which had obviously come from Santa when Mary-Anne was asleep.

Dad was softly singing his Irish songs while redding up the fireplace and setting the fire again. He was not going to work that day, oh, everything was all right now – Christmas was the best time of all. Mary-Anne with her auburn hair sparkling with the frost played in the snow in Littlejohn Street with her pals until Mum called her in.

It was soon time to eat the Christmas Day dinner. The weather was fine and the snow was crisp and although she could have played for hours in the street, it was so cold she needed her daddy to warm her up and most of all, she needed the suet dumpling that she had smelled all the way along the close and up the stairs.

That day the fireplace was a welcome vision for a change with strong, hot flames warming the tenement flat and lighting up the faces of all who sat around full-bellied, happy and not a care in the world. Dad had filled the fire with real coal and the coal bucket was full again for later. Dad was still here and never a word was said about the empty wooden 'hawker's handcart' or *'cartie'* as they called it he had stowed under the stair in the *closey*.

Tommy and two-year-old Joe were getting *crabbit* and neither of them dared to go to the outside lavvy halfway down the spiral stair, it was just too cold. Never mind, Dad was in a good mood today and he would empty the *po* in the morning and that would do fine. Time to sleep again now, Mary-Anne thought, and nobody was moving away from the fire, not even Dad, with his whisky.

John Murphy, hawker and mover and shifter of all things that could fit on a handcart for a small consideration was up and away to the railway station before dawn on Boxing Day. The air around the Crescent was thick again with the smell of jute and flax as the mills started up again after the break for Christmas Day. *All looks good for a new start today,* he thought, *and the New Year is just around the corner.*

Pushing his handcart through the rain and snow from the Crescent's Littlejohn Street to Dundee's West train station, his red hair and full set of whiskers dripping steam from his frozen breath in the gaslight in the street, his mind was on the purchases he'd made. He had a big delivery from Edinburgh to pick up from the train that would fill his *cartie* with pots and pans, soaps and brushes and keep his little business going through the New Year week. *Only five days to Hogmanay,* he thought and he daydreamed of a 'bliddy good snifter' at the New Year.

The 08.05 steam train was not due in for another half-hour. By the time he got to the station he was startled to see a crowd of other hawkers hassling the stationmaster. **'The NBR has closed the line due to snow and ice on the line at Ladybank in Fife and the 08.05 Edinburgh to Aberdeen is cancelled'**, a handwritten notice said. Ladybank was just a few miles south of the river at the other side of the bridge. *So close,* John thought. *So bliddy close.*

John was dejected. He had used all the money he had in the world on his order from the ironmonger's supplier in Edinburgh and the rest went on the bairns' toys and the rabbit and most of all, the warm, woollen shawl he bought for his wife, Annie. He needed to start selling goods again today for food at the New Year.

This Boxing Day in Dundee the mills were open and the

millworkers were moving through the snow-blown streets of the Crescent. The men with the snoot of their bonnets pulled down over their faces, the women with shawls over their heads leaving almost nothing of their faces exposed to the biting freezing wind were on the way to work. John had no work to go to and worse, had nothing to sell from his *cartie*. The next train might or might not be in today so he couldn't go too far from the station.

It was bitter cold already and the word was that there might be some line clearing by noon. John went back to Littlejohn Street to keep warm more than for any other reason but the bairns were indoors because of the cold. Annie was attending to redding the house up and now with the news that his consignment was delayed; John and Annie found each other just too much to put up with after such a disappointment.

At half past one John pulled his *cartie* out from under the stairs, reached into the back of the sack he kept there and took out his New Year's bottle of *Bonnie Dundee* whisky, just to keep warm, if he needed it. He then stashed the *cartie* back under the stairs and went back to the station to wait. At three o'clock, the stationmaster put a new sign up informing that the passenger train had been turned back to Edinburgh as the snow was drifting on the line with the gathering storm. The freight was unloaded at Burntisland to be picked up there or wait for the next passing passenger train when the weather turned. At four o'clock, darkness fell on Dundee and the weather worsened. John opened the bottle and took a mouthful. At half past six he passed out. An empty bottle lay smashed on the cobbles. Annie and Mary-Anne found him at ten o'clock halfway home at the bottom of the Lochee Road, no delivery, no *cartie*, no whisky.

For two days, John had no way of getting to Burntisland in Fife and recovering his goods. Even if he could get there, he had no way of transporting such a consignment in a handcart. He would have to wait on the train. In their flat, they had burned all the coal down to ash in the fireplace.

By the morning of the twenty-eighth of December, the bairns were cold and starving. John silently hid Annie's new shawl and one of Mary-Anne's Christmas dollies under his waistcoat and slipped out the door of the tenement flat and made his way to the pawnshop in St. Andrew's Street. *At least the bairns will no' starve tonight,* he thought before heading for the train station.

*

John Murphy was sheltering from the wind while watching for a train on the bridge at the railway station in Dundee. He was sober and alert with the news that his packages had been picked up at Burntisland and stowed on the luggage van on its way to him.

Gale-force winds blew down the Tay from Perth and the frozen girders of the bridge creaked and moaned in response. Violent storms whipped up a vortex around the steelwork and the bridge strained to withstand sporadic blasts as the steam train from Burntisland to Dundee began to make its way across the Tay.

Steel wheels misaligned by the power of the wind on the steel structure that held the rails, made sparks fly in the engine carriage as the wind hammered into the bridge. At the Wormit end, a terrified signalman was transfixed as he watched flashes of flame all along the undercarriage of the train.

Then, as the train bore down on the high girders it happened! With a piercing screech, the roar of distressed metal on metal, and a groan of the girders, the thirteen spans formed of inflexible cast iron catastrophically failed all at once. The train left the bridge and plunged into the icy river, taking the high girders with it. Suddenly, it came to an end and total darkness fell on the Tay Bridge where the train had been.

A half-mile downriver, the HMS *Mars* training ship pounded and panted against the wild waves as she lurched and stretched the mooring lines of the buoys she was tethered to. Nearly four hundred incumbent boys inside cowered in fear and gathered under the top deck ready to jump the bulwark and swim for it. They heard the pop of steel rivets loud and clear as they failed to hold the high girders of the bridge. They heard the screams of the people inside the train as it left the bridge.

Moments before the bridge fell, all communication with the signalman's cabin at the Dundee end of the bridge had been lost. At approximately 7:13pm on 28th December 1879, the new Tay Rail Bridge collapsed.

The stationmaster at Dundee sent a telegram to the North British Railway Company:

"Terrible accident on bridge one or more of high girders blown down – am not sure as to the safety of last train from Edinr (Edinburgh) will advise further as soon as can be obtained"

– **National records of Scotland GD1/556/8**

The disaster killed 75 people and destroyed the much-admired, brand-new, longest bridge in the world. Along with the central section of the bridge, the train was lost and all possessions thereon, including John Murphy's vital supplies. In the aftermath, the smell of death and methane rose up from the river, horrifying the population of Dundee.

CHAPTER 2

The Murphy Brothers

On the morning of Hogmanay, Annie Murphy stood in line with the other hopefuls at the back door of the *Verdant Works* low mill. The gaffer needed help with jute packers on a day-to-day basis owing to the number of deaths in the workforce caused by seasonal flu. As she waited for the gaffer to appear from the jute mill, Annie breathed in the reek from the coal fires of the surrounding tenements and the jute *stoor* from the mills that swirled all around the streets. Annie had worked there before on occasion when not wet-nursing her babies or when John had gone off on a drinking binge with his Irish brothers in Lochee.

The thing about the packer's job was that it paid by the day and, if nothing else, she could take home a few shillings at the end of the shift. She felt angry and sorry for John at the same time. Today would not be easy but the family was starving again and she needed this job. The gaffer recognised her; she was lucky and he started her at noon for a twelve-hour shift.

John left Tommy to mind Mary-Anne and Joe in the tenement flat. He went downstairs to his handcart and wheeled it through the *closey* to the back courtyard. Over and over again for days he had agonised on the next move but now with Annie being away for hours he knew he would get it in the neck for what he was about to do. The empty clay pipe in his mouth, John Murphy had had enough.

His family was starving, he had no job, he had nothing to sell from his *cartie*, and he had nothing with which to buy anything. He had failed and he had nothing left. He knew what he had to do. He raised the *cartie* high and charged at the tenement wall with all his strength, smashing the cart into pieces on impact. He had lost faith in providence long ago and his anger burned as the red mist came down. He picked up a few broken pieces and again drove what was left of the wooden box into the wall. Again and again he destroyed his only remaining possession into burnable pieces. When he had finished, there was not one bit of the *cartie* recognisable. John picked every lump and splinter out of the snow and carried them upstairs to the bairns. He lit the fire and they felt heat again.

Tommy was seven years old and big enough to look after his brother and sister for a few days, John thought. He left the house and headed towards Lochee to find his brothers and go for a drink. He didn't have to go that far as when he reached the West Port and he looked into the Scout bar in Temple Lane, there they were, waiting for him. "John, over here," they beckoned him to their place at the bar. John took the first drink of the day and started to tell them his story. Soon, he had used the last shilling he was keeping from the pawnshop but they kept him in beer and whisky to drown his sorrows with his brothers for the rest of the day.

The Murphys meeting up was a rare occasion but when they had a reason to meet, it was always spectacular. Peter and Wullie Murphy were shocked and saddened to hear what had happened to his goods on the train over the bridge and all three agreed that it was bad Joss and nothing else. He confessed right there, to his brothers, what he had done to his cart and the justification for it. They wasted no time in commiserating with him and more drink started to flow.

After an hour and a half they became louder and louder as the pub filled up with revellers. John looked around through a haze of booze and smoke to see who the arseholes were that were laughing and singing, all this on the day he had lost everything including his future.

His blurry eyes fixed on a table of five drinkers making the most noise. He made for their table and bumped the arm of one of the men, spilling his beer on the people around. "WATCH IT, YE IRISH BASTARD," someone said at the table.

John and his brothers squared up to them shoulder-to-shoulder and scowled menacingly. "You bunch o' bliddy *kettle bilers* are looking and laughing at me 'cause you think ye're better than us. Stand up, ye bastards, till I rap yer puss," and the three of them launched themselves into the men at the table, punching and kicking heads on the way in.

Peter went down first with the thud of the barman's cosh on the back of his head. John engaged with two at a time, punching and kicking, driven by drink and adrenaline from the atmosphere and roar of the pub. Wullie had a man down on the floor and was kicking the life out of him when the cosh came down on his head as well. John was the last Murphy standing, bleeding and missing a couple of teeth and the top of an ear. The bobbies rushed him at once and he belted them with all his might and anger and his strength was subdued when the batons came down. He never knew another thing until he woke up in the DRI with a bobby guarding his cot on the third of January.

He was released a week later, remitted to the Bell Street cells and charged with police serious assault on three counts. He was before the sheriff in court on the tenth of January and sentenced to six months' hard at Perth Prison before he knew it. His brothers were admonished and were seldom to be seen outside Lochee again.

Annie Murphy came in at ten minutes past midnight to see her children huddled on the floor in front of the wood fire that Tommy and Joe had kept stoked for her. "Happy new year, Mum," he said.

CHAPTER 3

The Parish

Mary-Anne soon got used to staying indoors all day without her mother but as she had moved into the big bed in the bedroom, she had newfound privacy from her brothers. Tommy said that if Mum stayed away all day that was a good thing because she got shillings to do that and she could bring food in because of that.

One hot Sunday morning the following year, Mary-Anne sat on the cribby in Littlejohn Street, drinking her *sugarelly* water from a Keillers' jam jar. It was her favourite drink made from liquorice stick and sugar that her mum made up for her. She shook it for what seemed hours to darken it before drinking because that's how it tasted best. She, and the rest of the bairns from the crescent were waiting for the horse-drawn '*scootie*' water cart to come along Littlejohn Street so that they could chase after it and play '*scooty-hoi*' in their bare feet.

The horse and cart eventually came along, spraying water on the dusty cobbles to keep the *stoor* down, and sprayed the bairns running after it at the same time. Of course, they all got completely soaked in the process but it was free entertainment, kept them cool and was great fun. When the cart had gone around the crescent and onto the Lochee Road, she put the jar down on the pavement to play the next game to help dry everybody off.

The other children started playing *'cattie and the battie'* and she joined in. Trying to catch the cattie, before the other kids, they all banged into one another and landed flat on their posteriors. From her position on her bum, she watched helplessly as a big boy deliberately kicked her jar off the cribby, smashed it, and she saw the contents run down the *cundie* at the side of the road.

Crying in sympathy with Mary-Anne at what she had seen, a little girl took hold of Mary-Anne's hair in the hands. "Never mind," she said then. "Look, your hair's all burnt!" Mary-Anne stood up with fright; both girls turned and ran up her close to Mary-Anne's home in tears.

"What's happened?" Annie asked in distress.

"My big brother John Garland kicked her *sugarelly* water down the *cundie*!" shouted Catherine, the girl next door.

"Oh, that's terrible," Mary-Anne's mother said.

"It's no' that, Mum, my hair is all burnt! That girl said my hair's all burnt!" she said, pointing a finger at Catherine Garland.

With relief, Annie scooped her up in her arms, saying, "No, no, that's not what she meant, she said it was auburn! Auburn is a colour," said Annie.

"What do you mean, Mum?"

"It's the colour of your hair! – It's called auburn, ye silly wee thing! It's braw and there's nothing the matter," she said, as they lingered in each other's arms as though they had just been saved from a disaster.

"Can I get another *sugarelly* water, Mum?" asked Mary-Anne.

"Me too, please," said Catherine.

Mary-Anne was growing up fast. As time passed, with her mother working in the mill all day, she began to take on the day-to-day running of the house and taking care of her brothers' daily needs. In between the housework, she played in the streets of the Crescent when she could. It would be a game of tig at first with the other bairns of her age, then boxies, and scraps, but shoppies were her favourite pastimes. If she could find more time to spend playing with the other girls around the Crescent she would but she knew her brothers needed her more.

She was aware that her dad could come back at any time and what would he say if she wasn't being strong for Mum? Helping her with the housework? What would he say if he found that she had not been looking out for her brothers and keeping them well fed? What would he say if she never made sure they went to St. John's school every day? How would she explain that she had more time for her pals on the street than her brothers? No, he could never know that or see these things, not if she could help it.

Gradually, Joe became very quiet and independent for a wee laddie of five years and missed his mum terribly when she was at work. Tommy, aged nine, accepted the way things were and never changed his attitude toward their father one bit. He had never liked his dad and never missed him. Eventually, Mary-Anne won her brothers' confidence and loyalty, even when Annie was home.

The days in Littlejohn Street were the same from morning till night. Only the weather changed as the months rolled into years. Annie noticed with sadness that her children were slipping away from her but she carried on the role of the breadwinner.

Annie was now a trained and proficient spinner in the mill and her work became the most important thing in her life in the knowledge that Mary-Anne was keeping the bairns happy at home. She also noticed that Mary-Anne was changing into 'a wee madam' with her bossy ways, getting the boys to do their own share and redding up after them. She also saw her transforming into an adolescent facially and physically.

She was a beauty with her deep auburn hair and marble-white skin framing the big hazel doe eyes. *Almost a woman,* Annie thought. She would have to watch that one. At 13, Mary-Anne was able to leave St. John's school in Park Place for good and stand in line outside the mill back doors in the mornings to try for a day-job as a helper in the batching departments. Sixpence a day was good money for a school leaver.

In the summer, Annie would be able to work early shifts and spend the evenings washing and cleaning and drying the hand-me-downs that her children wore. The school was very strict about that. Joe had been in trouble at school for fighting in class and she was aware that the lack of cleanliness was the reason. The last time Joe had nits he was sent home to an empty house and waited outside the door silently until Annie came home. Joe handed the note from the school nurse to his mum at which she burst into tears at the thought of the humiliation and hurt he had been feeling without her being there to take care of him.

At that point, Annie realised she was failing her family because of her need to work full-time and reluctantly she turned to the Parish for help and went on a begging mission to St. Andrew's Cathedral parochial board so that she could reduce her hours. Even though she wasn't a Catholic, her estranged husband was, and she believed that technically, that entitled her bairns to partake in the handouts.

She was aware of the *Poor Law* in Scotland that was recently introduced. Catholics were referred to the Parish who had a system of handouts, controlled by the *Society of St. Vincent de Paul* to assist in alleviating poverty. If they were poor enough, and passed the interview, benefits would be applied for, and administered by parochial boards.

In Annie's case, as her husband was Catholic, and had deserted her, she decided to apply for the relief. She was helped in filling in the application at the cathedral and a week later, the Parish's *'Inspector of the Poor'* interviewed Annie at home. He looked over her living environment, looked at the food cupboard and then the bedrooms for clothing contents. He took the names of the children, her marital status, religion and details of any previous applications.

To Annie's great relief, she passed the interview and was approved for help with food and clothing for the children but not for herself. It was ongoing and only subject to an inspection at home every month. *That will do us,* she thought.

One summer's day, Mary-Anne and her friend Catherine were out for messages for the family. She thought she saw her father walking along the Overgate and into Bell Street. She said nothing to Catherine but was bothered by what she thought she saw. However, she doubted herself because he looked like a workingman. In reality, it *was* her father and he was paying another fine at the police station.

A year later she caught a glimpse of the same large, red-haired, bearded man again in the same street and the warm and fuzzy feeling came back; it *was* him! It was her dear dad. She followed him this time at his pace and watched as he walked straight into the police station again. She waited a few minutes and he came out and turned back down Bell Street, the same way as he came, without noticing her. She continued to follow, secretly hoping he would actually see her and if he did, she would run to him but this time, he sped up his pace out of sight.

When she got as far along Bell Street as Jock Thompson's pub; the door was open and there, inside the pub, was her dad. She was looking at her father's broad shoulders from the back. From where she was standing, his red hair looked too long and curled around the droop of his bonnet. He was drinking beer and laughing with men she didn't know. She wanted to go into the pub but bairns were not allowed so she waited and waited outside.

Darkness fell as she caught a glimpse now and again of the father she had not seen in nine years and missed so much. Hunger overcame her and she decided it would be best to come back another day. She ran home and told her mother why she was late and who she had seen in Bell Street. Annie sat her down and told her she knew about him and his drinking habits in Dundee, and also, that for the last two years, her father had been helping out with cash.

In fact, Annie and John had been in regular contact for two years but they dared not tell anyone for fear of the Parish finding out. If that got out, all who knew her in the Crescent would chastise her and she would lose the benefits of being a Catholic's wife while claiming desertion favours. The neighbours were so nosy and everyone wanted to know everyone's business. It seemed like uncovering secrets was the only excitement in their lives in the Crescent.

The next month, Mary-Anne came home from school one day to find her dad standing in the *closey* with her mother, waiting for her. Mary-Anne couldn't take it all in. Her shock was tempered by the changes in his face. Older and greyer, weather-beaten and lined with the scars of fistfights and the effects of drink, he was not the dad she used to know. The day ended under a cloud in anger for Mary-Ann with John moving back into the tenement flat. How could that be? It all became clear when Annie announced that she was pregnant and that all was well with the church because she didn't need to go back to the Parish anymore as John had secured a steady job in the new Caledon Shipyard boilershop at Carolina Port as a Boilermaker.

He moved Mary-Anne's things into the press at the foot of the bed in the room that the boys slept in. Mary-Anne was relegated to the same bed as the lads, top-and-tail style. John moved back into the bedroom and the big bed. Mary-Anne became a rebel that day and hated her father from that day on. She had grown close to her brothers and felt responsible for them more so than her mother did, especially Joe with his sad eyes and his dependence on her.

She cared less about her mother than ever now and, in time, thought even less of her new baby sister Grace, when she came along. By way of payback to the Parish, John and Annie had Baby Grace baptised in the cathedral after her birth on 1st March 1888.

John worked six days a week in the boilershop and was hardly ever seen at home in daylight. He was always sure to be found in some pub or other from Saturday noon until Sunday night and always came home drunk and frequently with a black eye or new bruise here and there. Each time he claimed he fell over due to the heart condition he had been diagnosed with while in Perth Prison; he had better be careful next time, Annie always said. On the rare occasion that Annie remonstrated about his behaviour, she got the back of his hand; a new regular occurrence grew into a way of life.

CHAPTER 4

Tam Pepper and the High Cheekers

The Crescent was an assortment of streets of tenements in which flats were occupied as dwellings, but usually the people of Dundee referred to the flats, as 'houses'. Littlejohn Street was one of these streets in the Crescent that formed a cul-de-sac. It was laid out on what was originally a drying green for the whole of Dudhope Crescent. It only had houses on the north side therefore the numbers of the tenements ran consecutively along the street.

They started electrifying the cities in Scotland and electric lighting began to take over from gas light in Dundee in 1894. Dudhope Crescent, from the Lochee Road was illuminated fully for the first time ever that winter. From Dudhope Crescent Road through the Crescent and up the Parker Street steps to Garland Place was becoming a shortcut thoroughfare for the population to get to and from the infirmary and, straight across Infirmary Brae to Dudhope Castle in the Barrack Park and its occasional fairground.

The travelling fair was pitched in the grounds at the back of the castle three or four times a year. The crowds were drawn in by the noise from the fairground rides and the hurdy gurdy barrel organ for the young men, women and bairns that roamed the night streets. Tam Pepper, the *Barker* at the boxing booth, staged boxing matches for the entertainment of the drunks and punters.

Dundee began to be seen as a destination for trade incomers and visitors alike. Mary-Anne Murphy and Catherine Garland had both left school at 14 and Mary-Anne's mother got them both into the *Verdant Works* at the Scouringburn across the Lochee Road as helpers in the bleaching and dyeing department of the mill. Catherine's mother and father had split up and her father had left the Crescent, leaving her mother, Catherine, and her brother John to live in their flat – if they could find the rent.

For 35 hours a week the girls could each take home three shillings and sixpence a week. After paying her board, Mary-Anne was left with nearly two bob a week to do with whatever she wanted.

As her early adolescent years passed in the mills, she became a sharp young lady, confident in and around the boys and girls of the Crescent. She was now of courting age and with her auburn hair tied up in the Victorian way, she spent much of her spare time with her best pal Catherine and the older girls from the Crescent in and out of the fairground set up at the castle grounds in the Barrack Park. Mary-Anne loved laughing and joking with the McDonnells and the McKees, the boys and girls from the Crescent and the men around the fairground.

Catherine Garland's big brother John, in particular, stood out as the one who thought he was the bee's knees. To Mary-Anne, he was the one who looked like a tinker with his hair cawed forward and a fag behind his ear at all times. It was strange how he was suddenly always around them and he always made sure Mary-Anne knew it. Secretly, Mary-Anne always remembered him as the big boy who kicked over her '*sugarelly* water' in the street when they were both young.

The fair was run by the 'high-cheekers', they were the tinkers and gypsies that circulated around Dundee throughout the year, from

Brechin to Forfar in Angus, from Perthshire to Fife and over the Tay on the Fifie – the ferries that transported people and goods before and after the fall of the Tay Bridge. With their horse-drawn stalls and caravans they slept at the fairground when the fair fell silent during the night.

C.T. Brock and Co. held the licences for the trading activities within the travelling fair and employed Tam Pepper to manage and take on staff as and when required. The franchises of these activities were all held by Tam Pepper, who oversaw the sale of entertainment, food and drink that drew the crowds night after night where the carousels and the big wheel worked hour after hour all day and under the new electric light at night. From April until October it was the most popular venue in Dundee.

The booming voice of Tam Pepper, over all other sounds, called for all comers to take on his team of fighters at the boxing booth. Pepper was a well-known showman in Scotland who came from Dundee and never travelled with the fair's people, but rather lived in a big house up by the Swannie Ponds on the Clepington Road. He had boxing booth franchises in other locations and ran them with the use of the high-cheekers, the travellers that followed the fairground rides throughout the land. He had men working for him in the fairgrounds and boxing booths of Glasgow Green, Leith Walk in Edinburgh and Aberdeen, but Dudhope Castle fairground in Dundee was his own pitch.

He stood there on the platform in his waistcoat with gold watch on show, the bowler hat pushed to the back of his head. Pepper sported a magnificent black soup-strainer of a moustache that never actually moved whenever he spoke. The fairground was licensed to stage daily and evening events including 'music, rides and other attractions'. Alongside the boxing booth, of course, was the booze tent, his beer tent, discreetly tucked in at the back of the boxing booth in the corner against the castle walls where the east and the south walls met and, of course, well disguised under canvass.

That's where the legal and illegal drink was consumed, when the fair was in town, especially on a Sunday when the permanent hostelries in and around Dundee were closed due to the licensing laws prohibiting such ungodly activities on the Sabbath! The beer tent was virtually invisible to the public and that, is where you would find Mary-Ann.

By the time Thursdays came around she was generally skint. There was no fun to be had at home in Littlejohn Street at any time of the week so she would spend her 'poor days' at number 9 Littlejohn Street up the next *closey* in Catherine's house. Catherine Garland was a coothie wee blonde lass, ages with Mary-Anne and always dressed in the same style as her. She adored Mary-Anne, would do anything for her and was always by her side.

The McKee family also lived up that *closey*. The parents, six brothers and two girls all lived in that house. Both Mary-Anne and Catherine would often find themselves surrounded by the McKees, all happily ambling up the Parker Street steps. At the top of the Crescent they were into Garland Place and from there, to the Barrack Park and the Dudhope Castle fairground tents just to meet the rest of her pals.

Catherine Garland was the younger of two siblings at number 9 Littlejohn Street. Her older brother John Garland was a streetwise lad three years older than Mary-Anne. He had an eye for the girls, stood a foot taller than Mary-Anne and had spent a couple of years longer in the mill than her. He seemingly had his own money to buy his own Sunday best clothes which he wore all weekend, every weekend. John had known Mary-Anne for as long as he could remember but until

Catherine brought her into the house he had nothing to say to her.

Ultimately, when the girls came back to Littlejohn Street on Saturday nights, he always appeared around midnight with a half-bottle of 'Old Tom' gin and shared it with the girls before they ended the night in a stupor. In general, the McKees, Garlands and the Murphys had their spats but all grew up together in harmony and in general looked out for each other.

Mary-Anne spent her 18th birthday at the stalls at the fair with her pals and the lads drinking Old Tom gin and laughing the night away. She never made it home to number 8 Littlejohn Street that night and was absent from work the next day. She only woke up at the foot of the Parker Street steps under a pile of discarded old jute sacks around eleven thirty next morning with a hangover and a swollen face, bruised from top to bottom but, she had no idea how she got there or how she got her bruises.

She dare not go home because her father would see her face like that and would leather her for sure. She went to Catherine's and waited until she could get sneaked in when no one could see her. Catherine was sent next door to Annie to collect a change of clothing and some rouge for Mary-Anne. She was supposedly 'working all weekend in the mill due to the huge backlog of jute to dispatch for the army contract'.

The weekend was actually spent with Catherine at number 9 who tried to fill in the gaps for her, explaining that she and her brother John left them at midnight. Mary-Anne was last seen at the fairground just before midnight with a Russian sailor called Boris who she seemed to like very, very much.

She told the gaffer on Monday she was very, very sick on the Friday last week and couldn't have come in like that. It would never happen again she assured him and she was better now. The following Saturday, however, she was off work again and she was sacked the next Monday.

The jute and flax industry was booming by this time as the British army was buying up all the hessian sacks that could be made. Scott Brothers who employed Catherine, employed Mary-Anne on the spot that week and a full-time job was offered as she had reached the age a spinner needed to be. She trained and passed the test in a week and her parents never knew a thing.

CHAPTER 5

The Recruiting Sergeants

By October 1892, the Black Watch and Seaforth Highlanders had established a permanent booth in the Dudhope Park fairground representing the British army. Recruiting sergeants from both regiments were appearing daily at the boxing booth entrance in the fairground and it was so tempting for the young men fuelled by the booze and fights and full of aggression to sign up for a four-year stint in the army there and then.

Two of the eldest McKee boys, Billy and George, took the queen's shilling at the fairground and enlisted into the regiments; George joined the Seaforths and Billy, the Black Watch and both of them left Dundee together on November 1st 1893 and were off to Aldershot in Hampshire for recruit training. John Garland was tempted to sign up with the McKees but in the end he stayed at home in Littlejohn Street because he had other interests, one being money he earned in the mill and the other being Mary-Anne Murphy.

A year later, at the start of December 1894, Billy and George were both back in Dundee together for some home rest and recreation before leaving on the 4th for the East Indies. They had spent a year in the army and had both grown physically and mentally.

With their fair hair and white skin, they could have been twins but for height. Billy, the eldest, was a big man and stood six foot tall, strong as an ox and intelligent. George was three inches shorter, with an identical build but he was not the brightest spark. They were joined on the pub-crawl by Mary-Ann's younger brother Joe, who looked older than his sixteen and a half years and was the shortest but the stockiest, built like a bull and a match for anyone regardless of size. They met up with John and Catherine Garland and Mary-Anne and her other brother Tommy, for old times' sake.

The group from Littlejohn Street made their way to the Lochee Road and caught the horse-drawn tram, as was their usual start of a weekend in the old days. From the tram, Mary-Anne spotted her Uncle Wullie coming out of the Albert Bar or 'Kiddies' on the Lochee Road as it was locally known. At Tommy's suggestion, they all alighted and caught up with Uncle Wullie staggering in the shadows on his way along the top of the Lochee Road.

"What's the celebration for, Uncle Wullie? It's only six o'clock!" asked Mary-Anne.

"I've been at the futba' match at the Craigie Ground," her uncle shouted. "Dundee FC played their first ever league match against the Glasgow Rangers today and we drew three-all," he added. "Some Irish pubs were promising a free drink to every man who supported the Dundee against the Rangers."

"Really?" Mary-Anne asked incredulously. "Where are we going next then?" Mary-Anne laughed but was quite serious at the same time.

"The Whip Inn along the Liff Road if ye want to come," her uncle continued. "I'm meeting yer faither and yer Uncle Peter there then we're going into Lochee for a drink wi' the Irish," he said in his fading Irish brogue. "If ye dare let him see ye in a pub, come wi' me."

Why not? Mary-Anne thought. "I want him to meet John Garland anyway and what can he say to me with all the McKees there as well?" she asked her pals. By the time they reached the Whip Inn they were all agreed.

"Aye, come on, then, let's go in!" said Billy. The Whip Inn was full by the time they all rolled in and John and Peter were at the singing of the Irish songs in the corner.

"The City of Dundee welcomes you!" John McGinnes, the proprietor announced. "And, IF you were at the match, the first drink is on the house, ladies and gentlemen."

"Yes, we were all there, and it was a three-all draw," the McKees lied in harmony.

Anything for a free drink, Mary-Ann thought. "Me too," she said.

Mary-Anne positioned herself between her father and Catherine and John turned to see his daughter sipping gin with her friends. "What the hell are you doing here? You're too young to get into a pub!" he bellowed.

"I'm 18!" said Mary-Anne. She was sitting with John Garland at her other side, feeling inspired and scared in equal terms and sheepishly whispered to her father that she and John Garland were going steady!

He glowered and bellowed again, "What for are you wanting a man? And at your age you should be helping your mother and me with the bairns at hame."

Mary-Anne felt the rage beginning inside and blurted out, "That's YOUR job, no' mine." She went on furiously. "I am a grown woman and I'm working now, and I've got a lad." To end the conversation, she yelled, "If you don't like it, I'm leaving home when me and John get our own house and you're no' stopping me!"

John struck her across the face, the blow knocking her to the ground where she lay dazed and confused. "Get out of here, you wee besom, before I take my belt to you!" cried Mary-Anne's father. John's brothers held him back to prevent him giving her more of the same.

The McKees and John Garland pounced on John Murphy and his brothers. The blows rained in with fist and boot like lightning. The Murphy brothers had their hands full all of a sudden and it was Billy who stopped it with his bulk in between them. Mary-Anne hazily watched the confrontation while Tommy sheltered and comforted her but took no part in the fisticuffs.

She was transfixed as she watched her father fight off the attack and acquit himself adequately. His brothers fought in the same style, head down, windmilling punches flying in all directions. John Garland and the McKees, however, were younger and faster but most of all sober.

The Littlejohn Street pals were out of the Whip Inn and back on to the Liff Road within minutes of entering the pub. The oncoming tram was almost at the stop and they all piled on and back into Lochee High Street before they realised it.

They were also only here because the two McKees were due to rejoin their units for the East Indies in the morning and there was a good crowd in the High Street when they got off the tram. All of the Dundee-Irish locals resided close to the Whip Inn in the middle of Lochee. Once the group got inside the Burnside, the next pub of their choice, they mingled and drank with many of the hard-drinking locals, some with pure Lochee accents but most with Irish twangs. They were some of the many jute immigrant workers who had made Lochee home. They came mainly from around Athol Street in a new low-cost housing scheme that came to be known as 'Little Tipperary'.

The scheme was also owned and managed by Cox Brothers' mills of the Camperdown works, now the biggest jute mill factories in the world.

The next pub they came to was the Pentland Bar in Lochee High Street. Most of the locals in that pub that night were also part of the Irish immigrant mill workers employed in the area but not all. The Irish contingent, of course, was seething at the presence of travelling Rangers FC supporters in the pub. The rest were Dundee soldiers on leave like Billy and George. They recognised half a dozen faces from their Aldershot base and struck up a blether while Joe immediately checked out the pub for troublemakers. They relaxed in the company of their fellow regimental comrades and got stuck into the drinking, recounting and embellishing their affray in the Whip Inn. John and Mary-Anne went along with the pseudo-celebrations but in truth the feeling of guilt thoroughly gutted Mary-Anne for disobeying and defying her father.

John Garland followed her grieving process dutifully even though he had mixed feelings about the whole family affair. Beer after beer and whisky for the lads, gin and more gin for the lasses. That's how it went in Lochee in every pub that night. The Irish started their rebel songs and the Rangers started theirs. Of course, the Black Watch and the Seaforth being in town were not going to be outdone. The 'Watch' piped up with "Wha Saa' the forty-second…" And, with that, the first punch was thrown. The tinderbox was lit. Two locals jumped on the bar to give better purchase at kicking the Rangers drinkers in the head; they were felled by a torrent of blows and pint glasses from the floor and the pub erupted into a total rammy. Blood and beer flew in the air and men and women joined in, every one. Bottles were broken on heads and glasses were thrown in every direction; fists, heads and boots went in to the mêlée time and time again. Someone who thought it a good idea to keep the police out locked the doors of the boozer and the fight seemed to ensue forever.

The locals eventually managed to escape through the storeroom windows and onto the street. The cops finally got in that way and the pub emptied out the main doors. Miraculously, the police were told that all the fighters were friends and amazingly, none of them saw who the perpetrators were.

CHAPTER 6

A Pound a Round

Mary-Anne had seen virtually nothing of her dad at home since the fight in the Pentland in December. She had deliberately chosen to work the early shift at Scott Brothers as long as her dad was steady dayshift in the shipyard. The only time they ever saw each other was if by chance they happened to be in the same street at night at the weekend. Annie, Tommy and Joe preferred it that way as they all dreaded the next confrontation – if there was to be one.

John Murphy was, by this time, showing a side of him that Annie had never seen. Inside the house and outside, he drank, he got violent, he got violent, and he drank. The same pattern was repeated week after week and not a word was said in complaint in 8 Littlejohn Street. Annie believed it was the loss of his hawkers' business that was killing him inside, but he had found another way to bring in the money, from the shipyard. John Murphy was an honourable man, she knew that, he had integrity and she loved him for it.

By this time, John Garland and Mary-Anne Murphy were officially going steady. John Murphy and Garland never spoke but acknowledged each other's presence when they encountered one another in the Crescent by some quirk of bad fortune. John Murphy kept an eye on him from a discreet distance. Everything that young ne'er-do-well was doing with his daughter in tow was suspicious.

Murphy had seen him with other girls when Mary-Anne was at work. *Sniffing around them like a fly around shite,* he thought. *He's not to be trusted.*

Both Mary-Anne and John Garland were skilled up to a point in millwork but with John, only when it suited him did he stick in at a job. They both worked in the mills to earn a wage but Mary-Anne was a steady worker, John was not. The money they earned between them brought them all they needed for the good life, as and when they needed it. In spite of the potential to work steady jobs, he picked and chose when and where he worked, blaming the noise, the gaffer or the distance he had to walk to get to work as the reason not to work. Whatever the problem with the mills, the lack of money always came into it to some extent.

Like many thousands of households across Dundee it was the women who worked. The men were happy at home keeping 'the kettle boiling' so they say, and they became known as 'Kettle Bilers' throughout the Forfarshire area. Mary-Anne and John Garland's relationship was heading the same way: John was often out of work but Mary-Ann held down a job constantly.

With no other responsibilities, John Garland was happy to see Mary-Anne work all day in the mill and meet up with her after work. She would spend her money on him and to some extent it made Mary-Anne happy too, or, as much as she could be, in the stinking, poverty-blighted streets of the Crescent.

The real John Garland, however, was a leech who lived off other people – unless he had to work for the things he needed to survive. Surreptitiously, he prowled the Crescent and the local pubs and beer halls for easy people. People who, at first sight thought they could trust him. The same people who gave him their time, their friendship and their money for drinks, fags and loans for a Garland sob story that was never paid back. John Garland was a predator all right and Mary-Anne was his most productive prey. He took everything she had and he wanted more. In spite of that, John Garland always dressed well and looked like a man who had property whenever he was seen in public. John Murphy was right about him; Garland was a spiv and everything he represented was abhorrent to Murphy. In truth, everything Garland wore was on tick and Murphy suspected that the debt was mounting up week after week. *Bloody Conman,* Murphy thought. *He'll amount to nothing, that one.*

Mary-Anne spent her days at work and the summer evenings with her lad in the Barrack Park or in his house. Inevitably, as the summer nights closed in, Mary-Anne and John Garland always made their way around the grounds of Dudhope Castle, drawn in by the arrival of the travelling fair. Ultimately, each visit ended up in the beer tent at the boxing booth.

They were in the tent drinking with the usual crowd late one Saturday night in August of 1894 when Tam Pepper, the boxing booth barker and beer tent owner, was calling for challengers to take on the resident pugilists. "Come on, boys, who'll be man enough to step up here for a pound?" Over and over, again and again he shouted, "A pound a round for a heavyweight, that's what we're giving you, a pound a round if you stay the course."

Mary-Anne was ignoring the muffled noise next door as much as possible as the usual crowd shuffled into the boxing tent next door. She and John were drinking with the high-cheekers who ran the fairground stalls in the summer months then disappeared to where the caravan took them for another year. She felt at home with these people, safe and part of their culture. *I must take it from my father,* she thought. She liked the style of the hawker life her dad had lived and these people were cut from the same cloth.

The roar of the crowd grew louder and Tam Pepper was shouting something through the megaphone. She stood up suddenly and cried, "Did you hear what he said there, John? Did I hear him right?" They stopped and listened at the canvas wall of the tent and it came through again.

"And now, introducing our heavyweights, 'Boilermaker' John Murphy takes on Jed 'the Gypsy' Pace, the English boxing champion from Norfolk."

"That's my dad!" Mary-Anne exclaimed incredulously.

John and Mary-Anne had to go in to see for themselves what was going on. They paid their shilling each and slipped into the rear benches of the boxing booth, taking care not to be seen under the electric lighting. Her dad was in the ring stripped to the waist save his vest. His brothers Wullie and Peter were with him in his corner. After a rowdy reception, and a furious discussion with Pace's corner, both fighters agreed to discard the gloves and make it a bare-knuckle contest for twice the purse. With that, they closed and buckled the canvas doors to keep out anyone who might cause problems. The crowd roared their approval and the bucket came around for the extra shilling per head. This time, however, they were betting illegally on the fighters and another bucket was beginning to fill up in both fighters' corners.

"What's going on, John?" asked Mary-Anne with a tremble in her voice.

"Winner takes all," he said, "and anything you bet gets doubled if your man wins. Can you lend me a half a crown, Mary-Anne?" John Garland gave Mary-Anne that look and she reached into her purse and produced the extra cash with a look of fear and anticipation. He gladly chucked two more shillings and a sixpence into the bucket and roared along with the crowd.

Mary-Anne was horrified. First her heart thumped hard and fast when she saw her father and uncles getting ready for the bout. Now with the bare-knuckles terms her heart sank in fear for her dad. Now she realised for the first time how her father had got his cuts and bruises over the years His opponent was the Champion of all England and a well-known dirty fighter. The look of Jed Pace alone was enough to make her feel sick. Tattooed and craggy, his body bore all the hallmarks of a seasoned fighter, scars all over his face and hands as a result of his trade. John Murphy was getting the adrenaline flowing on the back of the frantic crowd spurring him on.

Tam Pepper doubled as the ref for the bouts. "New rules, gentlemen… No gouging, biting or kicking," he said to the fighters, loud enough for all to hear. "If a man goes down, let him up. If a man doesn't get up, he loses. Understood?" Both nodded in agreement. They returned to their corners for some last-minute advice from their seconds.

"You can do it, Murphy! Knock his frigging head aff, Murphy!" the crowd bayed.

John took a last mouthful of whisky from Peter's hip flask and with that, turned round to face his enemy. "Ready," he gestured, and the fight was on.

The bell rang and John Murphy launched himself into the middle of the ring in round one. Pace came out slowly and took up the pose of a professional but Murphy tore into the Englishman like a man possessed. John threw the first flurry of blows, some landing on the champ's forearms, the others skilfully swerved and ducked by Pace. Each time Murphy swung a right hook at the head of the champ, he missed by a long way. Pace threw the left jab to the jaw and another to the throat of the challenger. Murphy took a step back and Pace closed in, bouncing a punch off Murphy's skull. Stunned and dazed, Murphy caught him by the arms and, like a bizarre dancing couple locked in furious embrace, they stumbled and fell with Pace landing on top of Murphy, his back to the referee; Pace stuck the head in, cracking the bridge of the nose of the challenger.

Pace let Murphy up and, breathless and bleeding, he caught Pace on the chin with a right hook. The crowd erupted and shouted for blood but Murphy was slow to capitalise and took a crushing body blow and doubled up as he went down again. Mary-Anne cringed with each blow that landed on her father. The tears were rolling down her cheeks by the end of the first minute of the first round.

On the break by the ref, Pace caught Murphy with a left hook to the floating rib and another right hook to the ribs on the other side. The crowd roared and raged instructions at Murphy who heard none of it. The pain started in his torso and travelled through the middle of his chest to his throat and lower jaw. He couldn't catch a breath for the pain and Pace belted in a flurry of head punches, half of them illegally to the back of the head. Mercifully, the bell sounded the end of the first round and John slumped into his stool in the corner. Mary-Anne was calling for her daddy to come home with her now; John Garland was roaring for Murphy to get back in and "kill the English bastard."

"You're doing great, John!" said Peter who was clearly drunk and completely forgot to feed John with water in the break. Wullie, on the other hand, saw the pain on John's face and the pallor that was taking over from the blood-soaked upper half of John's body. He was worried that his brother was hurt seriously and fleetingly thought to stop the fight there and then. They cleaned John up and he was breathing better again so Wullie let him go back into the fight. Money was money, John Murphy thought and he summoned up all the anger and strength he could muster. Pace ripped into him with another left hook to the ribs and another right cross to the jaw. That did it! Murphy dropped to the canvas like a sack of spuds, out like a light and lay like a corpse for what seemed to Mary-Anne like hours.

Pace paraded around the ring, his seconds draped his Champ's belts over his shoulders and the crowd erupted in excitement of the fight and the win. They exclaimed in unison their appreciation of the fantastic performance they had just witnessed regardless of the fact that John Murphy was spark out in the ring before them. They had got the blood show they wanted and had paid for.

The Murphy brothers slowly carried John to the corner of the ring. "This is serious!" Wullie tried to tell Peter who was grieving more for the money he had lost than for his brother John. When they couldn't revive him, Mary-Anne and young John Garland took over. They wasted no time in lifting the big man off the canvass themselves. Time was of the essence, she told John Garland and they appropriated the wheeled stretcher from the fairground and dragged John onto it. She made them run as fast as they could across the fairground and over the Barrack Park into the emergency ward at the Royal Infirmary.

On arrival, the hospital staff nurses couldn't get a pulse and the young doctor worked on his chest, pumping and pumping up and down, up and down like he had been trained. John Garland took fright and took his leave from the situation. He left the hospital and went right back to the beer tent. Mary-Anne, however, stayed close to her father throughout the emergency, willing him to wake up so that she could see for herself that the man she knew to be her hero when she was a little girl was indeed still that man.

The first thing the medics tried was to warm the patient with hot water bottles on the chest and abdomen – that only succeeded in scalding the skin. In an effort to clear the airways, they forcibly removed all foreign objects with fingers and swabs from the throat, which included blood, mucus and whisky in a mixture of red glut. They turned the bed down at the head and up at Murphy's feet which elevated him by forty-five degrees. Then they applied pressure to Murphy's abdomen by having two nurses lean over him at the same time, applying pressure. They raised his bed horizontally and tried releasing air into his mouth using a pair of bellows and tickling his throat at the same time – still no pulse.

Finally, they were left with no choice but to get the 'smoker' in. This involved the rectal and oral fumigation with tobacco smoke, known as the 'irritant method'. They drew the smoke from burning pipe tobacco by the bellows and blew it down into his chest by his bloodied mouth and throat, then they changed the tube and they drove it directly into the anus and through the intestines. The bellows were worked for a full five minutes and suddenly there were responses in the eyes. This method was only ever used as a last result on the "almost dead" and amazingly, John Murphy woke up.

The police were called in by the hospital staff who were all alarmed at the injuries their patient came in with. The coppers said "he's been doing this bare-knuckle boxing for illegal betting for years. The doctor told Mary-Anne that night that the coppers said they knew her father well from the Bell Street cells for the same thing, common assault but usually drunk and disorderly.

John Murphy was clearly in both cardiac arrest and anaphylactic shock that night they brought him in. On top of that he nearly died from the blows alone to the skull causing blood clots to the brain and inducing the heart attack he had just suffered. The doctors said he was lucky to be alive. They knew when he came in it was touch and go. "If he came in ten minutes later, he would have been a goner now," the doctors told Mary-Anne later that night in the intensive care unit. She stayed with him until the morning then went to break the news to her mother.

After a fortnight in intensive care, the police interviewed John Murphy who had nothing to tell them about the injuries he endured or of the fight in which he sustained them. Jed Pace was arrested the following night. He was bound over in court not to fight again.

John Murphy was an invalid from that day. A heart attack and apparently being a diabetic was too much of a risk for the shipyard. He was paid off instantly with no recompense as he was 'unfit for work'. He never worked again. Hard work, hard living and hard drinking had ruined his health and he was confined to the Littlejohn Street flat for the rest of his life.

CHAPTER 7

The Smell of the Crescent

Mary-Anne paid her board and young Tommy, who was working in the mill now, paid his, albeit a pittance. Annie had no option but to reduce her hours in the mill further in order to care for John and the growing family with three younger bairns. Joe, however, was becoming really problematic. He drank, he fought, and he worked on the fairground rides and the boxing booth. In the tattoo tent, he even got a tattoo on his arm, not a name of a girlfriend or a mother or even a place, but a tombstone that epitomised the story of his life and death, to him.

It was back to the Parish again for Annie for handouts and they were glad of it because there was no other legal way of paying the rent. The Parish eventually paid for John's hospital treatment again. The charity negotiated the costs for the DRI with the Dundee Welfare Committee that operated the Dundee poorhouses – the same charity Annie had gone to for a midwife to care for her every time she had given birth at home. By then, the Murphy family had grown with the birth of Nellie and finally baby Willie. Mary-Anne was present at each birth subsequent to her own in that flat and knew the routine.

In each case the priest was always the first to visit and give Annie a round of the guns for not adhering to the 'rhythm method', the only birth control method permitted by the Catholic Church. Then she would promise to have the child christened and raised, as a Catholic as usual, which seemed like a small price to pay for the help, she supposed. After each birth, the Parish would continue to send a midwife or a nurse to see her and make her promise not to be so selfish again in future. Annie always dutifully felt guilty and complicit in equal measures at these visits and promised never to let it happen again. John never spared a word about Annie's wants or feelings. These were the times when he could have comforted her when she felt the guilt that the church had made her feel. He admired Annie for her strength to withstand the chastisement of his church but, although he wanted to tell her that, he just couldn't say it to her.

John Murphy spent his days mostly at home 'minding the bairns' in the two-roomed tenement flat that was now housing a family of eight. On top of the overcrowding, they had the use of one WC outside on the *plettie* halfway down the tenement stair but eight families up that close shared that toilet.

John was responsible for emptying the po and the buckets into the midden at the *backies* in the morning before the family rose and also for bringing in fresh water for the day from the bowser that arrived every second day from the Lady Well at the Wellgate, where it meets the bottom of the Hilltown. There was piped water to the flats but it needed to be boiled on the grate before use, as without this it was undrinkable.

Throughout Dundee and especially all through the streets of the Crescent, a permanent feature that only made a crowded house worse – was the smell. Regardless of what time of the year it was, the smell of effluent, escaped gas, raw jute and worst of all the thick acrid smoke or *reek* from the chimneys of dozens and dozens of jute mills filled the air.

Still, Annie would work all day for four and a half days a week. Each Friday the week ended for her with the wail of sirens all over Dundee as the mills sounded their one o'clock bummer getting everyone started again. Not for Annie though, that's when she picked up her wages and was off for her weekly messages. That was when she would always reward John with a half-bottle of *'Bonnie Dundee'* and that, was as much as he could actually manage without fainting with the effects of diabetes. There was no known cure for diabetes other than a diet of costly nutritious food and fresh fruit – and no drink.

CHAPTER 8

Marriage

By July 1895, all the jute mills were busy again and Mary-Anne was regularly working a 14-hour day as a spinner in the mill. By the age of 19 she and John Garland were spending all their spare time comforting each other and making plans for their future together.

There was no place in the Crescent where they could have the privacy of a courting couple except in the shadows around Dudhope Castle in the Barrack Park late at night. They took the opportunity when they could and they made their love in the deep and darkened doorways of the castle walls, or outside at the back of the beer tent in the shadow of the castle. On cold nights they never even noticed the drop in temperature.

By this time, Mary-Anne had had enough of her life at home. One night after making illicit love and more out of despair than love, she spoke of her frustrations and her wants as a grown-up woman. John agreed without argument. Both she and John Garland decided to marry as soon as they could.

The venue of a wedding was a sticking point as religion was important to her father but not, apparently, to John Garland. But they had to marry because they couldn't carry on doing this for much longer, they were sure to be found out or she was going to get pregnant. There was no question of living together in sin, not in 1895.

They used all their money to get a deposit together for a rented flat.

John Murphy and his wife Annie had been waiting to hear what was going on with Mary-Anne and young John. They had been left a note by Mary-Anne under the gas mantle by the door of the flat that John Garland was coming to see them at seven o'clock that night. It sounded important and John and Annie thought they knew what was coming and they resolved to stay home.

When the knock came to the door, Murphy looked gaunt; his red hair had turned white long ago and he had lost half his body weight. His head was splitting and he was as white as a sheet, as he opened the door for them in trepidation.

To his relief the couple announced that they were to be married. They emphasised that if she moved out Mary-Anne would actually be helping her parents by giving them back some space in the flat to bring up the bairns. Her parents said nothing except congratulations. Annie had the feeling it wouldn't last, John knew it wouldn't but this was not the time to say it. In order for the wedding to go ahead, however, they needed her parents' permission and also some money.

John Murphy stiffened because he knew what was coming next. John Garland came right out and asked Murphy for cash to get the marriage done as swiftly as possible. "I'm out of work, John, can you help me out?" he asked.

John Murphy hadn't worked in a year and was skint permanently. This would make it even worse. On top of that, Murphy was annoyed because he knew that Garland could have been in work. He had never trusted him and he bore grudges. He remembered the fight in the Whip Inn on the first night they met.

John Garland was not his choice for a son-in-law; he saw a weakness in him that reminded him of himself, and he drank everything away that he could earn and then took it from Mary-Anne. In addition, unlike him, Garland was a womaniser. He had seen him hanging around the bottom of the Parker Street steps to the Crescent with the young women who only appeared at night and inevitably, he disappeared into the shadows with them. Garland was untrustworthy, he thought, and unreliable. He would love to end this tryst to his daughter but now he had no way of stopping it.

Murphy, however, begrudgingly felt the responsibility of a father of a bride-to-be and reluctantly made a promise to the young couple that he would 'cover the cost of the wedding'. As he walked out the door with his girl, John Garland 'let slip' that he needed a new suit for the wedding and a new bowler would be "just the ticket to set it all off". John Garland added, "Oh, and a few quid would help, when the day comes."

John Murphy was raging inside but what could he do? His eldest daughter was getting married and he would never be forgiven if he let the family down again. Off he went to see his brothers in Lochee again and came back with a promise of a loan of thirty pounds. Hurriedly, arrangements were made and they were married in the Manse at Albany Terrace according to the forms of the Free Church of Scotland. John Murphy was bitterly disappointed, but this way was cheaper than a big Catholic church wedding.

It was a small family-only affair. Mary-Anne's side of the family was well turned out and her brother Joe, who had just joined the Cameronians, was resplendent in his kilt. Her uncles, Peter and Wullie, were suited and booted and appeared as requested, more than anything else to see what their money was spent on.

The venue and a party held at the church hall was a pound alone; the cost of the food and drink, and a wedding dress for Mary-Anne which made her look like a princess, was worth every penny paid, thought John Murphy. Of the thirty quid he borrowed, the balance of four pounds went to John Garland. John Murphy was indebted to his brothers but John Garland was looking like a toff, on the day.

The Murphy brothers had made their minds up within ten minutes of meeting John Garland formally. "He's a bad'ane, John, watch him," they confided. The red mist was rising but John Murphy kept a lid on it… for later. The wedding was a subdued affair – in fact there was a sense of menace in the air all day.

The Murphy brothers drank beer and watched John Garland like a hawk. He paid more attention to the two mill girls invited by Mary-Anne than he paid to his new wife. *A perfect opportunity to give Garland the message,* Peter Murphy thought. The wedding ended with the Murphys taking the girls up for the last dance and then escorting them home. Young Joe Murphy went back to his unit the following day.

The newly-weds had found a one-roomed 'single end' flat in the area to rent and moved into number 10 John Street, the adjacent street of tenements to their families. At least their move left space for the Murphy family just as Mary-Anne predicted. In her new single end home, she looked around at the stark surroundings. "A couple of gallons of white distemper on the walls will make all the difference here," John said as he lay in bed. He stayed in bed the next day and Mary-Anne went to her job in the mill.

"Have you any money left from my dad?" Mary-Anne asked nonchalantly, when she returned from the mill.

"Nah, that was all spent yesterday, see if yer mum could help out sometime." Mary-Anne felt sick in the pit of her stomach, the way it used to be when her father went off on a binge at the weekends in her youth. John said, "I'll see if I can get a start at the Verdant Mill next week, that should do it." He lit another cigarette.

There was not a stick of furniture in the single end to begin with but John did get started in the Verdant and, with a joint income of two pounds a week they were able to buy a bed, a wardrobe and a table with two chairs on tick. Annie gave them some bedding and she also made them a quilt by stitching a myriad of two-inch squares of discarded cloth together. She stuffed it with raw jute for extra warmth on the cold nights. Mary-Anne saved up and bought a new hand-woven rush carpet that fitted in front of the fireplace over the waxcloth on the floor.

They were happy beyond compare – for the first six months, and then the old feelings of a young, carefree, unmarried couple crept in. Back to the fairground at the Barrack Park they went if the fair was there, getting through all the cash they had earned between them by the Thursday of each week. "Never mind," said John. "Tam will give us tick at the beer tent."

Christmas was coming and they had each other in the dark days and nights of winter 1895, but between them they never seemed to have enough money to get through the week – or get the walls of the flat distempered.

The single end was at the top of the tenement. It was March and still the cold and icy streets were a daunting challenge for Mary-Anne. She was in two minds whether to go to the mill or stay there and try to get over the hangover and the tummy ache she had been bothered with for a week.

No doubt the drinking water is bogging again, she thought. "It'll be a bug again as usual," she told John as he went out to work. A wave of nausea came over her and she fell back into bed and curled up like a foetus. In the afternoon, she went to her father's house to see if there was any medicine there that she could have to help her get better.

Wee Grace Murphy was out playing on the cobbles of Littlejohn Street, bouncing the ball off the wall. "Johnny the Barber shaved his father wi' a roosty razzor," she sang in time to the bounce. "The razzor broke and cut his throat OH! For Johnny the barber." She finished her game. "Hiya! Mary-Anne!" she shouted to her big sister as she shuffled along the street.

Ignoring Grace, Mary-Anne climbed the stair and smelled the toast her father was making inside for the bairns and she suddenly felt ravenous – she had to have some. Inside the flat, her father was piling up a plateful of toasted bread for the tea in front of the fire but in she went, scoffing all the toast that she could get in her mouth without so much as a 'by your leave'.

"What are ye doing? That's for the bairns!" John exclaimed.

She had her fill and slumped down into the comfy chair her father used. "Doesn't matter, I'll make them more," said Mary-Anne – "After," but not today, she thought, then she felt very, very sorry for eating the toast and sitting in her dad's chair so she rose to leave when Annie walked in the door.

Mary-Anne burst into floods of tears on seeing her mother because that is exactly what she wanted, to sit and talk with her mum to find out what she thought might be wrong and what could be done for her. John discreetly left the room. *Up the stick?* she thought. *I canna be, but then, I suppose I could. How can I tell John? How can I tell my father? Will he be angry?* Mary-Anne needed time to think about this and begged her mother not to tell anybody for fear of it being wrong.

Mary-Anne winced when she remembered the times when her mother was about to give birth, it always remained in her memory that nearer her mother's due date, the midwife would supply the essentials to expectant mothers of painkillers and carbolic soaps, the smell of which hung about the building for weeks after the birth. This was natural childbirth at home in every sense of the word. She remembered vividly that eventually, Annie would go into labour with only the midwife and Mary-Anne in attendance and Mary-Anne would always get the water on, boiling and the cleaning cloths ready for the steamie for afterwards. The screams and sobs of Annie's pain had been terrifying for the bairns in the next room but there was nowhere else to go. Mary-Anne disliked the routine intensely and vowed it would never happen to her! And now it had!

After waiting another week, she did like Annie had told her and had seen the nurse in the DRI maternity department. The nurse said the baby was coming in October and the choice was hers: if she wanted the baby to be born at home then she could get help from the Parish.

On the other hand, if she wanted to have it in the hospital in the maternity ward she had better get her name down and pay the registration fee of ten shillings. The nurse said the full cost might only be as little as four pounds depending on her husband's income and she would be in there for two weeks. She and John had never seen as much as four pounds before. How could she get it, she mused? "I'll have to speak to my mother, she'll know."

Another week went by and Mary-Anne went to see her mother again. "I need ten shillings, Mum, the baby's coming in October and I want to have it in the DRI," said Mary-Anne.

"The DRI?" Annie said with surprise. "Are you serious? A hospital birth costs a lot of money," her mother reminded her, "and ten shillings will not cover it."

Mary-Ann responded, "No, that's just the registration fee, it'll just be four pounds."

Annie rolled her eyes. "We never had the money for any of OUR bairns to get it, what's so special about yours? There's nothing wrong wi' having it in the house!" said Annie in an effort to change her mind.

"Mum, we live in a single end, one room and nothing else!"

Annie scoffed at the idea of paying for the birth in hospital. "What does John say? How can he pay for it?"

"He doesn't know yet, and you'd better not tell him either, not until I have spoken to him about it. You're not helping, Mum!"

Annie reluctantly fetched the piggy bank from under the Belfast sink and emptied it into Mary-Anne's lap. "If ye can find ten bob there ye can have it. But don't come back for more, Mary-Anne, please, we don't have it."

Mary-Anne began to sob. "All I want is to do the best for this bairn and you don't want me to," she said.

"But you've no money and we can't help ye because after I've paid our own costs, and bought yer father's diabetes food, we have no money left either!" said Annie in despair. Mary-Anne ran out of her mother's flat in tears. John Murphy saw her from the street but said nothing to her. He knew what was going on all right, he had seen all the signs before, every time Annie was pregnant in fact.

John Murphy sat Annie down and interrogated her until the truth was out. *Mary-Anne is pregnant and they don't have a pot to piss in!* he thought. "Hospital birth, is it?" he said. Garland would be tapping him for more money no doubt and he still hadn't paid him back for the cost of his suit for the wedding let alone the cost of a birth. John felt the red mist rising again: "That little bastard Garland has done this, wait till I see him," he murmured to Annie. "God give me strength – I'll sort him out."

How can I tell my man? Mary-Anne thought. *Will he be angry?* They never planned for a bairn so soon and she would have to stop working when the bairn came. Her mother was right – they had no money for a hospital birth, unless, what if they just kept on working all the overtime they could get! That seemed like the only thing for it. *Yes I'll do that!* There was plenty work in the mills just now so that's what she would do: keep working.

Mary-Anne sat with John Garland that night and explained the situation. She hoped he would be happy with it but doubted it. She explained that she was sorry about it but what's done is done. It was happening and there was nothing more to say.

Additionally, she said she was having the baby in the DRI. It would cost them some money but they were both working and had time to save for it. She explained that although most babies were still delivered at home, the nurse had said that if they could pay something, the new maternity ward at the DRI was the best because they used 'the Twilight Sleep' method. Mary-Anne added gently that they gave the mother doses of morphine and scopolamine. It put mothers to sleep for the entire birth! That's the way she wanted it.

"How much?" asked John.

"Four Pounds and ten shillings, for everything including the antenatal and postnatal care."

He couldn't take it in. His first thought was why didn't she do something about it? Get rid of it or arrange to give it away for adoption or something? "We can't afford that, Mary-Anne," he said. "And we canna bring up a bairn in this stinking place. We could live here as a couple for a year or two but we couldn't keep a bairn in a single end with the money we have to live on!" he argued.

"Maybe my mum could mind it," she said with tears in her eyes.

"With your dad at home all day, he'd have a fit! And your mum's got to work all day. Who'll mind it?" he said.

"Wee Grace," suggested Mary-Anne.

"No, I don't want it!" John bellowed.

"Well I do!" Mary-Anne bawled. "And I've been to the DRI and paid the deposit."

John's eyes lit up. "Ten bob! You've paid it?" he said in despair.

"Yes, I've paid the deposit and we need the rest before October so get working!"

He threw his hands up in the air. "You silly bitch!" he exclaimed. "I don't want it, you are not having it and definitely not in the hospital."

She spat back, "You try to stop me. I'll stab you, ye pig. It's yours, yours and I'm not having it… here!" She pointed to the floor with both hands.

She was frantic and flew at him like a vampire bat on its prey, sinking her teeth into his nose, blood spurting in all directions from the instant contact. "All right, all right! Don't go yer dinger at me, Mary-Anne," he pleaded. "Just get aff, I'M BLEEDING! Let me up!" he cried. "Ye're getting more like ain o'they bliddy high-cheekers every day!"

CHAPTER 9

Growth of the Empire

Dundee was booming with the growth of the population it had gained and, by the volume of the production of jute and flax, Dundee was 'Jutopolis'. In fact throughout the 1890s over half of Dundee's workforce worked in the textile sector and Dundee supplied the whole world.

The British Empire had colonised the Indian subcontinent originally to exploit the spice trade. As a side product, the raw materials of jute and flax were grown in abundance around Calcutta, nine thousand miles away from Dundee. Dundee, having the weaving skills, mainly due to an influx of Irish people and the mills to weave in, became the destination for the merchant ships carrying the cargo of jute and all other valuables from the Indian subcontinent.

The mill owners in Dundee had to deal with Calcutta for costing of the harvesting and exporting of raw materials from Bengal ports. The problems of safeguarding and securing the trade routes and timely voyage to Dundee were obvious.

In earlier empire campaigns, British sailing ships bound for the colonies capitalised on the trade winds traversing the globe across the Atlantic from east to west and return. For the Indian trade routes, however, it was necessary to move the jute-carrying vessels from north to south around the African continent and back without the benefit of trade winds.

This was the time of the British Empire; an empire four times greater than that of ancient Rome, and Britain was firmly in control of the Indian subcontinent. All the resources in India were there for the taking and the British took it, not least the jute barons of Dundee.

The only problems that remained were purely logistical: How to recover the raw material and how to transport it to Scotland in the quickest time possible in order to keep the mills working. The answer lay in new technology – and more empire building.

Maritime technology had advanced, since the days of transporting people by sea travel under sail alone. By the 1860s British merchant seagoing shipping was able to make use of steam power across the empire. It is a fact that a high-grade coal had been extracted from the African interior since 1865 and that was of obvious interest to the empire makers of Whitehall. The answer clearly was for the British government to provide fuelling stages for the merchant steamships around the southern tip of Africa, the Cape of Good Hope, from the Bay of Bengal. The opening of the new Suez Canal in 1869 with the first ship being HMS *Newport*, a British naval ship, signalled control of the short route to the Indian Ocean and access to the South African coastal coal ports. In reverse, the jute steamships invariably crossed the Indian Ocean to Southern Africa and put into the Indian Ocean ports of Durban, Richards Bay in Natal, or Port Elizabeth in the Eastern Cape. There they replenished the coal fuel and water bunkers and took on provisions for the rest of the journey.

The same logistic stops were used on the way back; this time the vessels were full of saleable trade goods, including jute products for military contracts. South Africa, therefore, became strategic safe havens for the loading of coal and bunkering of British merchant and naval vessels similar to the British-dominated Cape itself. South Africa also became a strategic foreign protectorate for fuelling shipping that carried raw materials to Dundee and, as an afterthought, as a money mountain to scoop out from the gold and diamond industries.

So important was coal, however, that a new unique coal-mining town in Natal was named *Coalopolis*. It was funded by private enterprise rather than by British government handouts. Coincidentally, in time the town became known as *Coaltown of Dundee*. By 1891 it was producing eighty percent of the total output of Natal and, at the same time, became officially known as Dundee, South Africa.

By 1893, fifty thousand British hopefuls had settled in the Cape of Good Hope and Britain began to benefit from the fledgling minerals industry opening up there. There was a need for the empire then to occupy southern Africa in numbers sufficient to safeguard investments and with adequate force to protect its British subjects and strategic stockpiles of fuel for the royal and British merchant navies.

CHAPTER 10

John Garland's Job

John Garland started off well. He joined Mary-Anne at the *Verdant Works* at the Scouringburn as a jute preparer. The jute boom was on and weavers and spinners were in demand. Mary-Anne started work early every day and the noise consumed her thoughts. She heard the weavers' looms start up at eight in the morning and run until seven in the evening when the mill workers changed over for the nightshift.

Blocking out her thoughts, the shuttles ran loud and fast like lightning back and forth, back and forth, on and on. *Clack, clack, clack,* the noise went on all day but strangely she felt in her own world, not having to think about anything else while she was in front of the looms.

The day he started work again, John spent the first hours learning the ropes in the *Verdant Works*. When it was over, he left at five knowing Mary-Anne was there until seven. He walked back to the Crescent and along John Street and into the close at number 10. John Murphy stepped out of the shadow of the stairwell at the end of the close and Garland shook with fright. "Hello Faither," he said to Murphy almost silently.

"You little shite," Murphy said. "There's a bairn coming and your wife is doing all the work, I see."

"I… I'm just learning the job this week, John, and I'll get the overtime next week."

"You're a hoormester, Garland, and now you've got Mary-Anne in the family way," Murphy said angrily. "You're no' likely to get her the money she needs any time soon, are ye?" he said. "I'm in debt because of you, and now she's depending on you to pay for the birth o' the bairn!" he said aggressively. "The way you've been treating her is not good enough and I'm no' having it!" John Garland went dry in the mouth, he tried to say something but couldn't. "Have you got that money for her before the bairn gets here? You'd better, or so help me God, I'll do ye in," said Murphy. "I'm watching you, Garland, and if you bugger it up I'll do ye in for sure. Got it?"

"Th… that's not so easy done, Faither. Mary-Anne wants to have it in the DRI and it'll cost a fortune!" replied John Garland, sheepishly.

"That's your problem this time, Garland, sort it – and don't call me Faither! – If ye were mine I'd wring yer frigging neck!" Murphy replied.

John Garland prised Murphy's fingers off his collar and slithered up the stairs. "John, John, ye're no' well," he said, knowing Murphy would not come up after him. John Murphy was getting older and weaker and the diabetes was beginning to take its toll. *Auld fool!* Garland thought and under his breath he muttered, "And she's got no chance of that money."

Spending his days in the same mill as his wife was not John Garland's idea of a good job. There was too much sexual tension in him and temptation with a mill full of young female weavers and spinners all around, and, he knew that John Murphy was watching him. No sooner had he served his trial week, he packed up again because it was 'too noisy for his ears' and he said he would see what his mates suggested at the beer tent this week; he would get something to suit him better.

Mary-Anne said nothing but just hoped that would be true. She needed him to save money for the bairn now and not spend it. At least she was in a steady job, for the time being, she thought, but she was going to have to tell the gaffer at some stage in the summer.

John found a few labouring jobs in various mills over the next six months but each one was 'not right' for him. He was spending more nights out at the Barrack Park than at home as Mary-Anne grew visibly bigger. *That at least keeps her inside,* he thought. *So there's something to be thankful for about this pregnancy,* he concluded.

Money was getting tight and John knew that this idea of a hospital birth had no chance of happening. "She will be having the bairn in the house like everybody else in the Crescent does," he told his pals in the beer tent.

Six weeks before her due date John went to the DRI and explained to the matron in the maternity ward that they had changed their mind about a hospital birth. He told them his mother-in-law had convinced Mary-Anne to make other arrangements for the birth and it would now happen at home.

He was most grateful to the DRI for their understanding and for their refund of the ten shillings deposit his wife had made earlier. So grateful in fact that he made a donation of a sixpence to the maternity ward charity box on the matron's table in the office, in full view of the matron and for all her staff to see. Back in the beer tent, he began to think of how he was going to break it to Mary-Anne.

John started to distemper the walls in the single end and make it bright and peaceful. *It's a single end,* he thought. *There is only so much that you can do to make it into a family home.* He decided he would get a couple of toys for the baby when it came but there was no point in spending money on that stuff now. *Not until it's here,* he thought. *Maybe her mum will bring it some things,* he thought. *That's a good idea, I'll wait and see who brings the toys.* He might not have to buy them after all, he thought. He had held a job down for a few weeks now and he was loaded for the first time in months. *That'll be needed to wet the bairn's head with,* he thought.

*

The horse-drawn tram dropped her off at the omnibus stop in front of the entrance of the DRI. It was only a month until she was due to have the baby and she wanted to know why they had never been in touch. She needed to make sure everything was organised with the hospital and nothing would stop them from keeping their side of the arrangement. Most of all, she wanted to see inside the mattie ward and how it looked.

The doorman helped her climb the stairs to the entrance and sat her down in the waiting room. "Matron Watson, please," she said. "Can you tell her Mary-Anne Garland is here to see her at three o'clock as arranged?"

The doorman looked puzzled. "Are you sure, Mrs. Garland?" he asked.

"I am!" she said. "I've got an appointment."

"Well… it's just that she is busy with another lady right now and I know she has another appointment with another lady at three!"

"Oh, I'll wait," said Mary-Anne, "there must be a wee mistake," and settled down to wait.

A few minutes before four, another couple came in and went

through the same routine with the doorman. "A four o'clock appointment, of course, it's in the book," he said. Mary-Anne was suddenly speechless, she felt hurt that her appointment had been overlooked for the second time.

The Matron walked into the waiting room and asked, "Which of you is Mrs. MacGregor?"

Mary-Anne stood up slowly and said, "I'm afraid you've made a mistake, I'm Mrs. Garland, and I have an appointment with you – at three?"

"No, I don't think so," the Matron said, looking at her schedule. "Mrs. Garland, right, it was on the list but it looks like, yes – it was cancelled a fortnight ago – by your husband I believe! And," she said, checking the notes in the book, "he was given a full refund of the registration fee." The Matron closed the appointments book.

"My husband!" Mary-Anne suddenly felt unable to carry her own weight and slumped back down in the chair. "Of course, it was…" Mary-Anne reluctantly accepted it as she again struggled up and out of her seat.

With head bowed, she silently and slowly walked out of the waiting room and out onto the street. Standing there, alone and pregnant in the cold rain, she made herself a promise, and she knew her life was about to change forever. As she moved out of the hospital grounds, in tears, her wet eyes transfixed on shimmering rain on the cobbles, she considered her future without John Garland, working out how and when she could get him out of her life. It had been a slow realisation and too late, that marrying him had been a mistake. Carefully and slowly, she shuffled down Infirmary Brae and down further to the top of the Parker Street steps at Garland Place. She leaned on the railings and looked down into the Crescent. *This dark stinking place won't be MY home for much longer,* she thought.

Mary-Anne returned to her single end, totally deflated and shattered. She had heard the words but couldn't digest what had just been revealed to her at the DRI. She said nothing to John Garland about the money he had appropriated as she tried to process the change in her head. She had come to understand clearly, though, that he was the reason that the birth would now take place in their single end. Sadly, she felt the beginnings of resentment for the child growing inside her as well as disgust for her husband and any empty words he could offer. At that point, Mary-Anne shed not a tear. She knew she had no option other than to stay with Garland and make the best of things until the baby was born.

On Joe Murphy's next home leave he met Mary-Anne by chance in their mother's home. Something had changed in Mary-Anne and Joe was left in no doubt that his beloved sister's relationship with her husband had changed. That night, Joe went to see John Garland at the beer tent before he returned to the army. "I may be leaving the Crescent, Garland, but I'm here to tell you that if you step out of line and upset my sister like that again, I will come back and do you!"

John Garland shook visibly because he knew what Joe was like and what he was capable of. John immediately agreed to be the perfect husband and father. His first job was to go and see the priest at St. Andrew's Cathedral and ask – no, beg – for help from the Parish for the cost of the birth. Joe left Dundee for his unit in Inverness the following day, hatred for John Garland burning inside him.

Father Sullivan was clearly cross. "You left it too late, you know. Mary-Anne should have applied months ago, these things take time."

"Yes, but my wife did not want to bother the church with this, you see, and we were going to have a hospital birth, but when she went to see them they were all full up," he lied.

The priest believed him without question, adding, "I understand. I don't trust the DRI births system and they couldn't organise a raffle, I'll see what can be done with the Parish at short notice."

The routine was well known to Mary Anne and she recognised the midwife when she let her into the flat. "That wall is wet!" the midwife said, looking at the distemper running off the plaster. "Where is the other room?" asked the midwife.

"It's a single end," said Mary-Anne, dejectedly. "This is where I'll be having it, er, the baby."

"Hmm … Hot water boiler and the coal in the grate to boil it on?" the midwife demanded. "Where are they?" She looked at John.

"I… I don't have a boiler, only a kettle and we don't cook anything in here," he said sheepishly. "We usually eat at the buster stall or from the chip shop."

Mary-Anne added, "My mum is bringing everything that we need for the birth and for the baby in a day or two. "I just forgot to tell him," said Mary-Anne.

The midwife looked from one to the other, shook her head, and said, "You're not prepared for this baby, are you?"

Mary-Ann darted a glance at John who stood there like a fool. "We have both been working full-time up until now and we just haven't had the chance to go shopping for these things yet," he said in his defence.

"You will need clean bedding, towels and baby clothes, buy them now!" the midwife instructed. "You can't set the clock by the baby's due date and you never know when it will arrive, it could be here any time now."

The midwife left them with a list of essentials and John went off to the High Street shops that were preferred by the Parish and who took the vouchers from the church. From her window in Littlejohn Street, Annie saw John Garland heading towards the High Street, and she made her way up to Mary-Anne's.

The midwife had talked her through the birth and Annie went over it all again also. She made sure Mary-Anne was fully aware of the birth process at home. Still, it was hard for Mary-Anne to accept that she had to go through giving birth physically and mentally in her single end in John Street. "I'll never forgive him for this," she seethed to her mother. "Never!"

Sad. That was the only word for how she really felt. So sad that she wished it was all over and done with but most of all she wished she had never got pregnant in the first place. Mary-Anne knew nothing about 'pre- and post-natal depression' or *'Melancholia'* as they called it, until the midwife went through it with her but even then, surely, once the baby arrived the problem in her head would go, she thought. Still, she felt so sad that she wondered if she was becoming depressed with *Melancholia.*

John Garland changed over the next few days and he filled up the flat with everything from warm clothing to nappies for the baby. Sanitising soaps and towels, linen and new clothes for Mary-Anne were provided – just in time. On the 31st of October at 4:50pm, baby Jessie Garland was born in the single end, at number 10 John Street. Only the midwife was in attendance, John Garland was in the beer tent.

Mary-Anne cradled her baby and the depression set in. John was working every day now but began to stay out after work rather than come home to see her and his child. Annie would come round every day when John was at work, to keep an eye on mother and baby but inevitably, she ended up taking Jessie from Mary-Anne to let her sleep. Mary-Anne was failing to bond with her baby, Annie could see that but denied it and told Mary-Anne it was normal and "it was just what happens with the first baby" and, that "all mothers get sad, it will pass very soon."

The midwife was concerned that Mary-Anne was not eating the right foods and she was sure that was the cause of the baby's fractiousness. "All the medicine in the world won't make any difference to the bairn if you're not feeding yourself with the right things. Fruit, milk and grain and vegetables – that's what you need," said the midwife, "but most of all, stay off the drink."

"It's just a wee drop of gin that John brings me on a weekend," Mary-Anne said. "That's not going to harm Jessie, is it?" She looked up at the midwife with her big hazel eyes.

"If you keep on drinking, I'm going to have to tell the Parish," the midwife said sternly staring into the sad eyes of Mary-Anne. "Then I'll not be able to come back and help you. So it's your choice – do what I say, or reap the consequences," warned the midwife earnestly.

"But I need the money, we can't all live off John's wages, not after he spends what he wants at the beer tent," she said in tears. "Don't tell the Parish, please," Mary-Anne sobbed.

The midwife's warnings made no difference to Mary-Anne. She kept on drinking the cheap gin John Garland brought home for her; sadly nothing escaped the midwife's notice. The letter arrived on the same day as the midwife was due. Typed on Parish headed paper, which told Mary-Anne it was from the St. Vincent de Paul Parochial Board, it was clear:

As a result of your less than perfect behaviour involving the consumption of alcohol in a confinement period, we are concerned that your child is at risk. In the event that this activity is not ceased forthwith, the Parish intends to withhold all benefits currently granted to you with immediate effect.

Mary-Anne was distressed beyond belief. "I canna take this from these rotten bastards!" she screamed. *Wait till that midwife comes back, I'll show her!*

At four o'clock Mary-Anne was steaming drunk in bed again. The baby was crying for her feed and there was no fire in the grate in the cold room. A bottle of *Old Tom* was nearly drained dry at the bedside and the midwife walked in. Expecting a change for the better, the midwife was horrified at what she saw. Mary-Anne flew at her immediately and a torrent of foul-mouthed threats and accusations intended for the midwife rang out loud in the air. The midwife picked up Jessie and Mary-Anne started slapping and punching the woman to a torrent of violent swearing. Protecting herself and the baby from this mad woman, the midwife bundled past Mary-Anne, knocking her back to the bed where she lay screaming.

The midwife walked to Annie's house and sat down, shaking with shock and fear. She handed the baby over to John Murphy and said, "Look after this one, it's your problem now."

"I'll take her from here," said Annie, after listening to the vivid description of why the Garlands were to be barred from the Parish and benefits thereof. Annie and John comforted the midwife and assured her that the baby would be fine in their care from that point onward.

John Murphy was livid. He knew that his grandchild was at risk and was angry with himself more than anyone else. *There is no going back to John Street for this wee girl,* he thought. "She's staying here with us!" he told Annie. In truth, they both knew that they could not keep Jessie from their daughter without a legal reason. "That'll come," he told Annie. "That'll come."

Annie and John expected that their daughter and her husband would make an appearance later that day and they prepared themselves for it. They were right. John Garland knocked at the door at half-past ten at night and stood there, at the door, half drunk. "Have you got Jessie here?" he asked.

John Murphy couldn't help himself. "Are you seriously asking me if we have your baby? Don't you know where she is?"

John looked at him in the eyes, man to man. "No."

He turned to descend the stairs when Murphy shouted, "Come back here, you bliddy piece of shite," and then, "of course she's here. Do you think we would leave her with that excuse for a mother you call your wife? You've been cut off from the Parish and all you can do is get blootered!" John Murphy roared at him in the stairwell. Garland had nothing to say to that. "You and Mary-Anne are just a pair of drunkards who don't deserve a bairn," said Murphy. "What would you people do if we were not able to look after her? You would never see her again because the council would put her in a home and jail the two of you," Murphy raged.

"Can I see my wee baby?" said Garland, fake tears in his eyes.

"No, you cannot – not in that state. Come back when you're sober and we'll talk about it, now get out of here!" said John Murphy, pointing down the stairs.

John Garland could be heard sniffling and crying all the way down the tenement stairs. "Oh Mary-Anne, Mary Anne, what have you done?" he said over and over. Then, "That bairn is more trouble than she's worth. How can we live without the money from the Parish?"

he said aloud on his way out of the *closey*.

The only way Mary-Anne saw her bairn again was to feed her, three times a day at Annie's place in Littlejohn Street. Annie supplemented the baby's feeds with powdered baby milk, which she could ill afford. Jessie stayed with the Murphys for the next six weeks before John and Annie were prepared to let their daughter have Jessie back again.

Mary-Anne knew that without the Parish help, she needed to get back to work quickly and she knew that her own mother was watching for any sign that she was drinking again. She kept up her good behaviour and was convinced she had cured herself of the depression by staying off the drink and working hard. It wasn't to last as John Murphy had forecast. Jessie was getting bigger and more demanding. Mary-Anne was just not up to it.

CHAPTER 11

Teething

The Crescent was silenced under a blanket of overnight snow and Jessie was very tetchy and irritable. She was going through the usual teething steps all babies of four months do, but Mary-Anne was going through all the trials and tribulations that all troubled new mothers do – only in her mind, it was worse – much, much worse.

She begged John Garland for money so that she could buy some medicine for the baby. Better still, she asked him to go to the priest to get money for a doctor. "Her gums are sore and one cheek is so red with the pain."

"Give me an hour to get some sleep in peace," he said, "and I'll go, but it's Sunday morning and I'll have to waken them up at the priests' house," he said through a hangover and only two hours' sleep. He moaned.

"I've not had any sleep for nearly two days, John," she said through the tears again, "and you've not been here to help me with Jessie in all that time. Look at her, John, she's been crying all night and her mouth is dribbling all the time. She's rubbing her ears, and her face is very red on the one side." Mary-Anne was going on and on but John knew that Jessie wasn't in that much pain. "She's having an awful time so hurry up, John!" Mary-Anne said.

John Garland had had enough. He dragged himself out of bed and shouted at the bairn, "Shut yer mouth, ye stupid lassie, I'm needing MY sleep!"

"She's just a baby, John, don't speak to her like that," said Mary-Anne, inconsolably crying as she spoke.

"That's it!" he boomed. "I'm away from here. You go to the Parish or the priest or whatever the hell ye want, but don't ask me, I'm no' going!" With that, he got dressed, still in a drunken stupor and muttering about leaving her and the bairn for good. He packed a bag and stormed out of the door.

Mary-Anne had no option but to get up with Jessie and go to her mother's house in the next street. "Can you mind her for an hour, Mum, 'til I see the Parish for help?" said Mary-Anne almost incoherently. "John Garland's left me and the bairn's no' well – I'm going to ask them for the doctor now," she said in a daze and in confusion for the want of sleep.

Annie knew instinctively what the problem was. "She's only teething," she cried out to Mary-Anne but Mary-Anne was gone in a flash, down the tenement stair and back out into the snowy streets. Annie had seen teething children many times and had nursed them through it the only way she knew how. "I'll help you, Jessie, you poor wee thing, I'll help you," she said as she comforted and hushed the baby.

She wrapped Jessie in a warm blanket and turned to her husband. "John, I'll be back in a half an hour," she said on her way down the stairs, with Jessie in her arms. She made her way out of the Crescent and along the Overgate where the hawkers in the stalls of Paddy's Market were just setting up. She knew all of them by name and quickly found out which of the girls were breast feeding at that time.

Mary O'Rourke was actually feeding little Jamesie at the back of the second-hand clothes stall when Annie walked around her stall. "This bairn needs a feed, Mary, can ye please help us out now?"

"Aye all right, Annie, I'm as sore as hell but in full flow anyway so bring her on!" Jessie sunk her gums onto the full teat and guzzled it for all its worth.

Annie had the market stalls to herself for a full half-hour before they opened to the regular Sunday customers. She picked up all the clove oils, aspirin and creams she needed to take the pain away. She also bought enough infant food and milk powder to feed a baby for a week. John Murphy was looking out the window for them when she got back to Littlejohn Street, Annie – laden but looking in full control; Jessie – full and fast asleep.

It was still snowing heavily when Mary-Anne reached the priests' house next to St. Andrew's Cathedral. Knocking on the door loudly she was abruptly stopped by the housekeeper who stared aggressively down her nose at her. "What do you think you're doing at this time on a Sunday morning?" the housekeeper, Mrs. Smith asked, without waiting for an answer. "Get out of here, you bliddy heathen!" She recognised Mary-Anne and said, "I know you, you're Mary-Anne Garland, are ye not? And you're barred from the Parish so ye won't get anything here anyway."

"I'm not here for the Parish, missus, but I need some money from the priest and a doctor for my baby, she needs some medicine, she's not well, ye ken," Mary-Anne answered.

"How dare you!" Mrs. Smith said. "Father O'Farrell is holding mass in the cathedral and the other priest has gone away to another mass in Kirriemuir, so he can't see you either, not today at least."

"I need the doctor for the bairn now!"

"What's wrong with the bairn?" Mrs. Smith asked, fearing the worst.

"Her face is all red on one side and she's crying and dribbling all the time. I think she's teething – it's terrible," Mary-Anne said through tears.

"If she's teething just rub some clove oil on her gums, she'll be fine."

"No, no! I need the priest for money to get a doctor for her now," said Mary-Anne, imagining the problem to be much worse than it really was. Mrs. Smith couldn't believe what this young woman was saying to her.

"Have you no family you could turn to?" the housekeeper said.

"Yes, the bairn is with my mother – she is minding her for me."

Mrs. Smith added, "There ye are then, you won't need the priest, then will you? Now away with you and don't be bothering him on a Sunday," said Mrs. Smith and gave her a sixpence to get rid of her, thinking to herself, *This woman's lost her mind.*

Mary-Anne turned away and started walking. She walked into the town and along the Nethergate. Apart from the Sunday morning churchgoers, no one was moving, and nothing was open that she could take shelter in. Still, in a daze, she kept walking in the snow, not knowing where she was going but she did know that she wasn't going home.

The bairn is with Mum, she reminded herself. *That's true, so why do I need to go for the doctor when my mum can take care of her anyway?* she asked herself. She kept on walking and walking. She walked up Thorter Row and along the High Street then found her way up the Wellgate and into Dudhope Street and eventually, Garland Place, heading for the top of the Parker Street steps.

When she reached the steps and looked down on the Crescent, knowing her baby was safe with her mother, she stopped. *There is nothing to go home for,* she thought and kept on walking. Ten minutes later she was in the Dudhope Castle grounds, desolate and overcast. She knew the fair was over for the winter but she also knew that Tam Pepper would be opening the boxing booth and the beer tent around the back of the castle without the permission of the law, as he always did.

In the freezing cold, she trudged through the ankle-deep snow, soaked to the skin. Looking for shelter she automatically went to the dying embers of the night watchman's brazier, vacated when daylight came in. The residual heat made her so tired that she hunkered down and fell asleep, there and then. After an hour, Mary-Anne awoke in front of the now-cold brazier. She moved as if in a dream; she knew where she was going all right, to the place where she had always gone with John Garland in the past. She reached the closed beer tent and found a way around the back.

Under the guy ropes of the tent was a hollow in the canvas where she had lain many times before with John. Dry, and out of the cold wind, she slept again until Tam Pepper opened up the bar and the boxing booth. "Pound a round," she heard him call. "A pound a round."

She needed something to keep the cold out and she knew what would work. She surprised the barker. "Tam, Tam, I'm waiting for John and he's got my purse."

"Mary-Anne, we haven't seen you for months, are you all right?" Tam Pepper asked. "I heard you had the bairn," said Tam.

"Aye, aye, I'm fine but I'm freezing, can you just give me a wee drop o' Old Tom gin, Tam? I've only got a tanner on me, Tam but, if ye can make it a half bottle – until John comes… on tick?" she lied. "Before the high-cheekers come in?" Then Mary-Anne said, "Actually, Tam, can ye make it a full bottle? He's going to be some time."

John Garland saw her at one in the morning, still in the beer tent drinking gin with the high-cheekers and he went straight up to her. "What the hell are you doing here? Where's the bairn?" he demanded. "Is she OK?"

"What is it to you?" Mary-Anne spat back at him, drunk and clearly brewing the flu. She had all but forgotten about the bairn and her teething trouble. When she opened her shawl, while remonstrating with her husband, he noticed the damp patches on her breasts and he realised she was lactating and she never even knew it.

"The bairn is none of your business; you said it when ye walked out this morning!" said Mary-Anne.

"You mean YESTERDAY, you drunken bitch!" he threw back at her.

"Wha… What time is it?" she asked her drinking companions.

"Nearly closing time," shouted Tam Pepper, "and your slate's full, Mary-Anne, we're closing."

"Tam, will ye just let me have a bottle of Old Tom then, just to keep the cauld out?"

John Garland and Mary-Anne walked home to the Crescent in silence… but together. He, sober and angry; she, drunk, depressed and deadbeat. Neither of them particularly missing Jessie. They reached the Crescent and tried to avoid being seen descending the steps together, then they went straight to their single end in John Street and slept together until the next day.

The baby had been tended to and cared for perfectly well for the three days since her parents went missing. John, Annie and wee Grace had it all to do but they all fussed over baby Jessie who never wanted for anything… except her mother.

They made up a cot of sorts in the corner of the big bedroom and Annie and John cradled and soothed her in turns in the night. During the day, young Grace would feed her with a bottle and help change her nappies and clothing they got at Paddy's market. The place was always warm at least, John Murphy had seen to that with the sticks and the bits of coal he scavenged from the railway sidings at the train station every day. He was not a well man, though; he felt the cold going right through him these days regardless of how many layers of clothing he had on. His eyesight was going and with no appetite, he lost more weight every week. John Murphy hated to be like this but his strength was going and he truly was an invalid. Still, he had a growing hatred for John Garland in his heart that would keep him going until he was sure Mary-Anne was free of him. How and when that was to happen he did not know. All he did know was that Garland was going to get his comeuppance – or it would kill him in the process.

Wee Grace kept her father well informed of what was happening at number 10 John Street. He also knew Mary-Anne was last seen drunk and incapable in the beer tent on Sunday night past. He was aware that Garland fetched her home from the beer tent and, that they had both disappeared for the next two days. He knew that his daughter had been back to the beer tent again on the third day presumably to pay back her tick bill and start another one.

John Murphy had the baby in his arms when he answered the door the next morning, Grace at his side. It was Garland. "Garland! What are you here for?" he questioned. "Where's Mary-Anne?"

Garland replied, "She's at home, John, she… she hasn't been well but I'm looking after her and she's getting better."

"Why, what's wrong with her?" Murphy asked worriedly.

"She's got a terrible flu and we didn't want Jessie to get the same," said John Garland.

"Is that why you have been missing for three days, the pair of ye?" roared Murphy. John Murphy handed the baby to Grace and told her to take Jessie inside as the red mist rose in him.

When she had closed the door, Murphy turned round to face Garland and booted him in the gut so hard he doubled up with pain and onto his knees. A second kick caught him square in the face and Garland flew backward down the stairs. The satisfaction on Murphy's face said it all.

Garland lay there dazed and bewildered, not knowing how it happened or why. Annie stepped over him when she came up the stairs and she thought, *I knew that was coming. You deserve it, Garland, you bastard!*

Four days after she left her baby with her mother, Mary-Anne sobered up and made herself look decent and acceptable to her parents. In real fear for her life she had had a little gin and gargled with peppermint water to take any trace of it away and then, putting the last days out of her mind, she took a deep breath and knocked on the door of her parents' home.

Flowers in one hand, baby food and clothing in the other, she put on the sorriest face that she could muster. John Murphy answered the door with a start; he had been waiting for this. "What are you after? You had better no' be looking for yer bairn!"

She felt the pain of the deepest sob in her heart. "I am… I am back for Jessie and I'm sorry Dad, I meant to come yesterd—" John

Murphy slammed the door shut in her face. "I don't know what I was thinking… But I know what you think now!" she wailed at the door. "I know that I'm a bad mother and I left my baby, but I was sick with fever!" she cried. "And I think I'm no' well with that *melancholia – depression* ye get after having a baby."

Annie called from the inside, "Go away, Mary-Anne, you'll fleg the bairns. Come back when ye stop drinking!"

Mary-Anne was completely shocked. *They know I've been drinking!* she thought. *How can they know that?* Shattered and bewildered, her mind raced through all the possibilities. *Tam Pepper would never tell them, the high cheekers wouldn't tell them and I haven't seen the girls in the mill for weeks,* she thought on. *Wee Grace!* It dawned on her. *That little bitch!*

Jessie finished teething without much more drama. She was toddling before she was one year old and by the age of fifteen months, she was still staying at her granny's. She knew her way down the tenement stairs and out into the cobbles and watched wee Grace and the big girls playing *really-foe*. She joined in happily with the games like shoppies and scraps when she was allowed. Living at her granny's was a pleasure for Jessie, who seemed to like her grandparents better than her parents.

Mary-Anne started back at the mill in March of 1897, a full month after her mum and dad first kept her baby from her. Since then she had gone through hell for months without a drink, but her resolve was strong. She was able to get off the drink and whatever made her do these things and she was ready to get her bairn back. She realised, her real problem was John Garland, he led her astray and she followed like a child. *How can I leave him?* she pondered without answer.

*

Jessie stayed with her grandparents for nearly a year before Annie and John Murphy were satisfied that Mary-Anne was well enough to allow their granddaughter to go back home. Annie knew what she had to do and had no choice other than to hand the child over. John Murphy was in pieces knowing that Jessie was leaving.

"You look after this wee girl, Mary-Anne, or we will take her back again," Annie said with tears in her eyes.

"And if you canna look after her or if you do anything to harm her, you're going to lose her – for good the next time," her father said.

Mary-Anne gathered up the toddler and a few toys and took her back to John Street.

The millwork was hard for John Garland on the backshift but that was the only way they could both look after Jessie and work at the same time. Mary-Anne struggled to keep him out of the beer tent at night when he finished work and, of course, she struggled to get him up in the early morning to take over minding Jessie to let her get to work.

After a year of sporadic millwork John Garland had had it with the lot of them. He had been whining and moaning to Mary-Anne about the bairn since she came back to live with them. "I don't see why I've got to mind Jessie when your mother and sister are doing nothing other than sitting in their house in John Street." They would be glad to have her, he figured, "So, why the hell not?" he demanded.

Mary-Anne finally gave in to him. She agreed to ask Annie for her help again. Mary-Anne dressed Jessie in her 'going out' clothes, gathered up all the child's toys and bedding she could carry.

John Garland followed with a box full of baby food and medicines and her spare shoes and everything else that they associated with Jessie and they all walked around the Crescent to number 8 Littlejohn Street. When they arrived at the *closey*, John Garland walked as far as the bottom of the stairs, and put the box down on the stone floor, turned around and left for the beer tent without a word of goodbyes.

Mary-Anne climbed the two flights of stairs to her mother's house and chapped at the door. "We're here!" she shouted as she carried Jessie over the threshold. John Murphy was silently elated at the idea; he had fallen for his granddaughter and his heart melted at the thought.

"I'm no' a wet nurse OR a kettle biler," Garland roared at Mary-Anne when he came back from the beer tent that night. Mary-Anne was in floods of tears.

"Mary-Anne, you can see her at yer mother's on yer way home from work but I'm not going near that mad auld man o' yours so ye can forget that."

John Garland stopped working in the mill all together and, could be seen hanging around the fairground with the high-cheekers helping out in the beer tent or in the boxing booth for beer money. That was his contribution to the family coffers.

Mary-Anne was distraught and falling deeper into this depression she had worried about. She was desperate to leave him and, if she could find a way of walking out of the marriage, she would. John Garland had no intention of going back to the mills on account of the noise officially but, in truth, he couldn't take being told what to do by the gaffers. He also had no intention of babysitting Jessie ever again. His wife was back working, *And that is that,* he thought. No need for him to go back to the mills – ever.

He decided he'd carry on working with the high-cheekers until something else came up; he thought he might even go with them the next time they go on the road. Anything would be better than "biding in a single end with a screaming wife", he told his mates at the fairground, although, he never told them he had given his daughter away. John Garland was nowhere to be seen again that summer but Mary-Anne visited Jessie regularly on her way home.

CHAPTER 12

Wee Grace in the Jute Mill

Grace Murphy started the summer school holidays in July as usual, but she told her mother she was more interested in getting a job than playing in the street for seven weeks. Annie relented and took Grace to the mill across the Lochee Road. She was ten years old now and legally allowed to work part-time after school and during the holidays. The weaving mills were busy as usual and the Verdant took her on as a helper for the weavers. She learned the job quickly and happily took her three bob that she worked 15 hours a week for. *That would be fine,* Annie thought, *and especially as Grace is growing up so fast.*

With her jet-black hair and big brown eyes, *She will be looking to make the best of herself,* her mother thought.

Annie could see that Grace was beginning to need new clothes and she would be thrilled to be able to buy the new fashionable clothes and shoes for herself that she spoke about. *That lassie will do well, starting to work at her age, bless her,* thought Annie.

By the time the summer holidays were over, Grace started working after school and went directly to the mill at one o'clock each day. She was so familiar with the looms that by this time, when the gaffer wasn't looking, the weavers would give her a shot at shifting the bobbins up and down the loom to the other end and back again, then sending the shuttles along to the opposite end of the loom by hand when the spun jute for the weave was finished in the weft.

Annie knew that she was in good hands with the weavers and anyway, this part-time job was keeping Grace away from Mary-Anne when she was visiting the bairn at home. Annie had felt the animosity between them when they were in the same room and, *You could cut the atmosphere with a knife,* she thought. Anything that could be done to keep them apart was done with relish, so Grace's job was a godsend, and, she was bringing in her own keep.

The noise was something she got used to but the speed of the shuttle flying back and forth frightened her. At that point, she couldn't help but close her eyes when it approached her hands. The problem was that the shuttles were all moving fast at once on all the looms. The shuttles slowed down at the end of each run across the weave when the spun jute ran out. Grace, in a moment of confusion went to catch the shuttle in the loom but it was not slowing at the end of the weaving, it was in full flight and Grace's hands were inside the machine.

Grace wasn't thinking about the loom, she had been thinking about her sister and her baby when the shuttle hit her. She never felt a thing. All she saw was the spray of her own blood spurting high above her head. Bits of the shuttle exploded on impact with her hand and splinters flew in all directions. Through the haze of the jute fibre in the air and the noise of the looms and shuttles all around her, stunned, she sat down on the floor of the mill and was mildly amused at the shrieks of the weavers above the noise, who saw it all. She looked at her left hand; it was fine except for the blood. She looked at her right hand and was puzzled at the shape of it. There was a huge swelling in her palm and what was left of her fingers.

A deep cut ran across her fingers except for her index finger. A river of blood flowed from the forefinger of her right hand and… it wasn't there. It was severed at the second knuckle and that was the source of the steady flow of blood. When the shock wore off and the pain hit her, Grace was left in agony, writhing on the mill floor.

The gaffer wrapped a huge blanket over her hands and carried her to the waiting works ambulance outside the sick room. At the DRI they cleaned the little girl up and stopped the bleeding when they could but most of the finger was gone. "It's disappeared," they said, "in the mess and confusion with the bits of the shuttle that exploded."

Grace spent the day in the accident and emergency ward in the DRI. They stitched her hand and put it in plaster to keep it still. With a huge bandage, she was given a sedative and kept in for observation overnight. Annie was fetched by the girls at work and told of the accident. She and John took young Jessie to John Street where Annie left John in the street and ran up to the top floor with her. "There." She forced the toddler into John Garland's arms. "You take her and keep her until I come back for her," she cried. "Grace has had an accident and I'm away to the DRI to see her."

John and Annie took the tram to the hospital where Grace was being treated and the feeling of dread came flooding back to John when the memory of the last time he was in there, sunk in. They stayed well into the dark night and only left when they were sure Grace was sleeping soundly.

"We'll come back for you tomorrow, my wee lamb," Annie said and with that they left for the Crescent. They walked the familiar steps down Infirmary Brae and down the Parker Street steps.

John said, "I'm just going to see how Jessie is doing up at Mary-Anne's flat," and with that, he climbed the four flights to the front door of the single end.

He caught his breath and knocked at the door but got no answer. He knocked again and this time, the door swung open. Inside there was no gas light on but he could hear Jessie crying in the room. Fumbling for the gas mantle, he struck a match and lit the gaslight and, looking down, saw Garland fast asleep on the bed and the empty gin bottle beside him.

The red mist came back to John Murphy. There was no sign of Mary-Anne and, hurriedly in a panic, he picked up the bairn and turned to face the door. The pain hit him in the middle of the chest and shot to his throat. John Murphy managed to sit Jessie down on the floor and tried to shout for Annie. As she stooped down to help him, Annie could see that her husband was dead at her feet. Jessie stopped crying and John Garland kept on sleeping, oblivious to the fact his father-in-law lay cold and still in his home.

At 11:30pm on August 13th, 1898, Mary-Anne walked in the room to find the scene of carnage in her single end. Her mother was in tears, trying to waken John Garland who was comatose and prostate on the bed. Her father lay dead on the floor and the baby started to cry on seeing her again. Mary-Anne just did not know what to do first. She reached into her shoulder bag and took out the gin.

"At his daughter's home in 10 John Street," John Garland told the doctor who officiated. "Heart attack, I think, Doctor," John Garland said pretentiously.

"Er, h'mm, yes, thank you Mister Garland," said Doctor Jacob. "Cardiac failure and diabetes, no doubt – no suspicious circumstances," the doctor said as he signed the death certificate.

"That's fine, Doctor, thank you," Garland said in reply, and, "Yes, I was there when he passed away, it was my house, you see, and I was minding the bairn for him."

The next day, Annie sent John Garland to fetch young Grace from the DRI but he missed her. By the time he got there, she had gone.

She still had a huge bandage and her right arm was in a sling. *Nobody has been to see me!* thought Grace, forlornly as she walked down the steps into Parker Street. *I caused my accident and now my mum and dad won't speak to me again,* Grace thought. She had waited and waited until four o'clock and knowing they should have been there at twelve to sign her out of the hospital, she decided to sneak away without the nurses knowing and walk back home alone after the hospital released her.

Her mother was with Mary-Anne in the living room and the younger two were playing on the stairs when she got home. Mary-Anne was making sandwiches and there was a large plate of hot scones on the grate.

"Where's my dad?" Grace asked.

"Oh! Grace, John was just coming for you, really he was," said Mary-Anne.

Annie was sitting in her husband's usual chair and looking downwards, holding her head in both hands. Knowing something was wrong with her, Grace pushed past her sister. "Mum, where's my dad? Has something happened?"

Annie took her daughter by the uninjured hand and simply cradled her in her bosom. Slowly and softly, Annie said, "He's gone, Grace, he died… with a heart attack."

Grace looked at her mother square in the eyes and said, "Was it me? I mean was it my fault?" tears welling up.

Mary-Anne looked at her for a minute and scowled then dismissed her question out loud with, "No, it wasn't you – how could it be your fault?" She looked at Grace with sadness in her eyes. Annie said, "It couldn't be helped, Grace, his time had come."

"He's in the bedroom and people are coming to see him tonight. We're having a wake," said Mary-Anne without lifting her eyes from the task at hand. "Oh, how is yer hand, Grace?" she said loudly as if it were just a scratch.

"My... My hand is OK... What happened to Dad?" Grace asked both of them, imploringly.

No answer was forthcoming and she made for the door of the bedroom. Annie sprung to her feet. "No, don't go in there, Grace, it's not time to see him yet."

"But you're having a wake!" Grace said.

"Yes but that's when his brothers will be here and we can all go in at the same time," said her mother.

John Garland came out of the bedroom door and walked in to join them in the living room. "Ah, Grace." He smiled. "I went to the DRI but you were gone. Where did you get to?" he asked, not caring a jot.

"John, what are you doing in there with my dad?" Grace asked, not believing what she just saw.

"How's your arm?" Garland asked Grace.

Again, she replied, "OK... But it's not my arm, it's my finger," she corrected him. Irritated and confused, she asked again, "Why were you in there?"

"Just making sure your dad was looking well for the wake, that's all, Grace." John Garland was feeling good inside. He had just been looking at proof that John Murphy had truly departed from his mortal coil, as they say, and picked up almost a pound in change from

Murphy's personal effects at the same time. *Life is good,* he thought.

Mary-Anne's brother Joe walked in the door that night in his uniform. "I got the message from the Adjutant this morning. I'm home for the funeral."

John Murphy's brothers came in bang on eight o'clock dressed in their Sunday best, their bonnets in hand and they both carried flowers for Annie. A few friends from the street including all the McKees and the Garlands from the next close were next. By nine o'clock the flat was filling up with John's old hawker friends and a bunch of hard men bare knuckle boxers from the pubs. The Boilermakers were last to stagger in, representing the shipyard and that was the start of the wake proper. As requested, John Murphy was suited up and was looking better than he had been for years, thanks to the undertakers, Annie thought.

The open coffin was placed in the middle of the quilted bedspread on top of the bed. Annie, Mary-Anne and Grace were led in by John Garland and were the first of the family to see him in his coffin. Little Jessie trailed along hanging on to Grace's frock to stay close but couldn't see a thing of her dead grandfather.

Mary-Anne moved quickly past the corpse and out of the door to the grate. "I need to get the food out," she stated before anyone could think ill of her.

All who assembled in the bedroom around the coffin were treated to a version of 'I'll Take You Home Again, Kathleen' by the Murphy brothers who, by all accounts were well oiled before the wake started. They made their peace with the McKee brothers out of respect for the deceased but left John Garland out of the pact.

The bedroom filled up with the talk of men's deep voices and pipe tobacco and cigarette smoke. Between the four of them, the rendition was an assault on the ears of all in attendance but when accompanied by one of the hawkers on the mouth organ, became passable.

The men, lighting up their dog ends of Capstan full strength, some others puffing away on clay pipes, the hawkers joined in all the songs and started a few of their tinker tales in the background. "Get me a couple o' spoons, will ye Grace? He'll never keep the tune on that moothie," said old Jim McKee, a hammer man in the Caledon.

"And a bit o' paper for my comb!" shouted one of the other hawkers.

"Let's have *Danny Boy*, Mister McKee, you're good at that," one of the Boilermakers said and with that, the party started.

More Irish than Scottish songs were ventured and grew louder and louder as the night went on and as darkness fell. A warm and happy feeling descended on the room that night and the drink flowed freely but messily. Beer was spilled with gin and whisky all around including on top of John Murphy. "If that doesn't bring him back," Peter said, "then I suppose he's not coming."

The laughter resounded up and down Littlejohn Street into the night. Some were crying, some were singing, and some were getting cross at getting spilled on. John Garland was having a great time and, as usual, he sprayed drink onto everyone he spoke to in that inebriated state.

The drink took control and Joe Murphy took the opportunity of sticking the nut on John Garland at the best chance he had. "He's drunk," Joe stated in defence, "and he dribbled beer all over my uniform." Nobody thought that was out of order and the assembled let it go at that. Catherine Garland, his sister, voiced not a care about the head-butt nor, unsurprisingly, did Mary-Anne, his wife, who was more interested in the contents of a bottle of Old Tom gin at the time.

Blood flowed but the songs continued.

The Boilermakers' songs merged into the Irish songs and the pub songs grew louder than all the others. The smoke in the room got thicker as the singing grew louder. Occasionally, laughter rang out as stories of the hawkers and John and his *cartie* came out. The consensus was of how good a father and brother John had been. It was a good wake. Only Grace and Annie alone were not enjoying the event and they sat on the tenement stair in tears with Jessie and the other children until the wee small hours when the last of the drinkers left.

Together Grace and Annie quietly walked back into the bedroom to see John for the last time. To their total astonishment, they discovered the coffin was closed and covered with folding money. "What good friends John had," Annie whispered. "That's more than enough for a decent funeral." Her heart warmed with human kindness. They said a prayer and stood in silent testament to the man they both loved. The pain was beginning to ease in Grace's hand but not in her heart; Grace would never forget her father.

Annie spent an unnerving hour in the bedroom while the coffin was lying on the bed. She was thankful that in her absence, the Murphy brothers had been happy to oblige her with the task of nailing it down securely. She looked in all John's clothes and even under the bed where he kept suitcases and boxes of old personal effects and keepsakes. "I know he had some change in his pockets when we came back from the DRI after visiting Grace," she said to Mary-Anne and the rest of the family, "but I can't find it." She said, "John Garland was the only person in there alone but he wouldn't dare." Tommy and Joe looked at each other without saying a word.

Mary-Anne was beyond caring what her mother was saying to her. "I'm going home, Mum… unless you've any gin left then I'll stay with ye all night."

"No, off you go, lovie, and thanks for all your help today," Annie said wearily.

"That's OK, he was MY father as well ye know," she said, then she kissed her daughter Jessie goodnight and went off to see what her husband had done with the money he stole from her dead father.

John Garland denied it. "You can't think much of me if you believe I took money out of his pocket when he was lying in his coffin!"

Mary-Anne said, "No, I don't, and I don't think much of you anyway," and opened another bottle of Old Tom. "Where did you get the money to buy the gin then?" she quizzed him.

"Well, I did take a couple of ten-bob notes from the collection before the lads closed the coffin, just for my time and work with the wake and all that. The Murphys never seen a thing," John Garland said smugly.

Tommy and Joe couldn't bring themselves to tell their mother what they suspected but resolved to have a word with John Garland and Mary-Anne. "The funeral comes first," the boys agreed and kept the theft they suspected secret 'until the right time'.

Tommy and his mother went to see the priest at St. Andrew's Cathedral the next day. "Thank you for seeing us, Father," Annie said. "It seems we can change our plans and have the funeral from here, if you can do that?"

Father O'Farrell smiled kindly and, with a condescending frown said, "Well, I would be happy to oblige you Mrs. Murphy but, I'm afraid that will be very costly."

Knowing the Murphys had been habitual partakers of Parish

charity through the church for years, he was quite sure it was out of their financial reach. "A Catholic mass and a burial service, with hearse carriage, plus ground will run to over fifteen pounds." The priest went on, "Would you like to rethink your options on that basis, Mrs. Murphy?"

"No thanks, Father, we'll manage." Annie turned to Tommy. "Show the priest that we have the money, Tommy."

At that point, Tommy produced a wad of ten-shilling and one-pound notes. "Twenty-five pounds ten," he said. "How much is a headstone, Father?" he asked proudly.

At eleven o'clock on the 18th of August, the requiem mass was said in the cathedral with all the panache and flummery that the Murphys could get for the money. The horse-drawn funeral carriage was followed by another horse-drawn carriage, which held all the family except John Garland. Tommy expressly told him, "No room for you, John, you'll have to make your own way to the graveyard." The burial went ahead smoothly as planned at the new Howff graveyard in Bell Street. Joe Murphy had another week before he had to be back in Aldershot and he knew precisely how it was going to be used.

CHAPTER 13

The Jute Barons

Meanwhile, the jute barons of Dundee in Scotland were enjoying a monopoly on global jute manufacture. Baxter Brothers and Co. of Dundee had built their own batching plants and jute mills in Bengal, India, and managed them by loyal Dundonian mill supervisors. They were there to ensure a steady supply of raw materials to Dundee.

The workers in Calcutta made enough money for most people to live on. Bengal became a better place to be in general because the jute crop was in demand by the mill owners in Dundee. The workers in Dundee made the mill owners into rich jute barons mainly by way of the volume of military orders for the British Empire. The mills took all the orders for jute products they could get. On the back of the mill owners' wealth, the corporate taxation generated in Dundee mightily enhanced the British Government coffers by the sweat and toil of the Dundee mill workers in the most deplorable conditions for the least recompense.

Jute bagging and jute sacks from the Dundee mills were used to carry cotton from the American South, grain from the great plains of North America, coffee from the East Indies and wool from Australia. Jute was also the preferred material that the British army required for the containment of supplies to Southern Africa in support of the expansion of the next target of the British Empire: South Africa. In fact, Dundee jute was the preferred product and the jute barons' mills were the preferred suppliers for military contracts from opposing armies the world over.

After the India campaign, the gradual British annexation and occupation of Southern Africa was brutal and in obvious violation of all agreements with the Boers (or Dutch settlers who sparsely occupied the land). It had started in the 1860s with the need to secure Durban, then Natal, for the empire to secure safe passage for shipping on the Indian trade routes.

The discovery of gold in the Transvaal and then diamonds in the Cape Province created a stampede of diggers and miners from Britain so that the Empire simply was obliged to assist and help itself to the proceeds.

The more the Boers farmed South Africa, the more the United Kingdom scrambled for the land for its own exploitation of minerals within the ground. The Crown and Empire desired the shiny yellow stuff and diamonds to fill the coffers of Whitehall cheaply so that they could redress the cost of the loss of the New World colonies of the Americas after the declaration of independence of the United States.

The Afrikaner farmers or *Boers* as they were known, squared up to the British Empire and defied the British. Without a formal, regular army, the only way the Boers could defend their land initially was by political negotiation backed up by guerrilla warfare tactics.

British mining, engineering and exploitation of gold and diamonds were issues the Boers were prepared to negotiate but allegiance to the Union Jack was entirely another matter. From 1890 almost a decade of ongoing guerrilla war ensued in order to defend their legal rights from the British.

Britain, however, needed more strength and increased their force by the sweat and blood of their young men. In particular, Scottish regiments were ideal for the task; they were hard, loyal and most of all, expendable to the crown. The more the British army was deployed, the more guerrilla warfare continued in South Africa. The Highland Division including Dundee's own 2nd and 3rd battalion of the Black Watch was the instrument of choice in many of the brutal battles that ensued during the decade.

CHAPTER 14

The Beer Tent

Towards the end of 1898, the fair and travellers were on the move out of Dundee and the high-cheekers were heading for Brechin. In truth, John Garland wanted to be with them but his commitments to Tam Pepper in the illegal beer tent forbade that – in the meantime. His commitments to his wife and child, however, waned to nothing.

Tommy Murphy and his brother Joe walked in the shadows around the back of Dudhope Castle into the beer tent. John Garland was behind the bar and asked them, "How're ya doing, lads?"

Tommy said, "Remember that money you stole from my father when he was lying dead in his coffin?" He had surprised Garland with that comment and Garland's mouth dropped open. "Well I've come to get my share," said Tommy.

"And me," said Joe.

"Now wait a minute, lads! I never stole anythi—" He never finished the sentence.

From across the bar, Joe hit him with a right hook and Tommy caught him with a left, spinning Garland back again, to the back wall of the tent. Joe jumped coolly over the bar to finish the business while Tommy turned his back on the fight and stood facing the men in the bar, as if daring anyone to step in.

Joe made it an art of thumping John Garland into semi-consciousness. With effort, Tommy eventually pulled Joe off the comatose Garland and the men in the beer tent stood back and witnessed the most brutal beating of a man they would ever see. For once, Tam Pepper was impressed. His 'tache twitched but he never said a word. Neither did the men in the tent when it was over. Tam Pepper made a mental note to see Joe Murphy in due course about a job in the boxing booth in future.

Joe and Tommy walked out of the beer tent and straight down to the Crescent to tell Mary-Anne everything. Joe had a few more days' leave to take before he had to be back to the army base at Fort George in Inverness. He stayed with Mary-Anne to make sure Garland never returned to give her any more grief. They talked for hours about the good old days when they were small. It was the same each day until the time came for him to leave. He looked after his sister that week just like she had looked after him when she brought him up. His sister was the most important person in his life, and he would never forget that, and neither would she.

John Garland didn't surface for a week. Fear, pain and confusion kept him at his latest floozy's place hiding away from the young Murphys. Mary-Anne was nonplussed at his disappearance and kept on working and never spoke a word as to his whereabouts. *Hell mend him,* she thought every day he was missing.

He knew he was leaving Mary-Anne and Jessie, just as soon as he found somewhere to go, but most of all John Garland just had to get out of the Crescent.

CHAPTER 15

The Boer War

The Black Watch recruiting sergeants were doing a roaring trade in their stall at Dudhope Castle and when he could, John Garland spent his spare time with them, quizzing them about life in the army. They correctly advocated that there was no work in Dundee for young men but the army offered a good future for anyone who was unemployed. Garland was also informed that the British army intended to invade South Africa and that well over 400,000 men were being made ready for war on top of the 48,000 already there. The empire needed more young men there, like him.

John Garland's wife had shown no interest in him since the birth of the bairn and even the bairn didn't talk to him, or even know him! "I've got to get out of here, right enough," he said to himself. He spent another half an hour in the recruiting sergeants' tent, then he committed to three years and signed up to the Royal Highlanders, 2nd Battalion, the Black Watch. "There is so much going on in South Africa," he said, "and it looks like there's going to be another Boer War," he told Mary-Anne when he finally went to see her.

They hardly looked at each other when she let him in the door. "I've joined up, I'm going to get paid, fed, a free uniform and a gun," he said to Mary-Anne, trying to make a joke of it, but essentially, he was telling her he was leaving her. It was the only thing that made sense to him anymore. Life had been bad to him this year; he never had enough time to himself for working with Tam Pepper and he couldn't stand being with his wife in that stinking little single end.

He told Mary-Anne that she was better off without him and he said, "Mary-Anne, I've just got to do my duty for my queen and country and, I've just signed all the papers."

Mary-Anne wasn't particularly interested. "When are you leaving?" she asked.

"Tomorrow, I leave for Inverness on the steam train at ten in the morning," he announced.

"Will you see Jessie before you go?" asked Mary-Anne, indifferently, aware of his black eyes.

"No, she wouldn't like to see me like this and I don't want to get her upset."

"Alright," she said and drew a deep breath and then breathed a long sigh of relief. John Garland quietly left the Crescent with just a small valise over his shoulder and never looked back.

"Can I move back in with you, Mum?" Mary-Anne said at the end of the week. "It's just that I can't really afford the rent on John Street without John's money to help out, not that it made much difference. And now Dad's gone, I thought there might be space in your bedroom."

Annie replied, "Wee Grace is sleeping with me in the meantime, but we can get a bed made up in the front room," she said in reply before she had really thought it through. Annie didn't like the idea, but she did need time to spend with wee Grace to help get her fingers better. "OK, but you'll need to take responsibility for Jessie again. Do you think you can do that?" Annie asked.

"Of course I can, she's MY daughter," said Mary-Anne.

John Garland underwent a successful medical on arrival at Fort George Inverness barracks, in spite of sporting the remains of two black eyes. He completed recruits' training in 10 weeks. He trained hard and did well and excelled on the shooting range. Armed with the new short magazine Lee Enfield automatic rifle, mark one, firing .303 calibre rounds, he felt it was made just for him. All he wanted to do was leave Scotland and get into the theatre of war as soon as possible.

Garland passed the recruits' course and, at the rifle range, was awarded the marksman badge of honour. He was posted to Aldershot barracks where he remained awaiting an overseas posting. On arrival at the barracks, Corporal Billy McKee collared him in the mess and welcomed him into the regiment. Thereafter, much reminiscing about the Crescent ensued.

"Do you remember that night in the Pentland bar in Lochee?" asked John. "What a fecht Billy, eh?"

"I do," said Billy, "and we showed them not to bugger the Black Watch about that night, Billy retorted.

"Aye, quite right," John added, "but we'll go back and see what the Pentland Bar boozers think of the Watch when this South Africa shite is over, eh?"

"Dead right, John," said Billy. "Dead right."

Twice in that year he was allowed home leave but John Garland never went home. He tagged along with his new Edinburgh mates from his unit rather than go back to Dundee. He wore the red hackle with pride and, in his Tam O'Shanter headgear with his battledress and kilt, he felt every bit a soldier, and a different man.

He was going to make this adventure his own and he would return to Mary-Anne a hero and a changed man, he decided. All he needed was to put the time in and let his training take him through the next chapter of his life.

Billy McKee was going through the ranks. He was made up to sergeant just before his own leave was due and was able to make arrangements for himself and George in the Seaforths, to travel together back for an R&R weekend in Dundee before the regiments were posted to South Africa.

Mary-Anne looked at the calendar and suddenly realised John had been gone almost a year. Living at her mother's place was good in the beginning but Jessie was getting bigger and more demanding than she could cope with, for her liking.

When Grace returned to work at the mill, she carried on like nothing had happened. "She's a tough one," Mary-Anne said to one of the older women spinners, "she'll do well here." At home, Grace was behaving like a spy whenever they were all together but she was back at school for most of the time, then at the *Verdant Works* after school. All in all, it was a manageable arrangement with Annie keeping control of the purse strings in and out of the home.

It was, however, no small comfort to Mary-Anne when the McKees came home from the army on leave and she and Catherine Garland got back into the pubs along the Overgate with the brothers. Billy McKee in his uniform, now wearing his sergeant's stripes, looked the epitome of the man she had always wanted. "In the Black Watch," he told the ladies, "the men are hard and trained to do or die on command," he boasted. "Most importantly, they do it for the mothers, wives, and all the other Scottish women they know for they are the mothers of the future generations of Scots." The girls liked that and they were captivated by the life he described. He also told them all he knew of the conflict in South Africa that he had been briefed on, and that he was sure they were going to war.

They talked briefly that night about her husband and how surprised Billy was to see John Garland had joined up. Mary-Anne made it clear she did not miss him under any circumstances and Billy's interest in her grew. She was more concerned, however, with the life in the Crescent that John Garland had left her with, due to him not sending any money since the day he left, and also how she was currently struggling because of him. Mary-Anne described how incredibly boring her life was between mind-numbing work in the mill and playing happy families at home with her young daughter, her mum and her sister. And with that, they went on drinking and talking for the evening about anything and everything they could think of. Billy was getting very friendly with Mary-Anne and she was enjoying it.

She realised that Billy was very different to her husband in that he was listening to everything she said. Gradually, she began to relax and felt at ease again and then realised that she liked him very much.

George McKee, also on home leave prior to being transhipped to South Africa, was also getting very friendly with Catherine. *Must be the uniforms*, he thought. The foursome made a really good night of it and pushed the boat out. The soldiers treated the girls like special people, to be cared for and of course, spoiled them rotten.

They stood in the snug in the Ladywell Tavern and reminded each other of the Crescent where they had come from, but also of where they were heading in life. Mary-Anne and Catherine said they were dreaming of getting out of the Crescent and moving up in life, perhaps moving to Edinburgh, where the money was. It was like old times, the lads drinking beer and whisky and the ladies on the gin. Much more gin was going down than they should have had.

Then it all came out. Mary-Anne told them of the way her estranged husband John Garland had treated her. The plan to give birth in the hospital was explained, and how it was ruined by his lazy, greedy behaviour, and then, how her father really died was revealed. Catherine expressed her disgust at her brother's actions. Mary-Anne felt relief at the chance to tell someone who was able to rationalise and understand the facts from an independent point of view.

She also told them about the money they suspected John stole from her dead father and the money she knew he took from the coffin. She cried when she confessed she knew about that and did nothing. Billy McKee said, "And now he has joined my battalion of the Black Watch and he is in my battalion at Aldershot now. It'll be interesting catching up with him again in the field," said Billy.

The night ended as amicably as two professional soldiers could make it with two lady friends. Needless to say they were all still friends the following morning when they rose from their respective rooms in the Queen's Hotel.

Billy McKee and Mary-Anne Garland went on to spend the weekend together without a thought for the rest of the world. The couple shopped for anything Mary-Anne wanted in D.M. Browns, the new store that opened in Dundee. In Draffens, the shop that sold everything, he bought her a gold and enamel Black Watch sweetheart brooch for her lapel. Mary-Anne accepted it with great pleasure. This was a new experience for her and she loved it.

I can wear it every day and people will just think it was from my husband, she thought. Their day was completed with a meal in the restaurant of Draffens on the top floor. They sat by the window looking out at the Auld Steeple of the city churches on the busy Nethergate.

In the late afternoon, they climbed the Law hill, the extinct volcano that overarched the city. Above the dense smog around the dull grey buildings, they looked over Dundee and counted hundreds of mill chimneystacks, all of them, spewing out smoke, firing the boilers of the jute mills. The smoke and subsequent pollution fell on the streets and houses of Dundee, filling the lungs of the workers, unaware of the clear blue skies and fresh air above the clouds over the city where Mary-Anne and Billy made their love again. They picked out the Crescent and saw their old dwellings from afar; Mary-Anne was glad to be away from it. They saw the Lochee Road winding its way through the west end and into Lochee to the biggest chimney of all, Cox's stack, belching out smoke without a care. At least nobody in Dundee cared, they were all too busy working to survive in that poverty-blighted city at that time. The couple watched from the slopes of the Law, as the newly rebuilt Tay rail bridge carried a steam train over the river to Fife. Billy said, "I'll take you on that train to Edinburgh one day, if you wait for me?"

"I will wait for you, Bill, but I'm married, it seems we are doomed unless something changes," she whispered, sadly.

On Saturday night, they ate and drank at Caw's restaurant and bar in Panmure Street near Meadowside. Then, the cast of 'Pirates of Penzance', the new Gilbert and Sullivan musical comedy that was doing the rounds of venues, entertained them at 'Her Majesty's Theatre and Opera House' in the Seagate. Mary-Anne had never been to a theatre or, indeed, romanced like this.

She loved the excitement of the theatre and she loved being with Billy. The following day, the girls saw the McKees off at Dundee East Train Station.

"Can I write to you, Mary-Anne?" asked Billy as he leaned out of the open train window.

"You'd better!" she said as she reached up and kissed him passionately as the train began to move. She retraced her steps out of the station, deep in thought. The only thing that had spoiled Mary-Anne's perfect weekend, was the thought that she had fallen for someone she could not have, and, for that reason, she elected not to tell her mother her whereabouts for the past three days.

CHAPTER 16

The Highland Division

Billy was with the 2nd Battalion, Black Watch, the Royal Highlanders, who entrained at Aldershot on 22nd of October 1899. They arrived at Tilbury Docks in fog, which caused a two-day delay before they could sail. They embarked the SS *Orient* on the 24th, and made for St. Vincent, France, to take on coal, then set sail for South Africa without further delay.

Major-General Arthur G. Wauchope, or 'Red Mick' as he was affectionately known by his men, was the commander of the Highland Division. He was an Edinburgh man of 33 years standing with the Black Watch and was a confident and very capable man. The division he commanded comprised more than 4,000 men including his own 2nd battalion of the Black Watch made up of 1,011 men and 27 officers, all experienced, combat ready and optimistic.

Billy watched while the 2nd Battalion disembarked the Orient in Table Bay on 13th of November and transferred by tender to Simonstown docks, Cape Town the following day. The battalion then joined the balance of the Highland Division including a company of 60 men of the 26th Foot Scottish Rifles (Cameronians), of which Joe Murphy was one, now a trained and experienced rifleman.

Joe Murphy and his company of Cameronians were assigned to the Seaforths to assist in *'the defence of the railway line and protection of the*

British army lines of communication of the east coast of South Africa'. He knew John Garland would be with the recruits at the rear of the company and he picked him out straight away. Joe blended into the ranks anonymously as Sergeant McKee took the parade on arrival on dry land and marched the new men at double quick time to Cape Town railway station.

"Especially for you, Garland," shouted Billy McKee, "I've got a special job when we get to the end of the line," he bellowed, "to get you out of the sun!" John Garland was confused. Here was an old friend from the Crescent and he thought there would be at least a nod or a wink but nothing of the sort. Billy McKee seemed to be a stranger now.

They entrained again in Cape Town and alighted nine hours later at their destination, a desolate junction inland on the border of the Orange Free State and Northern Cape Province, midway between Cape Town and Port Elizabeth. They then undertook a 55-mile march to the Modder River.

Reveille sounded at six hundred hours and after breakfast, McKee ordered a kit check and ammo issue; the battle dress for the division that night comprised the new khaki jacket, kilt and khaki apron, and pith helmet. The Black Watch, of course, wore the red hackle on the left of the helmet secured into the cloth band around it. Every man carried his Lee Enfield rifle and bayonet and a hundred and fifty rounds apiece in ammo pouches. Soon, the Highland Division was on its way by train again from the Modder River, through the *Karoo* to *De Aar,* a newly formed divisional Headquarters in the vast expanse of scrubland in the sandy northern Cape.

John Garland was assigned by Sergeant McKee as assistant to the company mule keeper and his twenty native black volunteers. There were sixteen pack animals, and his detail was to groom, feed and health check his mules daily and of course, shovel the shit they dropped.

McKee put the pressure on Garland even more by calling him Rosie, a nickname he conjured up for John's humiliation and it was having an effect. All the company men joined in the humiliation by making 'Rosie' take as much of their kit as he could get the mules to carry once they reached De Aar.

Billy McKee kept up the pressure for the first week on the march then one night in the bush after ablutions, McKee called Garland into the sergeant's field quarters and gave him a warning about his attire and his unkempt presentation – all of it was complete lies, of course, just designed to break Garland. McKee wanted Garland out of the regiment and he wanted Garland to know it.

"I'm telling you this, Rosie, because I cannot see you making it in the Black Watch." Then, lowering his voice, Billy said, "Why don't you apply for the catering corps? I'll send you on a cooking course if you like, as soon as we get to Kimberley."

"No, not me, Sergeant," said John Garland. "I'm a trained combatant like you, and I want to see active service in the theatre of war, like you, Sergeant," said Garland.

"But you're NOT like me, are you, Rosie? You're a thief, a lazy bastard and a hoormester aren't you, ye little shite!"

Astonished at the tirade just thrown at him, he realised that he had heard these words before, in the Crescent: it was like listening to John Murphy all over again! It all came back to him in a flash. "Of course, you've been back to the Crescent on leave, haven't you!" Garland said. "You've been talking to Tommy and Joe Murphy, haven't you?"

"Wrong, Rosie, I've been talking to your wife, or should I say ex-wife!!" said Billy. "And she's gonna be with ME when we get back, not you!"

John Garland was speechless. It was all beginning to make sense. His old pal was now his enemy and he was talking about seeing his estranged wife in secret. Garland had no answer and no defence. Here he was, six thousand miles from Dundee and suddenly his actions in the Crescent had resulted in a horrible mess of despair and humiliation and there was nothing he could do about it. He stumbled to the door of the tented quarters. "I'll apply for the course when we get to Kimberley."

"You'd better!" said Sergeant McKee.

On the 19th of November, Wauchope received orders to move out to Colesburg to reconnoitre the Boers' strength and position. The Highland Brigade was made responsible for the safety and defence of communications and that included the single-track railway line that the British army depended on all the way to Kimberley.

Despite their 'amateur' status, the Boers had the distinct advantage of familiarity of the country and its climate over the British troops. Although they were outnumbered five to one, the Boer forces threw everything they had into Natal in an effort to reach Durban before the British had time to ship in reinforcements.

That effort by the Boers included fighting for control of the northern Cape, where the Highland Brigade was heading. Ironically for the Dundee men of the Black Watch, Dundee in Natal was a strategic target owing to its vast coal reserves much needed by the Empire to fuel the trains and the shipping, which kept the British army of the Empire machine rolling.

The Boers fought hard to win control of Natal, under General

Piet Joubert, another veteran of the First Boer War, twenty years earlier. His army had occupied Newcastle in Natal without significant resistance from the British in that State and he set his sights on Dundee for the value it held for the British.

The first battle of the Second or New Boer War had just taken place at Talana Hill outside Dundee on October 20th, 1899. Dundee in Natal was occupied by the British but was completely surrounded by the Boers. This disrupted rail communication to Ladysmith. Joubert, however, the son of a missionary and a devout Christian, never sought to exploit the success of capturing Dundee and allowed the British to slip out of the town and ordered his force not to interfere.

With Dundee taken, Joubert next turned his attention on Ladysmith, where the British army made an ill-conceived attempt to break the advancing Boers at Modderfontein. There, they lost 1,764 men, 1,284 of whom surrendered. As the survivors fled back to Ladysmith, Joubert refused to pursue them, telling his men: "When God holds out a little finger, do not take the whole hand."

Three British strongholds were therefore under siege in the area and the Empire had resolved to relieve all three of them: Kimberley, Ladysmith and Mafeking. Kimberley, however, was the priority to the Empire because it had been producing diamonds since 1865.

The Highland Division had arrived at the foothills around the Modder River, blocking the Boers' way to Kimberley around the river. The highlanders had come under fire from the Boers on several occasions, acquitting themselves adequately but losing significant numbers of men to the Boer sharpshooters. The Boers watched every move from the veldt they knew so well but remained almost invisible to the men of the Black Watch.

Eager for the fight, the Black Watch battalion surveyors checked out the ground that was, by and large, flat for a radius of six or seven miles around. The only high grounds of consequence were three ridges in a row: the highest was a hill in the middle of about 2,000 feet, called Magersfontein. That, Methuen, the British Commander-in-Chief told Wauchope, is where the Boers would be. "That is where we attack them," Methuen said. "We should put the observation balloon up first, sir, to see their position and strength," voiced Wauchope.

"Not to bother, old chap, I know they are on the high ground, because they got here first. Besides, we cannot waste time waiting for the observers to do their work," Methuen concluded.

On the afternoon of Sunday, December 10th, 1899, Wauchope received orders from Lord Methuen that the Highland Brigade was to clear the way to Kimberley for the army to relieve the ongoing Boer siege. In order to succeed in reaching Kimberley, Magersfontein hill, or *kopje* must first be cleared of Boers.

General Cronje, or Dark Piet as his Boers called him, was a wily sixty-five-year-old veteran of the First Boer War. He had been involved in action in the field and many guerrilla activities including the Jameson raid since then. He had with him eight and a half thousand fighting Boers, sharpshooters, every one, plus more than two thousand blacks, who worked as diggers and carriers for the Boers when they needed to entrench and dig-in. From his position at Spytfontein, close to Kimberley, they watched the British column move toward the *kopje* and knew instinctively what and where the action would be.

Cronje's second-in-command, Vech-Generaal (*Combat General*) Koos De La Rey, had gone to bury his son Adriaan, at home in Jacobsdal. The British shelling had killed Adriaan at the Battle of Modder River the week before. When he returned to the field force,

De La Rey immediately saw the danger of a potential hill battle and insisted that Cronje move his troops to Magersfontein to prevent the British taking the high ground. Cronje's plan, as always, was to dig-in to the front slopes of the *kopje* and defend the hill from the high ground. De La Rey disagreed with him for obvious reasons and went over his head to the president of the Boer Republics, Paul Kruger, for approval. In spite of Cronje's remonstrations, De La Rey took command. He knew the British were about to attack and took evasive action.

While the Highland Division was standing easy in the night rain, Joe Murphy found George McKee and took up his position by his side with their regiment, the Seaforths. Together, they made their way through the hundreds of Scottish soldiers to meet up with George's brother Billy for an hour. They had time on their hands while awaiting further orders and they found Billy with his battalion. In a moment of idle chat they remembered the days of their youth in Dundee and the nights in the Crescent.

Billy admitted to them he had fallen for Mary-Anne and spoke of the happiness they shared that weekend in Dundee. Billy McKee also told Joe, Mary-Anne's brother, that he intended to have it out with Garland and resolve the situation as soon as possible but he would pick and choose the time. Billy confirmed that John Garland had joined his battalion at Cape Town. "I don't trust that little bastard," said Billy. "I'll be watching your back, and you watch mine," Billy told George.

"You're dead right, brother, dead right," George replied. Joe remained silent.

Before he left to rejoin his unit, George reminded Billy that Garland wasn't to be trusted. "I'll deal with him in good time, George, but we've all got the Boers to kill first," he said with a wry smile.

"Come on, Joe," said George, "let's get back to the line."

Sergeant McKee was a well-respected soldier and proving to be a fine leader of men. He gathered his four sections of twelve men each in a huddle and communicated the situation. "The Boers are dug in on top of the big hill in the middle of the three. Our artillery is going to blow them to hell with the big guns, and the howitzers tonight. When they have finished, we are going in to wipe up what's left," said Billy, enthusiastically.

CHAPTER 17

Waiting for News in the Crescent

Back in Dundee, Tommy had left home. He had started working as a miner in the pits in Fife and after a month of travelling every weekend, he took a better paying job and was off to Glasgow working on the coalmines in Lanarkshire. Tommy made it clear that he was going for no other reason than he hated the Crescent.

With Tommy and Joe gone, young Jessie was living with her mother and Annie and her family at number 8 Littlejohn Street. Annie was disgusted and ashamed of Mary-Anne's behaviour, for going missing for a whole weekend after her husband had left for the war, but she felt obliged to make the peace and allow her to come back. Within days of Mary-Anne moving in, however, there was a bad atmosphere between them all at all times.

In many ways Annie was thankful that Tommy and Joe had both moved out of the flat and out of Dundee. The place was full of personal memories for Annie that Mary-Anne just couldn't see. Mary-Anne had resettled into Annie's flat, taking the kitchen bed recess with Jessie, and left her mother and Grace to the big bedroom each night. Willie and Nellie, the two little ones, shared a shaky-doon on the floor by the fire in the same room as Mary-Anne.

At least that was how it was supposed to be. To Mary-Anne, Jessie had become a burden again and more suited to the panderings she got from Annie and Grace. More often than not, Jessie slept with Annie and Grace because her mum was often out at night and up and away early in the morning.

In those early days, Mary-Anne received one letter from Billy to say that he was aboard a troop ship going to Cape Town and that he had made contact with her estranged husband. She replied immediately with affectionate words and a few suggestions as to what he could say to John Garland but never received a reply.

Mary-Anne was a twenty-four-year-old woman who had just experienced adulthood without her husband. She decided she wanted to be with Billy, not John. She resolved at that stage that she would do what she wanted, as and when she wanted, and nobody else could tell her otherwise.

As time went by, Mary-Anne began to feel the depression she used to feel after having her baby. She remembered what the midwife told her in an attempt to explain why people get depression. "When we know something's going to end, we tend to value it differently," and that is what she felt now. She never missed her husband but she did miss Billy McKee more now than ever. She felt her relationship with John was over, but now she felt that her relationship with Billy was also over. What would she do if Billy never came back? She sank deeper into depression as time went by without another word from Billy.

CHAPTER 18

Magersfontein

On the night of 10th December 1899, the Highland Division was formed up in close formation into a dense column, the Black Watch in front as usual. In the front lines of the battalion, good, seasoned soldiers in the first seven rows of one hundred men each row, reached back to the most recently recruited men at the rear.

In the relative safety of the rear rows of the Black Watch, John Garland had his own briefing from another sergeant. The Highland Brigade comprised nearly four thousand men in a quarter column as ordered. The order of advance was the Black Watch in front, and then the Seaforths, followed by the Argyles and then the Highland Light Infantry taking up the rear of the division. Expert riflemen of the Cameronians, including Joe Murphy, were strategically positioned in the column, peppered throughout the division. Positioned another two to three miles behind the column, was the addition of the artillery of 12th Lancers and G Battery, horse artillery and a howitzer battery. In all, there were four howitzers, twenty-nine field carriage guns and central to the artillery guns was a huge 4.7-inch naval gun, 'Old Joe' as the Brits knew it. The big gun was drawn on a carriage by thirty-two bullocks and attended by eighty seamen gunners; it was famed for killing all within 150 yards of landing a shell.

The bombardment commenced at 4:30pm on Sunday 10th 1899.

The huge gun cracked off the first fifty-pound shell and that exploded on the hilltop. Magersfontein shook and spewed rock and boulder. The artillery barrage followed in the knowledge that the attack was killing Boers with the storm of high explosives they had landed. The big gun relentlessly boomed with shell after shell, as did the rest of the artillery. No response came from the enemy on the hilltop at all. The heavy artillery bombardment ended after two hours and the Highland Division were readying for the sweep up. Not a movement was observed on the hill from the battalion positioned three to four miles away, but orders were orders and the hilltop of Magersfontein with the red boulders strewn all over it, was the devastated target. That is where the British thought the Boers were entrenched.

It was pouring rain by midnight and at one o'clock in the morning the battalion moved forward, tired and hungry, in the darkness and looking to finish the action quickly. Under his lieutenant's orders, Sgt McKee had his men stand and say a silent prayer for a few seconds then, raising his voice, "Are you ready, Black Watch?" And again, "Are you ready, DUNDEE?" he bellowed to the men.

A unanimous. "AYE, READY," was the response.

Finally, Billy yelled the words, "Steady, Black Watch." The men were suddenly pumped with adrenaline and ready for the fight. The Division started to move in the dark, densely packed into a quarter column and moved forward as one. They were led by ropes at shoulder height in the direction of the hill to prevent stragglers tripping and straying into the veldt. Billy McKee was in the second row from the front with his men.

Slowly the column advanced towards Magersfontein, keeping the thirty-two companies of the four battalions in the line one after the other. One hundred men in each line, and forty lines were moving in as close to lock step action as possible, all moving toward the *kopje*, in a single block, in the dark. With the exception of sporadic flashes of lightning lighting up the African sky, the night was pitch black. The soldiers stumbled forward over anthills, uneven scrubland and stones. Two strong lights shone at them in front, one at each extreme end. Presuming they were British lights, the column mistakenly blundered on.

An entanglement of planted pegs and wires stopped the front men and the column began to bunch up. Clearing their feet, they heard the sound of tin cans clattering and rattling all along the width of the front line as the front men tripped over and fell among the wires unseen in the ground. Billy and his men recognised the sound as an alarm to tell the enemy where they were.

At the sound of the alarm, the Boers opened fire on the front of the column at 400 yards from a multitude of hidden trenches at the foot of the hill. Accurate rifle fire ripped into the head of the British column, dropping them and pinning down the Dundee men of the Black Watch. Out of the darkness and the silence of the hill, blasted before them a thousand murderous flashes of gunfire that roared incessantly on and on from repeating German Mauser rifles from ground level. Another thousand rifles fired two seconds later, then another thousand more.

Red Mick Wauchope realised instantly that the Boers were not ON the hill but in FRONT of it. He saw by the light of their gunfire that Dark Piet had the Boers dug into long trenches about four feet deep and just wide enough to take a man and nothing else, providing maximum cover from artillery fire. Wauchope gave the order to extend the line but was blown off his feet by rifle fire and he was shot again as he lay scrambling for cover that never existed. He died with his men in the field.

The pipers immediately struck up with 'The Campbells are Coming', hurrying the counter engagement by the Scots. On his lieutenant's command, Billy McKee rose from his prone position among the dead and dying. With a nod of approval from his lieutenant, they fixed bayonets and he led the remnants of his row of about fifty brave but bewildered men right into the Boer trenches in front of them. He shot and killed one Boer and flushed more of them out of the trench with rifle fire before chasing them up the rise of the hill. The Boers in the trenches at ground level to the left of Billy's position continued firing into the jocks. The entire battalion returned fire instantly but the column was bunched up so densely that only the front soldiers could see the targets.

The Black Watch frontline, in a desperate effort to evade the oncoming storm of Boer rifle fire, was caught in a trap. Clearly, the Boer ammunition was the Dumdum type, the hollowed out warhead that exploded on impact causing horrific damage to human flesh. The battalion back markers couldn't believe that the remaining standing rows of the Black Watch were turning back and running into their own gunfire. From his position with the Seaforths, where some of the sergeants were shouting, "Retreat, retreat!" George ignored the command and, taking his promise to his brother quite literally, broke ranks and advanced. Dropping the guide rope, George raised his .303 and took aim; Joe Murphy did the same beside him. They both charged forward, towards Billy.

When they reached the trenches, George saw that Billy's men were at the mercy of the Boer rifles. His own battalion the Seaforths, and the Black Watch, were returning the fire, and inadvertently hitting their own men from behind. Regardless, George and Joe, side-by-side fired repeatedly at the Boers in an effort to give Billy and his men cover. It was all but useless because they were under horrendous incoming fire themselves.

Within five minutes of the action, hundreds of Scotsmen lay dead or wounded on the veldt. They either lay motionless or writhing in agony from a constant shower of lethal lead flying into them. Still, it seemed that half the battalion was retreating from the slaughter at the front line and the other half were still firing right into them. Billy McKee was shot in the right leg from behind. He spun round, looking back for help from his comrades.

The last thing he saw was the hundreds of flashes of the Highland Division's Lee Enfields firing in his direction at the Boers all around him. He never saw his brother George or Joe Murphy right behind him, but for an instant, was elated that the firepower he did see was in his support. At that moment, a .303 round from a Lee Enfield of his own column slammed into his forehead, and Billy was dispatched instantly.

The Boer onslaught continued, firing at the Black Watch from ground level now at 200 yards. To those watching, who could not help because they were out of range, the rifle fire was unbearable. As they ran forward, George and Joe continued fighting as they followed the line of downed soldiers to the right flank where some Black Watch had advanced into the Boer lines. They bayonetted and fired into the Boers' trench ahead of them. In a rage, George emptied his magazine into his enemies around him and while trying to eject and reload another, he knelt down to see Billy's face but he could see that he was gone. Joe was covering George's back as best he could, taking out the Boers in the trench with his rifle and alternately slashing with his bayonet and gouging into the trenches.

Standing over Billy and George, Joe took a .303 bullet in the back at his left shoulder; it went straight through and out the front and he crumpled to the ground. They heard the foreign roar of several Dutchmen, "*Skiet hulle dood te maak die verdoem engels Manse!*" (Shoot to kill the damned English men!) Then the lights went out for George. The butt of a Martini-Henry Boer rifle had struck him on the back of the head and down he went to his knees. Two pairs of strong weathered hands caught him as he fell into the trench and the choice was theirs, take a prisoner or leave him there dead. They took him. George was dragged screaming for his brother in one breath and yelling abuse at his captors in another. Up and around the back of the hill he was dragged and then slung into the back of an ox wagon alongside Joe and another thirteen Black Watch soldiers, all of them wounded or badly beaten and bleeding, but alive. For the next twelve hours, as the African sun rose, the Boer marksmen kept up the attack on the Black Watch. The dying and wounded were left on the veldt without tree, rock or scrub cover at the bottom of the hill to protect them. Those that were unhurt were badly burned by the heat of the sun at the backs of their legs beneath the kilt, as they lay prone on the veldt.

The Highland Division was severely mauled that night. Dundee's own Black Watch alone lost 355 men dead or wounded. It was exacerbated by the debacle of negative action the following day. The Boers held their positions with impunity at the foot of the hill because any ensuing British artillery fire flew over their heads and slammed into the hill harmlessly behind them, or fell short of the thin lines of trench defences in front of them. Subsequent to the battle of Magersfontein, a soldier of the regiment wrote:

Such was the day for our regiment
Dread the revenge we will take
Dearly we paid for the blunder,
A drawing room general's mistake

Why weren't we told of the trenches?
Why weren't we told of the wire?
Why were we marched up in column?
May Tommy Atkins enquire?

– Pte Smith, 2nd Battalion The Black Watch, December 1899.

In time, that desperate period for the empire became known as 'Black Week'. The Highland Division suffered the loss of 747 men killed or wounded at Magersfontein. Both McKee brothers and Joe Murphy were posted, like many others, as missing, presumed captured or killed.

George McKee and Joe Murphy were in fact prisoners of war. They both knew, however, that Billy was dead, killed either by the Boers or by 'friendly fire' – George didn't know which, but Joe was very sure he knew. They never discussed it further.

Speculation was that in the immediate aftermath of the initial onslaught, the Boers buried the fallen Black Watch men in the nearest trench. This allowed them to continue the action without the stench of human flesh rotting before them when the African sun rose. Those buried in the trenches though, were the missing men of the Black Watch never to be found again. In addition to the official casualties, seventy-nine men of Wauchope's Highland

Division were captured at the battle of Magersfontein. Fifty-five were Black Watch, fourteen were Seaforths and the rest, Argyles and Cameronians.

CHAPTER 19

The Courier

Mary-Anne's letter replying to Billy was posted to South Africa in late November and by the following month she had heard nothing.

In the week leading up to Christmas 1899, all of Dundee was shaken by the news of the Magersfontein battle. *'The Courier'* had published an early account of the action after pre-approval by the British government but no names or numbers had been published. On the 23rd December, *'The People's Journal'* finally published a list of Dundee men killed or wounded. The newspaper dwelled on each man killed together with his address in the city and a short obituary on the victim.

Mary-Anne and Catherine went through the names frantically looking for their men: 'Private John Hardie, Private J. McMillan, Sergeant T. Godfrey, Private T. Scullion…' the list went on and on and at this point, ninety-three Dundee men were named and venerated in turn. Then the names of the wounded with a similar status on their condition and a suitable homage to the injured men were published.

Buried deep in the middle of the paper, the *Journal* also published a list of those missing, presumed killed or captured. Both McKee brothers were on it, so was Joe Murphy.

After some serious talk with Catherine, they both decided it was safe to approach the regimental HQ with their questions. *Has Billy been killed?* she wondered. She felt confused and ashamed at the same time. *I am married to a man in the Black Watch, but I really want to know what has happened to Billy McKee, in the same regiment. Who can I ask though?*

Catherine agreed that they also had to find out what had happened to the others from the Crescent. It was inconceivable to the girls, but possible, that all three of their men from the Crescent who were missing might have been killed.

In late January 1900 both women received news from the office of the Black Watch at Balhousie Castle HQ. Annie Murphy had received a telegram that day indicating that her son, Private Joseph Murphy, Cameronians, was posted missing in action. Mary-Anne was advised by letter the same day that her husband, John Garland, was not mentioned in any of the action at Magersfontein and was currently safe and still with his regiment in the field.

By the time she walked into number 8 Littlejohn Street, the house was full. Her uncles Peter and Wullie and her mother's friends from her mill days were all there. Grace was crying and was staring out of the window with a telegram in her hand. "Let me see that," said Mary-Anne. She just focused on the text.

We have to advise that Private Joseph Murphy, Cameronians, was killed in action on 26th January 1900 in Transvaal, South Africa. Our sincere condolences to his family, Adjudant, 26th Foot Scottish Rifles, the Cameronians.

Annie was distraught and Grace was crying but Mary-Anne was devastated. Joe was her dearest and closest sibling; she had brought him up as a young schoolboy and saw him grow into a soldier. This war was the devil himself; she hated it with all her being. Catherine also found out that day from the neighbours that a telegram had been sent from the Seaforths to Mrs. McKee informing her that Private George McKee was missing in action at Magersfontein, and that Sergeant William McKee of the Black Watch was also posted missing, believed captured or killed.

Annie McKee was a middle-aged woman who lived with her family in the flat above the Garlands. Her seventeen-year-old son Jimmy opened the door to Catherine and Mary-Anne, and they asked to see his mum. Jimmy scowled when he saw them and aggressively, he demanded to know what they wanted. On the face of it, there was nothing unusual in a neighbour asking after another neighbour's sons but even so, with a frown, Jimmy let them in. "She is in bed but I'll get her for you," he said. After a few minutes Annie McKee appeared, her eyes red with crying, her face bearing all the hallmarks of a hard life. Already she had two of her sons missing in the South African war and a younger son Johnny, who was now fifteen, had been detained in Baldovan Approved School for juvenile misdemeanours and theft since the age of ten. "Oh dear, oh," Mrs. McKee sighed. "It's an awfy life!"

"We heard about George and Billy. How are you, Mrs. McKee?" said Catherine.

"Yes, I have had telegrams today," she said frostily. Mrs. McKee also said in a quiet voice, "They are missing in Africa."

"Missing? What do they mean, 'missing'?" Mary-Anne said. "How long have they been missing? she asked.

"Since the 11th of December," said Mrs. McKee as she lowered herself into the fireside armchair while removing a handkerchief from her sleeve and dabbing her eyes.

They left the McKees' flat after offering their condolences to the family and making Mrs. McKee a cup of tea. Jimmy McKee retained his scowl and mysteriously refused to speak to the women. Mrs. McKee's telegram had only confirmed what they had read in the paper and heard from the neighbours. "That might explain the look on Jimmy's face," said Catherine.

That night, Mary-Anne was frantic with worry and the following day she couldn't bear to keep her mind on her job. On the 31st of January 1900, both women stayed off work and went in search of some 'peace of mind' as Mary-Anne called it. As soon as it was opening time, they walked into the Scout bar in Temple lane that day and got through two bottles of gin before five o'clock. Mary-Anne got obstreperous with the bar staff and they were asked to leave.

As darkness fell, they made their way across the Westport and into the Globe, a pub that her father used to frequent in his fighting days. She wore her sweetheart brooch high on her shawl, so it was on full view to all. Mary-Anne got teary and drunk.

"Was your man at Magersfontein, hen?" the barman in the Globe asked her.

"Aye he was and he's missing," she said. "He is dead, I know it."

Catherine was all for heading back to the Crescent, but Mary-Anne ordered another drink and they stayed in the Globe drinking and fretting for the missing McKees. The more gin they consumed the more Mary-Anne's worries evaporated. An hour later, her worries were gone. "Come on, let's go up the Hawkhill and see what they say in the next pub," she said to Catherine, and they staggered out of the Globe. Catherine just followed dutifully in silence.

The Hawkhill, or 'Hackie' as the locals call it, was a densely populated tenement street festooned with drinking houses and other dubious establishments. It was an area that Mary-Anne was becoming known in, for all the wrong reasons. Owing to the icy streets and the frozen horse dung in and around the Westport, and the amount of drink they had consumed, they were unable to move very far, especially with the long skirts the women wore trailing in the wet. They slipped and slid on the road and only got as far as the foot of the Hackie and into Micky Coyle's pub, just around the corner from the Globe. By 9pm, both of them were shouting and swearing at the staff and the men in the pub, calling them "kettle bilers" who were "feared to join the army like their men did."

The police were called and arrested both women. They were detained in the Bell Street cells for the night awaiting their appearance before the magistrate of the Dundee Police Court the following morning. Knowing it would be in the papers, Mary-Anne told Bailie Muirison she was unmarried and gave a different address so as to protect her true identity from prying eyes of her neighbours in the Crescent: The 'Evening Telegraph' that night reported:

"THE RESULT OF A FRIEND'S DEPARTURE TO WAR"

"Mary-Anne Murphy, Millworker, Overgate, admitted being incapably drunk in Hawkhill yesterday. She received a letter from her brother, she said stating that he was going to the war. She absented herself from work on this account and expended three shillings which he sent her on liquor". The Prosecutor said it was not her brother but a very intimate friend of Mary-Anne's who had been called out. The Magistrate allowed her to go without penalty."

– Dundee Evening Telegraph, Thursday, 01 February 1900.

Annie was black affronted. She knew that it was Mary-Anne that 'got her name in the paper' and she knew what pubs the women had been in. "The paper says you have an intimate friend in the war," Annie said. "Your husband left you because you didn't want him around, so who are they talking about, this very intimate friend?" Annie asked Mary-Anne as she sat there crying in the flat. "You said yourself that John Garland was OK and never got hurt in the battle, it canna be him you are crying for, so who is it?" said Annie. "What is it all about then, Mary-Anne? Why did you get drunk and end up in jail, and who gave you that brooch?"

Mary-Anne answered without another minute's thought, "Billy McKee, that's who it was," Mary-Anne confessed. "It was Billy McKee, he was the friend, he gave me the brooch and he is still missing! I think he might be dead, but I don't know. I was depressed and I got drunk, OK?" said Mary-Anne woefully.

Annie was stunned. "How long has this been going on? Does John Garland know? What are you going to say to him when he finds out you've been in the jail all night?" asked Annie, crying.

"Questions, questions, always questions! No, John Garland does not know!" she shouted at her mother. "And he's not going to know, ever! Do you understand me?" roared Mary-Anne. Annie showed her shock, and then she too, burst into tears with the shame of it.

For the next year they all co-existed in number 8 Littlejohn Street in the Crescent. In all that time Mary-Anne was full of remorse and kept her nose clean. She knew what they all thought of her and she lived the life of a nervous wreck at her mother's home without a drink. Not a word came from South Africa about Billy. She worked every day in the mill like all the others for less money than she earned five years previously. She was living the life of a poor woman without money from her husband because John Garland sent nothing, not even money for the bairn's keep.

There was no argument with the mill owners. Dundee's jute mills' fortunes were on the wane and the mill owners blamed it on the lack of demand from the military. *I can't take much more of this life,* Mary-Anne thought. The Boer War raged on and still not a word was heard about the McKees. She was beginning to feel the loneliness of a grown woman without a man to complete her life. On the 22nd of January 1901, Queen Victoria died. In Dundee, the general consensus was that her death would bring a swift end to the Boer War. It was expected that the mystery of the missing soldiers would be resolved but, no, nothing changed, and the war raged on. Mary-Anne's hopes were raised again and then they were dashed once more.

CHAPTER 20

Prisoners of War in South Africa

The big Boer spoke in monotone, "*Gaan sit en wees stil,*" (Sit down and be quiet.) And then, "*Generaal Cronje sal met jou praat.*" (General Cronje will want to talk to you.) Five ox wagons in a row filled with Scottish soldiers moved along the South African veldt in the dark away from the battlefield and into the savanna of the North Eastern Cape. All day the wagons rolled northeast toward Harrismith and the Boers gathered around their prize. The wagon train came to a halt at the first watering hole and the animals drank. The Boer army doctor and his black medical assistants tended the wounds of the prisoners of war where they could. Medicinal products were in short supply but were given to the captured Scotsmen where possible.

Twenty or more horsemen trained their Mauser rifles on each of the wagons and made sure the jocks went nowhere. Each wagon was accompanied by about ten black men of various tribes, solely employed to keep the oxen going and fetch and carry anything that the Boers had so deemed. Until that point, they stopped for nothing except to eat or ablute. When fed and watered, they rolled on again, heading for the Vaal River. Two days later and eighty miles away from Magersfontein, General Piet Cronje and a powerful commando of 550 of his Boers arrived on horseback. They had caught up with them at the Vaalharts Dam waterhole in the Northern Cape region.

The blacks driving the wagons knew the spot well and took respite from the sun in good shade around them under the camelthorn trees. The highlanders were fed by this time and, after clearing the sable antelope and a herd of springbok from the watering hole, they were allowed to bathe and clean their wounds. After a pep talk in Afrikaans and a service by the Boer army *Dominee*, (preacher) the Boers were informed of the great victory they had achieved, and the damage inflicted on the heathen British Empire at Magersfontein. He finished with, "*Mag God met ons wees,*" (may God be with us) and, *"Ek moet met die buitelanders praat,"* (I must speak with the outlanders) to rousing applause.

Cronje turned and spoke to the Scotsmen in English; he addressed them as gentlemen for a reason. "Good day, gentlemen." He intended to impress on them the importance of high standards that the Boers held sacrosanct in front of the lord and his own troops. "I am glad to see you are all coping with the heat and are being cared for by the medics among us," he said. "You are heading for the safety of a Prison of War station in Pretoria. You will be held far from the conflict in our dear land for the duration of this godforsaken war."

Cronje went on, "The fact that your empire has brought us to the point where the Afrikaner republics are forced to take such action as you have just witnessed is testament to the criminality of your own government." He continued, "Your imprisonment therefore is right and legal in the eyes of our land and of our lord, Jesus Christ. It is far from our wish but that is what the good lord tells us we must do. If it be his will, we will do it all again if we must. That, gentlemen, is the choice your Queen and Empress has to decide. We are not her subjects and never will be." Cronje then asked the Dominee to say a blessing and dismissed the gathered prisoners of war without another word.

Cronje's words, slowly spoken and with passion began to sink into George's head. *My brother Billy has just been killed for that Queen and Empress, it cannot be for nothing that he and the others died,* he thought. *There must be a reason.* They rested overnight under the stars in silence and, sad as he was for the loss of his brother, and the trauma of the battle, George felt true peace overcome him for the first time in his life. Joe Murphy felt nothing but hatred for the Boers. His wounds were healing but not his heart. He endured the pain and remained silent. Cronje then ordered that the injured prisoners who required further proper medical aid be taken by horse-drawn field ambulance to the nearest field hospital for quicker attention. Joe Murphy went with them without a murmur.

The wagons moved on before the sun rose the next day and Cronje and his commando headed southwest towards Kimberley to re-engage the good fight. Every minute a *sjambok* (whip) cracked above the leading oxen; the natives stiffened in anticipation of it landing on their backs, but they kept singing the rhythmic songs that kept them and the wagons moving in harmony.

Every crack of the *sjambok* reminded George of the battle and of his dead brother. He was glad he was the lucky one that survived, and to feel the warmth of Africa, and the love of the lord. The jocks stirred awake at the crack of that whip regardless of how exhausted or physically sick they were. They were among the first prisoners of war the Boers had captured, and the Boers were not ready for them, for they never expected to take prisoners, ever. The wagons moved at a steady pace every day and the prisoners, like the Boers, were fed on biltong, a cured and dried meat strip of springbok or kudu, seasoned and hung for weeks in the still air of the veldt. By night, they circled the wagons and built a *braai*, a wood fire in the middle of the circle and roasted the freshly shot meat from the springbok or impala that crossed their path that day.

The Boer guards shot only as many animals as they needed to feed the people on the trek including the POWs. It was the richest, and most enjoyable food that George had ever tasted, even better than his mum's cooking in the Crescent. Even the smell of the meat roasting on the grid over an open fire was satisfying. Ironically, he began to like this country. By night, they bedded down under the stars of the Milky Way in silence save the occasional roar of lion or the rumble of buffalo or wildebeest.

The landscape was awesome, even at that time of year. They passed Harrismith in the night and reached Van Reenen's Pass, where, looking back, they could still see some snow-capped mountains of the Drakensberg in the distance. Framing the vast expanse of that sun-drenched land was the lushness of the green Kikuyu grass in the foothills hosting the baobab and acacia trees populated by troops of baboons. They saw wild animals roam and hunt in the bush and herds of kudu, hartebeest and springbok as they moved across the plains, followed by warthog families and of course, the inevitable hyena packs scavenging behind them.

The black Bantu 'volunteer' army of workers of the Xhosa who enrolled for the Boers in the northern Transvaal and the loyal and fearless Zulus who were picked up in Natal, and even the Ndebele from the north of the country, all engaged in their workday in the same rhythmic song irrespective of the tribe they belonged to. With relish, they sang out the choruses in harmony following the head or *boss boy* who made them pick up the pace of the chants on the flat ground and slow it down again on the hills.

They did it for the pay they signed up for, not for the morality or righteousness of the war they were involved in, but they did it without complaint. It was not their war; it was their job. For that reason, these blacks had no truck with the jocks in their charge, but rather, even exchanged words of clarification with them in order to get along and get through the laborious days. George watched how the Boers and the Bantu interfaced, it was all structured and respectful.

Themba, the big Zulu *Bossboy* was a proud man of about forty years of age. He took instructions from each Boer officer in charge of each wagon in the Zulu language and related it to the gangs of black men in *Fanagalo,* a mixture of a dozen tribal languages that was developing in the gold mines in the Transvaal gold reef. The blacks showed total respect and kept a straight face when taking orders from their bossboy but George noticed that they all smirked and sniggered when the Boers tried to talk to them in their own language.

This was especially the case when the wagon train commander, Schalk Van de Merwe, a second-generation Dutchman, fat as a pig and lazy as a fox, attempted to bark out the orders to the blacks in their language. They all referred to Van De Merwe as '*Mapoonpan*' (the big fat one) and even called him that to his face because he thought it meant 'Oh great one'. With his huge bush of a beard poking out from below his bush hat and clothing, he thought he looked terrifying, in fact he just looked like an overstuffed jute sack – with a gun. However, with his Mauser cocked and ready at all times and two full bandoliers overs his shoulders, he was just waiting for the chance to kill a Brit or a black, anyone, it didn't matter to him.

All of the gangs started every wagon in unison to the strains of the beautiful melodic 'Shosholoza', a work song with its origins in the gold mines of the reef around Johannesburg. It was in the form of onomatopoeia and the word 'Shosholoza' was imitating the sound of a working steam train. The word, in this case was understood by all on the wagon train to mean 'go forward' All in all, George was not complaining at his captivity in this magical land.

As the year 1899 was drawing to a close, the ox wagons approached the Vaaldam. George felt mesmerised by the slow rolling of the wagon and the song of the Bantu, as they reached the huge natural waterhole in the Transvaal. After the scouts waved the signal for *Alles Duidelik* (All Clear), the wagons rolled lazily along the banks of the dam for days and on to Vereeniging and then into Pretoria in silence.

The POWs lived under the same conditions as the Boers for the next two and a half years. They were kept in a *Boma* (shelter) at a place called Waterval Boven, about a hundred and forty miles east of Pretoria in the Transvaal. Each Sunday, the Dominee of the N.G. Kerk, would hold a service and the jocks were offered the chance to attend. It was all in Afrikaans and for that reason, the Boers and the Bantu actually helped the jocks with the language. That was how the POWs had a chance to learn what they were saying. The only way the POWs got any news, was by listening to their captors' conversations in their language. George soon learned enough Afrikaans to converse with Boers and their Bantu helpers.

The Bantu people who worked for the Boers were very good to the jocks, they made their lives bearable with their kindness and showed great respect for fighting men. In particular, George struck up friendships with Themba, the *Bossboy*, who always liked to discuss life in Scotland with him. There was no seclusion of blacks and prisoners except at night when the blacks had to sleep in rondavels outside the prison perimeter. The Boers who guarded the Scots, however, kept their distance unless they wanted information – then their piousness went out the window. God-fearing as they were, they could be brutal at interrogation times, George soon learned.

There was no chance of escape as the walls of the sleeping block were actually made of steel and barbed wire fences corralled the vast enclosure. "They treat us like human beings though," George summed them up in conversation with his fellow inmates. Throughout the two and a half years of captivity so far, he told them, he heard the Boers speak of the atrocities that the Brits had caused their families to bear and, with horror, of the concentration camps the British made their families stay in. Their wives and children were dying in the camps while the Boer menfolk were fighting a losing battle for their own country. George felt empathy with the Boers and began to understand why they went to war with the British Empire.

Looking out of the *Boma*, George watched the African veldt as the seasons changed the country from a dry brown winter to a lush green in the spring rains. After that, the Jacaranda trees on the hills all around the encampment bloomed their lilac leaves for the months of October and November. Such beauty was never seen or heard of in Dundee and, as he thought about it, he knew the folk at home in the Crescent wouldn't believe him. Themba spoke to him every day and they swapped stories of each other's homelands. Themba enlightened him in the ways of the Zulu and George was transfixed by their cultures and knowledge. George told him in return, of the cold and the snow that fell on the stone built cities and of the camaraderie of the clan system that prevailed in Dundee in the hard times.

All of the blacks, he learned, could each speak at least six or seven different tribal languages and most of them could speak English and Afrikaans as well. The paradox, it seemed to George, was that these highly intelligent people took their daily instructions from the Boers who, for the most part could speak Afrikaans and some only spoke a smattering of Zulu or Xhosa. This was not their land originally, but the tribes were gracious enough to live in beneficial harmony with the Boers who, for all their sins, brought prosperity to their homeland.

Themba saw that George was bothered by the peace he saw in the camp in the time of war and that his own homeland of Scotland was on his mind and it was far, far away. Themba watched closely as George walked around the camp perimeter every day for hours on end, just looking out over the land and wishing he was home in the Crescent. He came back to his sleeping area one day with a feeling of great sadness and homesickness. As he approached his prisoner cot, he saw that the whole bed had been raised by six inches all around. Totally surprised by this display of disrespect, he demanded of his fellow POW inmates, to know, "Who has been frigging about with my bed?"

Nobody spoke at first, then Themba walked forward toward him and said, "I did it, George, my friend." He spoke in English for all to hear. "You are clearly suffering from the *Tokaloshe*."

George was confused; he had no idea what Themba was talking about and, throwing his hands up in the air he said, "What the frigging hell is a *Tokaloshe*?"

Themba replied seriously but calmy that all of the Bantu people knew that the *Tokaloshe* was a mischievous evil spirit that can become visible by drinking bad water or swallowing a stone, or being struck by a sadness, enough to want to cry. He was, Themba said, a two-foot-high devil created by the *Sangoma* (Witch Doctor) to harm his enemies, and he was also known to bite off sleeping people's toes. Themba also said that he knew that the whites are not so well educated, and they knew nothing of the *Tokaloshe*, but, in this case, he would overlook it.

George looked at the bed and asked why the hell his bed was now sitting on top of four bricks at each foot. Themba explained that the *Tokaloshe* comes for these victims at night in their beds. Inexplicably, the victim may die after these visits unless the *Tokaloshe* can be stopped from getting into the bed. "Now when he comes for you, George, he will walk right under your bed now because he cannot reach you anymore. I do not want you to die so I have stopped him coming to you at night." George was speechless but his heart melted at the thought of this proud black man thinking he was trying to save the life of a friend. "You will be all right now," said Themba, and he turned and walked away.

Ever since that day, George found it hard to speak ill of the blacks or even the Boers of South Africa and, in truth, he was actually smitten by the country he had been detained in during the Boer War.

CHAPTER 21

Churchill in South Africa

Much of the news that reached the far corners of Britain was disseminated from the London tabloids of the day. In November 1899 Winston Churchill was a freelance journalist for the *Morning Post* covering the war story in South Africa and looking for personal glory and to launch his political career. Churchill, a failed Harrow scholar whose social class gave him three attempts at an almost automatic entry to the Royal Academy at Sandhurst, took temporary leave from the army and made the trip to the theatre of war for money. While most of the privates in the British army earned one shilling and threepence a day, amounting to less than two pounds a week, Churchill was receiving two hundred and fifty pounds per month plus expenses as a war correspondent. This was in addition to his army pay. He was determined to write the news by making it. A novel way to do it was to ensure he made the headlines himself.

On his first assignment in an armoured train, he was captured by the Boers and taken prisoner. He 'escaped' or was allowed to escape for the sake of dramatic reporting. Churchill eventually reported that he navigated 300 miles through enemy territory without speaking a word of the Afrikaans language. 'Impossible' and 'Money makes Money' was the consensus in the ranks of the army in that particular theatre of war.

In time, the British seized control of the Transvaal and Orange Free State. The two states were officially annexed by Britain as two different countries. The British army implemented a scorched earth policy that destroyed anything and everything that might be useful to the enemy. Afrikaner homes and livestock were destroyed, and women and children were imprisoned in the world's first concentration camps. Thousands of Afrikaners died of disease and hunger, especially the children. Churchill elected not to report this news. By the spring of 1902 the Boer War was going the British Empire's way as expected. The half a million *outlander* British troops who invaded the land had crushed an army of eighty-eight thousand Boers, all for gold and diamonds.

Toward the end of the Boer War, South Africa, originally unified by the Boers was split in two by the *bittereinders* (bitter enders) and the *hensoppers* (hands uppers). In the end the hands uppers won the argument and allowed peace to return to their land. The English language was formally adapted as an official language.

CHAPTER 22

A Stabbing Affray

Mary-Anne had known Henry Mitchell as a friend from the beer tent days. She knew he was a scallywag from the moment she had met him but she liked him, not trusted, but liked. They had been drinking in the Campbeltown pub up the Hackie all day. At the end of the session, instead of going back to Littlejohn Street, she was happy to stay at his rented place in Mid-Wynd, a little cobbled street off the Hawkhill. While in the pub earlier, she bemoaned her life and told him she had had enough; she wanted her freedom and just felt like walking out on her mother, her daughter and all the family that she lived with. That is exactly what she did. As far as Mary-Anne was concerned Jessie was her mother's problem now. She moved in with Mitchell as man and wife fully in the knowledge that Mitchell was a layabout and a thief.

On a cold December Saturday night, in the Westport, the couple went drinking in the Scout. In the course of the evening, they met and befriended some Russian sailors. Drinking heavily, Mitchell was seen leaning into Mary-Anne's ear talking to her as if instructing her. After leaving the Scout at closing time, outside, in an adjacent alley, Mary-Anne and one of the sailors were seen kissing and cuddling by passers-by. Drunk as they both were, the sailor was relieved of all the money in his possession by the deviousness of his new Dundee friends, he claimed. The sailor remonstrated but it fell on deaf ears as far as Mary-Anne was concerned. He summoned the help of the bar manager of the Scout, who called the police. Both Mary-Anne and Henry Mitchell were arrested. The Evening Telegraph reported:

FOREIGN SAILOR FLEECED IN DUNDEE

In Dundee Police Court to-day, a young woman named Mary-Anne Murphy, a millworker, living in Mid Wynd, and a labourer named Henry Mitchell were charged with having stolen a purse and five pounds and ten shillings from Gustav Olsen, a foreign seaman while in Temple Lane on Saturday night.

Both denied the allegations and at Mitchell's request, his trial was adjourned until Friday, bail being fixed at five pounds. Murphy's case was disposed of.

The complainer explained that he came from Russia to Methil with the ship John Morrison. He was paid off on Saturday forenoon last and he came to Dundee along with a fellow seaman in the course of the day.

He had seven pounds in his possession when he arrived in the city and expended about thirty shillings to his knowledge.

He had some drink with his friend, and on leaving the public house about half past ten o'clock in the evening he was accosted by the accused. She joined his company and while in a dark lane she went into his pockets and took his purse. Other witnesses observed Murphy handing something to a man after Olsen discovered he had lost his purse, but the money had not been recovered. Sentence of a month's imprisonment was passed

– The Evening Telegraph, Dundee, Monday 30 December 1901.

Mary-Anne was duly released from prison a month later and on arrival at Mitchell's house in Mid-Wynd, found that they had been evicted for non-payment of rent. Too ashamed to return to the Crescent, she found lodgings in the Overgate with another friend from the fairground, Mary Carr.

She was going out of her mind again with depression and out of control. Like a house of cards, Mary-Anne's home life was collapsing again. She only drank at the weekends in those days, and worked during the week (when she was not in prison). She was getting through the weekdays by working as long hours as the mill would allow but the weekends turned into drink and devilment time. She started drinking with her friends on a Saturday morning in the beer tent and ended with a different friend, usually a male, on the Sunday nights. Her housemate, Mary Carr, had no complaints with Mary-Anne's habits and both women usually made good profits from both bedrooms at the weekends from the men she would bring home from the beer tent.

She started work in various different mills in and around Dundee countless times but ultimately, she lost her job due to her wild and scandalous behaviour. During the week, the fear of poverty, the evils of drink and the shame of illicit sex, all weighed heavily on her and forced her to keep working for a better life, if she could find one. She started visiting Catherine Garland again in the Crescent, out of desperation for a real friend.

In June 1902, the newspapers told everyone that the war was over in South Africa and the army would soon be demobilised. *Where is he?* She still fretted to herself over Billy, still hoping to get to the end of the mystery. At the same time, she dreaded meeting John Garland again if he happened to survive and ever get back to Dundee. *Worry, nothing but worry,* she thought. *What else can I do?*

She was always tempted to visit the McKees' house when she was in the Crescent but resisted the temptation when she remembered Jimmy, the aggressive young brother and the hostile feeling he gave her when they went to see his mother. On these occasions she would slip up to her mother's at number 8 to see Jessie once in a while. Always with a drink on her, Mary-Anne would become argumentative and cause a rammy in no time at all. She was never welcome at her mother's place again.

One late summer's night when she had persuaded Catherine to accompany her to her mother's place to see Jessie, Jimmy McKee spotted the two women going into the *closey* at number 8 and ran in after them. "Mary-Anne Garland, I want to see you," he shouted.

"Me?" she said. "What do you want with me, Jimmy?" she asked innocently.

"You were carrying on wi' my brother Billy, weren't you? And you, are married to John Garland at the same time!"

"That's none of your business, ye wee shite," she fired right back at him.

"It IS my business, and you stay away from my house and away from my mother, she has enough to deal with, never mind a bitch like you bothering her," he blurted out. "Or you'll get this," he yelled, brandishing a knife, causing the women to scream in alarm. The women ran up and knocked on Annie's door in panic. Young Grace answered the door and let the women in.

Jimmy McKee waited under the stair for ten minutes while the women were inside, until he heard them coming down again. "I said I want to see you," he shouted at the bottom of the close. Again, he held the knife up to Mary-Anne, showing her that he intended to use it on her.

The red mist rose up instantly and Mary-Anne flew at him, fists flying to his head. Jimmy lashed out with the knife and caught her on the shoulder; he stabbed again and this time in the back.

Catherine rushed to her pal's aid and got in between the two of them and she too, got the knife shoved into her hand. They managed to get back into Annie's house and wee Grace was able to shut the door on McKee to keep him out. With blood all over him he fled the close, allowing Grace to sound the alarm and get an ambulance. The *Dundee Courier* reported the incident the following Monday:

A STABBING AFFRAY

Littlejohn Street in the neighbourhood of Barrack Park, was the scene of a sensational stabbing affray late on Saturday evening.

The victim of the knife was Mary-Anne Garland or Murphy, a young married woman whose husband is at present in South Africa. She, along with her sister-in-law, Catherine Ann Garland was proceeding to the house of her mother, Mrs. Murphy, at 8 Littlejohn Street, when she was accosted and followed by a man named James McKee, who resides in the locality.

A quarrel seems to have taken place between the parties for on the women leaving the house, McKee was on the stair brandishing a knife in his hand. Without any warning, he is alleged to have struck at Mrs. Garland, and inflicted a couple of wounds, one on the shoulder, the other on the back.

The sister-in-law went to the assistance of Mrs. Garland and in rushing between McKee and the woman, who had fallen back into her mother's house, she received a nasty cut on her hand with the knife. Mrs. Garland's wounds bled profusely and she had to be removed to the Infirmary where she passed a very restless night. The other assaulted woman was taken to the Police Office, where the information supplied resulted in the apprehension of McKee who will likely be brought before the court today:

– Dundee Courier, Monday 2nd June 1902

Mary-Anne was badly injured by Jimmy McKee and she was mentally shattered by the attack. She now knew why he had been so hostile to her at the door. He was clearly unstable. The weekend she spent with Billy must be common knowledge in the McKee household and Jimmy must have held that grudge for a long time. It also meant, she supposed, that his mother also knew about their weekend together.

She wondered if Mrs. McKee knew anything about her recent previous misdemeanours. Had she seen the papers with her name in the court reports section, she mused? If so, would all the McKees be against her, including Billy, if he was still alive? She hated the thought.

She moved out of Mary Carr's flat and into a small single end again on Blackness Road where she was able to recover quietly albeit in fear of her life. Incredibly, the Hon. Sheriff-Substitute Ogilvie in relation to the stabbing dealt with the case of a 'very brutal character':

DUNDEE BRUTALITY

SERIOUS ASSAULTS ON WOMEN

A sentence of two months' imprisonment was passed on James McKee who pleaded guilty to having stabbed Mary-Anne Murphy or Garland on the back while on the stair in Littlejohn Street, and for having stabbed Catherine Ann Garland on the right hand while the latter was endeavouring to rid her companion of McKee.

– The Evening Post, Dundee, Monday 9th June 1902

Life went on for Mary-Anne but living without Mary Carr had financial challenges for both of them and they both struggled with the basics like money, paying the rent was difficult each week but they had to stay somewhere. Before the year was out, she was in front of the sheriff again and the *Dundee Evening Post* reported:

At The Police Court:

Two women named Mary Carr and Mary-Anne Murphy, millworkers, were remitted to the Sherriff charged with stealing shawls from a draper's shop in the Overgate.

– Dundee Courier, Monday 10th December 1902.

CHAPTER 23

The Dundee Arms

On a cold and rainy Saturday night later in December 1902, Mary-Anne went off with Catherine for a gin evening in the city. After a few drinks they were leaving the Dundee Arms in the High Street to head home to the Crescent. Pulling their shawls over their heads in harmony to shelter from the rain, they turned into Thorter Row, a pedestrian alley leading to the Overgate. In the shadows she saw the silhouette of a soldier.

The shock of it made her come to an abrupt stop and, holding Catherine back with both hands, Mary-Anne whispered, "It's Billy." Instantly, Catherine looked up and saw the same unmistakable silhouette of Sergeant Billy McKee. Terrified, and in disbelief, Mary-Anne started to walk slowly toward her man. The gaslight strengthened and illuminated the face of the man as she approached him. "My god, I thought you were dead," she cried and ran to him. She stopped three paces away from the man and saw to her horror, her mistake. It was not Billy, but George!

He was amazed to see the girls in this state and this late in Thorter Row but elated at the same time. "I don't believe it," he said, arms stretched out to greet them both. Catherine threw herself into him, but Mary-Anne stood still shaking and crying.

"Where's Billy?" She waited for his answer.

"Billy is dead, Mary-Anne," he said softly.

The three of them had had a shock. They turned back into the Dundee Arms and returned to the corner table they had just left a minute before. George bought the drinks and sat down with the ladies. Catherine held his hand tightly as George told them what had happened at Magersfontein. "But they said he was missing," Mary-Anne said through the tears. "Your mother told us he was missing, not dead." Adding, "He was never on the list of dead. Just like you were never on the list of men that were captured."

George tried to explain it to her. "Some Black Watch men were buried in the trenches they were killed fighting over." George added, "I saw him, lying there, dead, on the battlefield." He went on, "It was the way the Boers dealt with these things; he was probably buried in the trench where he died." He added, "I was lucky, I was captured and kept in a secure *'Boma'* prison in the middle of the African plains." He told her, "There was no way I could escape and tell anyone about Billy, it was not like a real prison or even town jail to hold us, and there was no means of communicating where we were." He explained that they were in a remote settlement in the middle of nowhere, where the Boers and their blacks guarded them and prevented any news in or out.

He told the women that the Boers, being Christians, also tended to the prisoners' physical and spiritual health. "These men are not so different from us," and he added, "they are good and God-fearing people and they fought for their land like Scotsmen."

Mary-Anne said, "How can you speak so kindly of those animals, George? It sounds like you don't hate the people who killed your brother."

"Hate? No, I don't hate them, Mary-Anne, hate is a poison I

cannot take anymore and, anyway, I'm not so sure it was the Boers who killed my brother."

"What does that mean?" she asked.

George was silent for a minute, clearly thinking about the battle. "Nobody really knows what happened to Billy, but maybe you should ask your husband," he said. Mary-Anne looked at him intensely as George went on. "He and Billy were in the same fight, with the same enemy, at the same place. Funny thing is, he swears he never saw Billy at Magersfontein," George said. "I've got my doubts about him, Mary-Anne."

"Why?" she asked.

"He is a born liar and says anything he wants you to believe. Mind you, it was a shambles at the front, some of our lads did take friendly fire," he said.

"What does that mean, George?" she said, knowing the answer.

"It means that some of our own rifles shot our own men… in error. It is possible that's what happened to Billy, but no one who saw him die actually lived to say it." Finally, he said, "Even the Black Watch never knew what happened until I told them a week ago when I was released, and my mother never knew Billy was dead until I told her an hour ago at home in Littlejohn Street," he said sadly. "I have just left her, and it is hurting her even though I think she expected it. All I can tell you is that I tried to get to him when I saw what was happening, so did Joe," said George.

"What do you mean?" asked Mary-Anne.

"Joe Murphy was with me all the time at Magersfontein, he was wounded beside me when we reached Billy's body and we were taken prisoner together," George replied. Mary-Anne cried in silence.

"What happened to my wee brother, Joe? Wasn't he with you in the POW camp?" Mary-Anne asked.

"No, he was taken away to a Boer field hospital. That was before we reached Pretoria, it must have been just before Christmas in 1899," said George. He added, "I never saw him again or heard any more about him. I thought he might have been medevac'd out and sent home to the UK."

Mary-Anne spoke up. "We have been told he was dead too."

"Whaaaat! I never knew that. How?" George was genuinely shocked. "He was recovering the last time I saw him," said George sadly.

"What about my brother John?" Catherine said hesitatingly. "Have you seen him?" Knowing that Mary-Anne despised him, she kept her voice low.

"John Garland? Oh yes, I've seen him all right He's back in Dundee now as well," answered George. Mary-Anne stiffened as George explained that John Garland was on the same train back to Dundee with him that day and that he had had the misfortune to be within earshot of him all the way from Aldershot to Dundee with the rest of the demobbed soldiers coming home from the war. Turning to Mary-Anne, George said, "I know why you split up from that eejit now, he is aff his heid, ye know. All he talks about is how many Boers he killed with his .303." Jokingly, he said, "If he HAD killed as many as he said, the war would have been over two years ago."

Mary-Anne was so distraught; she had already lost her dear brother, and now she had been told that Billy was dead and he might have been killed by mistake. "How could they kill their own men by mistake!" she fretted in disbelief.

"I will never know why any of you even joined up and went to

South Africa in the first place! It has nothing to do with us," said Catherine.

"We went to defend our Queen and country," said George.

"Against what?" she said. "How can you defend your country if you are in Africa? What possible harm could the Boers do to Britain? None," said Catherine, answering her own question. "And the only damage the Boers could have done was stop the Empire stealing the wealth of their own country," she said.

"Well, we never thought of any of that, Catherine, we just wanted to join the army," George said defensively.

Mary-Anne then said, "George, can I ask you a question? Did your mum know about Billy and me?"

"Yes, she did, and she was very sure he was coming back for you." He explained that they both told the family everything before they left for South Africa. "He was very fond of you."

"Has your mum said anything else about me, George?" asked Mary-Anne after a few moments' contemplation as she sipped her gin.

"Not that I know of, but I've only been back a few hours," and to that end, he held his glass up. *"Goeie gesondeid, dames, dit is goed om jou weer te sein."* They both looked at him, bewildered. "It means, 'Good health, ladies, it's good to see you.' It's the Boer's language, lovely people," he said with a wry smile.

"Did you know that Jimmy stabbed me? Stabbed us both actually," said Catherine.

"What are you talking about?" he said. "All I know is that Jimmy has been inside and that he has left home now." He added, "Nobody seems to know where he is."

"We've got a lot to talk about, George," said Catherine, with a sigh. The discussion ended on that sad note prematurely and, being in a pub, it wasn't exactly private. Knowing Jimmy was no longer in Dundee, the women were happy to walk George back to the McKees' house in the Crescent that cold, wintery night, to continue the conversation.

They reached Littlejohn Street and George said, "My mother will be grateful for the company but be careful what you say about Billy, she's not taking it well." Slowly the three climbed the stairs to the McKee's flat and George quietly turned the door handle. He stepped inside and froze in disgust when he heard that voice again – John Garland was in mid-flow of telling a story. Mary-Anne looked at George in horror.

"And the Boers were firing at us in the dark and our sojers were just lying all over the place…" John Garland was holding court in George's mum's house. His mother was sobbing silently in the chair by the fireplace and her youngest son Robert was kneeling by the fire listening to every word. Cup of tea in hand, Garland turned round to see his estranged wife standing in the doorway beside George and Catherine. "Mary-Anne, there you are! What are you doing here?"

"WHAT THE HELL ARE YOU DOING HERE?" she asked.

"That's a great welcome home," said Garland. "I've missed you too," he screeched sarcastically. Then, realising where he was, he lowered his voice and, in a civil tone he said, "I went to the house in John Street but they said you had moved. Then, I went to your mum's and she also told me you had moved out, but she didn't know where!"

Forlornly, he looked at his wife. "I've nowhere else to go so I thought I'd see if George could put me up! Then you walked in and my prayers were answered," he said with a smile on his face.

George quietly told him there was no room there and he had to leave… now. That was enough to get Garland out of the house and on his way. Catherine gave him her key to her mother's house in Littlejohn Street. "You can stay the night but you're sleeping on the kitchen floor." John Garland really wanted to stay at Mary-Anne's that night but accepted the key and took his leave begrudgingly. The women stayed for an hour with George and his mother going over the future without Billy and what the future held for George and Catherine. Mary-Anne went home alone to Blackness Road.

Before Garland left, Mary-Anne had agreed to meet him at some stage to 'discuss' what to do about the bairn. She was absolutely physically and emotionally shattered. Mary-Anne fell back onto her armchair when she got her home in Blackness Road and sank immediately into the depths of depression once again. Like the last time, the only way ahead for her was to work hard during the week and drink on weekends.

CHAPTER 24

Grace and Johnny

Young Johnny McKee had been released from Baldovan Industrial School in May 1903 after doing five years for thieving from the crowds in the city. A former thief and a burglar, Johnny was always going to survive his own way in the Crescent. A tough laddie, he learned to stand his own ground and fight for his own space in detention.

When he was allowed back to his parents' home in Littlejohn Street, Johnny was welcomed back with a lukewarm reception from his mother. His older brother, James, had served time in Perth Prison for the stabbing of the girls in the next close. "You can sleep in Jimmy's bed until he comes home but not in Billy's," Annie McKee said. "He can appear here at any time and he'll need it when he comes back from South Africa," she said, not believing her son Billy was dead. "But only until James comes back, then you need to find another place."

His mother, Annie McKee, used to be the matriarch of the family but by this time she seemed to have lost the will to live ever since hearing that her two sons were missing, presumed dead at Magersfontein. She had been desperately ill and diagnosed with severe bronchitis. When George came back and told her that Billy was dead, she just refused to believe it. Annie McKee fell apart mentally, and her health deteriorated. She could no longer work or look after her family due to her illness. Johnny, on release from Baldovan, realised his mother was suffering from more than bronchitis, and at sixty, she died on the 6th of December 1903, believing to the end that Billy was coming home. George was devastated for the loss of his mother but relieved to be home for her passing. Unlike his brother, he had at least been able to return home to Catherine, his lady friend and his life was getting back to normal again. Johnny, his younger brother was home now, and at fifteen years old, tough enough to deal with it, being a very streetwise young man.

Grace caught up with him in Parker Street at the top of the Crescent and walked up the Parker Street steps with him. "What are you up to, Johnny?" she asked him as though she hardly cared a jot whether he answered or not.

"I'm going to the beer tent," he said nonchalantly. "It's where I work… sometimes."

"You're too young to work there so don't tell me lies!" she retorted. Wee Grace Murphy was also fifteen and had been working full time in the Verdant since leaving school a year earlier. She knew everyone in the Crescent and was a well-known source of gossip and secrets. She knew the McKees in number 9 had been through a lot of grief with the death of Mrs. McKee and the sons in the Boer War but she never knew much about their young brother Johnny, or why he had been put away to the bad boys school.

"Well sometimes I work there," he said, removing the woodbine from behind his ear. "Want a fag?" he asked.

"No!" Grace said.

"Where are you going?" Johnny asked.

"The Wellgate for messages for the house," she said. Then, "Want to come with me?"

Startled, he lit the fag, and said, "OK."

"I thought you were going to work in the beer tent, Johnny?" said Grace.

"Well, I only work there when I want to… sometimes."

She said, "You mean when Tam Pepper wants a skivvy. I've seen ye hanging about that tent waiting on something, now I know you're just looking for work," said Grace.

"I'm getting flung out of my mum's hoose," he said, "so I'm going to join the army, but first I'm going to be a boxer," he said to Grace as they walked together to Meadowside.

"Why don't you go to the mills and get a job there?" she asked.

"I did but there's no money in it," Johnny said. "I'm a strong man and I can do better things other than push bails of jute around for a living," replied Johnny.

"What do you really do for money, Johnny?" Grace asked.

"Anything that anybody will pay me for," he said back.

"What does that mean?"

"I've been getting money from Tam Pepper for getting the empty beer barrels out and the full ones into the beer tent," he said proudly.

"That's' not a job! That's just Tam Pepper taking a 'len o'you!" she said.

"Eh, but like I said, I'm going be a boxer, like your brother Joe when I'm sixteen," he said.

Grace stopped dead in her tracks and said, "What do you mean 'like my brother Joe'?" said Grace disbelievingly.

"Joe fights in the booths," he said, "and he's got a stage name, I saw him fight last week."

"You mean Joe Murphy, my brother? You're wrong there, Johnny, he's dead, he was killed in South Africa!"

"Naw he wisna', he's a boxer!" said Johnny. "He's in the boxing booths and works for Tam, fights at middleweight, been doing it for months and he's good."

Grace said, "Joe Murphy is not a boxer, my brother Joe Murphy, is dead. I can't believe you said that, Johnny McKee, ye're a wee liar."

"Well, if it's no' him, it's his double, let's go up there and see," said Johnny.

"I will, right after I've finished at the Wellgate and we'll see who is right," she said.

"Right," he said.

Grace was expecting it all to be a mistake and to find that Johnny was wrong. She waited and waited with him until after ten o'clock when the electric lights came on and illuminated the 'BOXING' sign on the booth. The crowd started to gather, then the fighters came out in single file. She saw a man in the line-up that looked like Joe from afar but needed to get to the front of the crowd. Grace and Johnny squeezed through to the front and were now looking at him from six feet away. She was overwhelmed, it WAS him. Her big brother was standing on a stage in front of the crowd with the other boxers… Looking up at him, she saw the difference that the years had made to his body. Toned, muscled and fit, he looked like a fighter in every respect. Aggressive posture, face scarred, his nose – big as always but now broken. She noticed too, the tattoo on his right arm that she'd seen many times before – a tombstone with adornment around it – so she knew it was him. Joe was standing in the line-up outside the boxing booth on the stage. "Come on, boys, Pound a Round," Tam shouted as usual.

"JOE… JOE!" Grace shouted and started waving her arms. His eyes flicked down to hers in the crowd then back up at the lights above.

Tam started to introduce the boxers: "Dundee's own… at flyweight," he roared into the megaphone, "Paul Brady. At lightweight we have Davie McCormack." Then it was Joe's turn. "At middleweight… Glasgow's own… Garland Fraser, "and finally…" She never heard the name of the heavyweight. She was confused.

"Tam has got that wrong… He's missed out Joe's name, why is that Johnny?"

"It's a stage name, Grace, like the entertainers do. I've heard him called that before, that's what I wanted you to hear."

The boxers stood on the stage in front of the booth for about ten minutes more and the benches filled up. Joe never acknowledged his little sister, and she was at the point of crying when he turned and went into the tent with the other fighters. "It's not him, Johnny, it can't be. If it was Joe, he would have recognised me and said something… surely?"

"I think it's him – that's why I told you about him, either that or it's his double," Johnny said. "Come on. Let's go and speak to Tam Pepper, he must know if that's your brother."

As the customers filed into the booth, Johnny said, "Tam, Tam, can we speak?"

"Johnny, there's nae empties in here, ye'll need to go speak to them in the beer tent if ye want yer money tonight, son," said Tam, dismissively.

"No, no, it's not that, Tam," he blurted out. "This is my pal fae the Crescent, Grace Murphy, I've told her that your middleweight is really her brother Joe Murphy but you call him by another name, some funny name, Fraser something or other. What is that boxer's real name, Tam?"

Tam caught his breath. He was clearly unsure whether to say something or not. The young couple looked at Tam and Tam looked down at his feet. "That's not Joe Murphy, lassie, that's Garland Fraser," he said. "My middleweight is Garland Fraser. Comes from Glasgow an'a, I think. Now then, if that's all, I need to start the bouts."

"Jeezeepeeps! Not a chance, Tam Pepper, that's my brother Joe and you know it!" Grace said indignantly. The realisation of what was going on there made Grace yell incredulously. "Yer a bliddy liar, Tam Pepper, standing there wi' that walrus mouzer talking a load o' shite and ye're telling me lies!" she raged, wagging her half finger in his face but missing by a mile. "And," she said, "ye're a worse liar than that bliddy Winston Churchill!" Grace shouted at him as he turned his back on her. "I'm going home to tell my mum."

Tam Pepper twitched his moustache and focused his attention on the few punters still outside the booth, roaring, "Pound a Round! A Pound a Round!"

CHAPTER 25

Blackness Road

Dundee was becoming a hard place to live after the Boer War because of a lack of work for the men on the dole. In general, it was becoming a poverty-stricken and drunken, grimy den of iniquity again and, in Mary-Anne's mind, Hell on Earth. It suited her mood to a tee. The de-mobbed soldiers were queuing up for handouts at the *Broo* (labour exchange) in Gellatly Street; the only work in Dundee at that time was the mills, usually for women and the wages were eroding.

Mary-Anne heard, however, that John Garland was trying to secure a labouring job back with his old employers Scott Brothers in Mid-Wynd between the Hawkhill and the Perth Road. That impressed her because she was sure he would never work again. As the mill was not far from Mary-Anne's single end in Blackness Road, he had cheekily suggested to her through his sister Catherine, that he would have a better chance of a job there if he lived with her in Blackness Road.

One Saturday morning, Mary-Anne had met with John Garland for the talk. They walked the length of the Blackness Road and had a civilised chat about the future. They could get divorced but the mutual friends and families and gossips of the Crescent would frown on that. In addition, a divorce would hold John and Mary-Anne to legally binding financial agreements and potentially take precedence over their meagre incomes. An agreement like that would undoubtedly bring Jessie into the equation. With her living quite happily at Annie's, if they divorced, they would be liable for maintenance to be paid to Annie. Both agreed that would be a complete waste of money. In addition, the courts could back charge both of them and monies would probably be owed to Annie. Money was hard to come by and so neither of them wanted that. The outlook, however, would be better if they could pool their resources. They even talked loosely about getting together and even getting Jessie back. They entered the Westport and conveniently, the Scout in Temple Lane was open.

By the end of the day, both were steaming drunk, and the plan had developed somewhat. Although Mary-Anne could see through it, John maintained his nice husband act, and, the drink was taking its effect. She was warming to him again somewhat just like she did in her teens. He confessed that he had overstayed his welcome at his mother's house, and she wanted him out as soon as possible. It was decided then, from that very night John Garland would be staying at Mary-Anne's, on the settee of course, to try and save money. Still legally married to him, but as far as she was concerned he had deserted her. Nevertheless, how would it look if she refused to let him come home with her that night after being with him all day?

In reality, in moments of sobriety it occurred to Mary-Anne that John Garland was NOT welcome at her place in Blackness Road, but she was in an impossible situation. She was doing this only to save money and, as they discussed, the possibility of taking Jessie back was there, if they were a family again. All of this was helping to put the death of Billy out of her head.

"Only one bed, Mary-Anne," John Garland said after he got

settled on the settee.

"That's right, it's another single end," she said.

"You live here alone, right?" Garland asked.

"Yes," she answered.

"And you can afford the rent on a spinner's wage?"

"Yes," she said, getting annoyed.

"Then why is there a man's shaving kit by the jawbox? Are you having an affair?" he demanded.

After all that had happened to her she wanted to kill him. "IT'S MY BROTHER'S," she shouted. "It's Joe's, he left it with me on his last leave and it has stayed with me."

"What brother? Joe is dead!" he said.

"You insensitive pig!" she shouted. "I'm telling you no more, John Garland, you buggered off and left me without any money – I can't even afford to bring up my own bairn, and you're questioning me about MY habits."

Then the real argument ensued.

"Where is the money you're due me for the last five years then?" she demanded.

"Oh no, I've no money, Mary-Anne; sojers don't get much to live on. I can let you have a pound."

Mary-Anne exploded. "A pound! What frigging good is a pound to me? What have you done with five years' army pay? I'm your wife and I want to know what you've done with my money. Answer that question and I'll tell you what you want to know when you pay me!" she said, shaking with anger.

The argument went on and on. Mary-Anne was exasperated

between the strain of being with John again and hearing his stories. At the back of her mind, and especially knowing about Billy's death, she knew it would never work. Now, even more unbelievably, her husband had wormed his way back into her home. What she didn't know, was that John Garland was fully aware of her weekend with Billy McKee before the war. He said nothing about that. Neither, of course, did she.

CHAPTER 26

An Annoyance to the Land

John Garland had been staying in Mary-Anne's single end for a month. He started work as a labourer at Scott Brothers low mill in Mid-Wynd. He was determined to make another new start in his life from here on. Although he slept on the settee for the first few nights, Mary-Anne actually found he was a changed man in certain respects and let him into her bed. He gave her a pound for housekeeping and another pound for herself. He bought her a box of chocolates and a packet of fags for her birthday on the 10th of April. All that put a slight smile on her face, but she was still secretly heartbroken. He knew she was hiding something but thought he'd better not push it.

Mary-Anne's birthday fell on a bright and sunny Monday and she had taken the day off at John's behest. They went to visit Jessie at Annie's house in the Crescent. The street looked better in the spring sunshine and cleaner after the snows and April rains had cleared the dust and grime away. Mary-Anne felt nervous about meeting her mum and her daughter again but secretly she stayed off the gin before the visit and just hoped it would go well and that the meeting would settle her nerves like all family get-togethers do. John brought Jessie a new gird to play in the streets with.

Mary-Anne and John Garland climbed the stairs of 8 Littlejohn Street together for the first time in five years, but to them, it felt like there was never a gap, until they saw Jessie.

Jessie met with her parents but never spoke to her father. She had grown into a lovely, eight-year-old lass and it appeared to all intents and purposes that she was perfectly at home there, and to her, Annie was the mother figure that she knew. Jessie recognised her mother but not her father. She took the gird and thanked them politely but had nothing else to say to them. Annie was decidedly frosty to them both. No tea was offered because all Annie really wanted to know was what they were after. Inside, Annie was upset at the thought that they wanted to take the bairn from her. Grace stood by her mum like a guard and made it clear they were not welcome. Jessie stood behind Grace and Annie instinctively.

The talk turned to the possibility of Jessie coming back to them and Annie quickly knocked it on the head. "You cannot stay in a single end with an eight-year-old lassie. Where is she to sleep? It certainly can't be in the same room, now can it?"

The conversation ran dry very quickly and Mary-Anne politely said they had to leave. Before they left, Jessie disappeared into the big bedroom and was not around to say goodbye. Jessie knew that the gird was not a well thought-out gift because it was a boy's toy and she didn't like it.

When they reached the pavement in Littlejohn Street, John and Mary-Anne Garland breathed a collective sigh of relief and he said, "Well, if it's not to be then it's not to be! Let's go down the town, Mary-Anne, and I'll tell you all about South Africa and the time I shot the Boers."

To keep the peace, Mary-Anne muttered, "I can't wait."

First stop was the Phoenix in the Nethergate, a pub that John Garland knew well before he left Dundee to join the army. To Mary-

Anne, it felt claustrophobic. The fact that it was across the road from St. Andrew's Cathedral made it worse, it brought back all the bad memories of the funeral and the melancholia she had when baby Jessie was teething. The old depression was descending on her again that day and it was as if nothing had ever changed, drinking with John, listening to his lies, his bragging and his ambitions. *Has it really been five years since he walked away from us?* she thought. *That was the last time my bairn and me had a life together.*

The more she thought about it the worse it got and she began to hold back the tears. John Garland noticed how upset she was, and he whispered in her ear, "Don't worry about Jessie, she's happy at your mother's, and anyway, we're better off without her right now but we'll get her back one day." He had misunderstood her entirely, again. She began to cry.

After a couple more in the Phoenix they moved along the High Street to the Royal Hotel. The crying got worse, and, as always, she became obstreperous. John and Mary-Anne were asked to leave. Eventually, they made their way back to the single end in Blackness Road. By the time they had arrived in their *closey*, the gin had taken hold. They were in full song when they got to the door of their house. "There was I, waiting at the church…" they sang through tears of laughter until her next-door neighbour, Mattie McGuire, popped her head out of the door and asked them to be quiet.

"Who do you think ye're talking to, ye old bag?" shouted Mary-Anne. "I'm Mary-Anne Garland and this is my hoose! I'll sing if I want, you'll not stop me!"

Matilda McGuire responded, "Well, we all know who you are but God knows who the new man is!" At that, Mary-Anne went for her, bursting into her house and grabbing Mattie by the hair, pulling her all over the room. John watched as his wife fought her neighbour, then he pulled her off the terrified woman. Matilda's granddaughter Maggie, who had witnessed it all, stood transfixed in shock as Mary-Anne, on her way out, belted the girl a full-fisted punch on the nose for nothing other than badness.

Mrs. McGuire went to the police that night and filed a complaint. They came to see Mary-Anne and gave her a warning. Early the following morning Mary-Anne was still drunk and seething and burst into Mrs. McGuire's door and gave her more of the same. The police were summoned a second time and resolved the issue their way:

'AN ANNOYANCE TO THE LAND'

A three-fold charge was preferred against Mary-Anne Murphy or Garland of 80 Blackness Road in Dundee Police Court to-day. The charge consisted of two disorderliness and one of assault. "The complainer was Matilda Swan Ogilvie or McGuire, a neighbour of the accused. Her statement, which was submitted by Chief Constable Dewar, was to the effect that Garland was much given to drink. And when under its influence was a source of considerable annoyance to the land". On Monday evening she was in this condition, and going into the complainer's house she began to curse and swear at her, and then seizing her by the hair dragged her about for a few minutes. As she took her departure she struck Margaret Ogilvie (11) a severe blow on the nose. Mrs. McGuire complained to the police, requesting that the accused should be cautioned. About six o'clock on the following morning Garland burst open the complainers door and behaved in a most outrageous manner on account of the police speaking to her about her conduct on the previous day. She continued her disorderliness until about noon, when Mrs. McGuire again complained to the police. Garland was ordered to pay a fine of one pound, with the alternative of fourteen days imprisonment.

– *Evening Telegraph, Dundee, Wednesday 13th July, 1904*

Mary-Anne asked for time to pay but received none. She turned to John Garland for a pound to pay the fine. "You are joking, aren't you? I've given you all you're going to get, and, after that performance, I am wondering if it's even safe biding with you anymore," he said. Mary-Anne paid the one-pound fine with the same pound John Garland had given her for housekeeping the day before. She was skint again and it was entirely his fault. After the latest court appearance, John Garland walked away from her and left her standing alone in the court. She ambled forlornly home about twelve noon.

She just wept in silence until she had no more tears. She was out of money again, out of tears and out of love; nobody wanted her. Ironically, when he came home, John Garland felt sorry for her and wrapped his arms around her. "It's OK, Mary-Anne, I'll take care of you."

She knew he was not serious but she needed someone's love to take away all her depressed thoughts. She calmed down and curled up in his arms like a child. "I know you will, John." She even fooled herself for the time being.

Two months later she hit him with a frying pan. "Take that, you useless piece of shite." She flew at him. "How can you walk out of a job a week ago and not tell me?" she screamed.

"I didn't want to upset you and… Ouch, stop that with the pan." He motioned to her with his fists. "I'm telling you, Mary-Anne, if you raise your hand to me again, I will do you," he spat at her with venom.

"You could'na do up a kipper," she shouted and took another swing with the frying pan.

"That's it, I'm leaving you again! – For good this time!" shouted John.

"Leave if you want to, I can live without you, John Garland, you know that, but be warned, I'll be right after you for money and, wherever you go, I will be looking for child maintenance."

John Garland drew his sleeves up readying for the fight. "Don't kid yourself, Mary-Anne, after all this time at your mother's, they won't make me pay maintenance for Jessie now," he said.

"Not Jessie, the NEW bairn," she bawled. "I'm pregnant, you bastard!"

John was speechless. "How the hell did that happen?" he said in genuine bewilderment.

"Use your imagination!" she cried.

John Garland shouted back at her, "After all the grief you've given me, now you go and get pregnant!?"

"Whaaat? It's yours," Mary-Anne said. "You, parasite, all you do is take, take, take, what do you give me in return? Another frigging bairn! Well, leave, ye bastard, go, frigg off," she wept. "It's all your fault, you got me drunk on my birthday in the first place."

"Your birthday was months ago!" he exclaimed. "That was the start my troubles with you – again." He gathered up all his things and stuffed them into the valise he kept under the bed.

Hearing the commotion next door, Matilda McGuire leaned out of the window that looked out onto the Blackness Road, looking down the road for any sign of Mary-Anne to see if it was safe to go down the stairs for messages. She watched John Garland as he stormed across the street to get away from his wife. He stood across the Blackness Road smoking and kicking his feet until Mary-Anne came down the stairs and reached the end of the close.

"Don't think ye are getting back in here, Garland!" she shouted across the busy road in between the trams and the horse carts.

"Don't flatter yersel'," he said. "I'm no' coming back to you!" Then he shouted back, "I only want the rest of my stuff and my kit bag and I'm getting on my way, far away from you, ya bitch."

Matilda McGuire never knew what was happening until Mary-Anne got back in the flat and opened the window next to hers from her own flat next door. She raised the window frame and fired his kitbag out onto the road. Next, she threw his shaving kit out onto the Blackness Road as far as it would go and, as if, almost by divine intervention, *splat!* A passing Clydesdale shat on it. Then, *crunch*, the back hoof of the horse drawing the jute cart flattened the steel shaving tin into the cobbles. "Take that, ye get! And never darken my doorstep again!" shouted Mary-Anne.

John Garland gathered up the remnants of his possessions from the road and looking at his shaving kit, kicked it as hard as he could into the gutter and walked away. He ambled around Dundee thinking over his options and, ultimately, he knew where he was going to spend the next few years of his life. He walked straight to Dudhope Castle fairground and into the recruiting sergeants' tent. John Garland re-enlisted in the 3rd Battalion of the Black Watch, the Royal Highlanders, for another four years.

Looking out the window to her right at Matilda, she bawled, "See what ye've done, ye auld witch! – I hope ye're satisfied now, that's my man and he's gone again!" Her temper was up and she was taking it out on her neighbour again. "I'm watching you, Matilda McGuire, just remember that!" Matilda slammed the window down and sat in her flat all day. Mary-Anne also waited until darkness fell, thinking, *I hate this place,* and wishing she was back in the Crescent again, then she sneaked out of the close and away, as far as she could get, for any pub to get her daily drink of gin.

CHAPTER 27

Garland Fraser

A week later, Joe Murphy knocked quietly on Mary-Anne's door at half past twelve at night. Mary-Anne shouted, "Go away!" He knocked again. "I'm no' letting you in, John Garland, you and me are finished." The knock persisted.

"It's not Garland, it's me, Joe."

"Joe who?"

"Joe Murphy, yer wee brother!"

Her mind started racing. *What the hell is happening?* she thought. *Am I imagining things? It sounds like Joe but it can't be. I must be going mad!* After a few long, terrifying minutes and another knock, she finally opened the door an inch at a time, to see her long-lost brother. "Joe, is it really you? I thought you were dead – you're no' dead, are you?" she asked, staring at him.

Joe was smiling. "It's good to see you, Mary-Anne, and no, I'm no' dead."

Mary-Anne was overwhelmingly relieved to realise he was not a ghost but real, and then she was desperately saddened when she saw his battered face.

"Did you know we were told you were dead, Joe?" she asked when they had settled in front of the fire with a cup of tea.

"Yes, I knew it. I let that happen for a reason. I'll explain, but you have got to swear you'll keep it to yourself." He told her that he had been back in the UK for about six months. He said he never felt as though he could get in touch until that day.

"Why not, Joe? Mum had a telegram that told us you'd been killed on active service, I've even seen it! How can the army have got THAT wrong?" she asked. "Even now, she still thinks you are dead, we have to tell her," said Mary-Anne.

"I can't tell Mum, that would ruin everything I've planned for. I'm using a different name now and I don't want anyone in Dundee to know I'm back, Mary-Anne, but, if I tell you the reason, you will have to keep it a secret," he said.

"Why, what have you done, Joe? You can tell me, I won't tell anyone, I promise," said Mary-Anne. She went on, "Did you desert from the army? Is that it?" she asked him.

He answered her, "That was a part of it, Mary-Anne, but it's much worse than that and I hope you will find it in you to forgive me, that's why I'm here." That was the most important thing to him. "As for the army," he told her, "they were secondary to me but," he said, the army would jail him for sure, for what he did, and he wasn't having that! "Even if they don't get me for murder, they'll jail me for desertion."

"Murder? Oh my god, Joe, who did you murder?" she asked.

"I'm going to tell you, Mary-Anne, but I'll be in the deepest shit if the army found out. I mean, I'm actually on the run and it could be the firing squad for me if I am caught," he said.

Mary-Anne looked at him as if he were mad. "Start at the beginning." She looked puzzled and said slowly, "OK, so why are you on the run?" she asked.

"Because of something that happened at Magersfontein – I would have been court-marshalled for shooting one of our own men. Mary-Anne," he said, "I shot Billy McKee."

Mary-Anne was speechless. She stared at Joe's face but never saw him; the red mist was rising inside her head. "You killed my Billy?" she stammered incredulously.

"Yes, but it was a mistake," he added. "I was trying to help him and somehow my shot was deflected."

"Joe, are you sure you shot him?" she said, tears in her eyes and her heart thumping.

"Yes, I am," he said. "I saw him hit the ground, and then, when we got to him, I knew he was dead," adding, "I know the marks of a Lee Enfield .303 fatality." He said it again sorrowfully. "It was a mistake, I was trying to shoot at the Boers around him, but in the crush in our column, my arm was bumped." He went on, "And that's when Billy fell."

Joe took a deep breath and started to explain that he too was shot. He slipped his shirt over his head and showed her the mark of the clean bullet hole in his back and a larger one out of his left shoulder in front. She winced at the sight of the scars. She noticed another healed scar on his right arm. "And this?" She pointed to a two-inch linear mark above the elbow.

"I'll tell you about that now," he said. "Anyway, I was captured at that point of the battle." Joe told her how he and George McKee were bundled onto an ox wagon as prisoners of war and held by the Boers after Magersfontein. They were driven away under armed guard and then, he told her, he was transferred to a Boer hospital in Wynberg, Pretoria, in the Transvaal Republic.

He explained that he was hospitalised with some English POWs and they were all kept together under armed guards. One of the lads was Arthur Jones, a private in the Lancashire Fusiliers. Arthur was wounded in a battle on a hill called *Spion Kop* (Lookout Mountain) near Ladysmith. This happened in January 1900, just after Joe was captured. They spent about three weeks together in the same Boer hospital, and, as they recovered from their wounds, they decided to break out of the camp. "We went over the wall one night and spent about a week on the run." He went on to say that the Boer trackers were out looking for them and, if caught, they would shoot them on sight. They were tracked to the banks of the Vaal River hiding in the scrubland around the Vaal Dam. He and Arthur decided to swim for it that night but the Boers were waiting for them and opened fire when they reached the middle of the dam.

"They started shooting at us from the shore." Joe went white when the memory came back. He said, "Arthur was shot in the head and I pulled him to the far bank." Joe went on, "He was dead by the time I got him there." Joe went on to explain that they all carried a glazed ID card in their breast pocket for identification. It was called an Army form B2067. The card listed all their details including name, rank and serial number and, gave instruction if a soldier was killed or wounded. "I knew the Boers would find his body and so I searched him for his card," he told her. "I swapped my ID card with Arthur's so that they would think it was me who died when they found his body," he said.

"Why would you do that?" asked Mary-Anne.

"Because I killed a Boer guard going over the wall," he said.

"What? How did you do that?"

"I broke his neck and I took a flesh wound in the arm from his knife in the process," Joe said. He knew that if they caught him, they would shoot him for that. He added, "The guards at the hospital knew me but these trackers didn't." He went on, "So, when the Boer trackers found Arthur with my card, they would think it was me, and report back that I was dead." Mary-Anne recoiled in shock.

After some thought, she said, "Holy Mother of God." Then, "Good! That was good thinking, Joe, but how did you get back to the British?"

He explained that a troop of Kitchener's Fighting Scouts had been on patrol around the Vaal Dam and, hearing the shots, outgunned the Boers, "And they got me out of there."

Mary-Anne asked, "But why not tell the British your real name was Joe Murphy? You were at war, the British army won't be after you for killing an enemy, will they?" She looked at him with a glint of hope in her eyes.

"No, they won't, but they WOULD be after me if they knew I shot Billy McKee. I just couldn't tell that to the British army, and that is why I pretended to be Arthur Jones until I got out of South Africa." She was stunned into silence, so Joe continued. "Remember, I had Arthur's card on me when the British picked me up." Joe went on to explain that he was cared for at a British dressing station and was eventually shipped back to Liverpool under the name of Private Arthur Jones, but he couldn't keep that up for long.

"Why not?" she asked.

"Well, do I look and sound like an Arthur?" he said, almost cracking a joke. He added that he drew a new uniform from the quartermaster's stores and travelled with a detachment of Royal Irish Dragoon Guards, none of whom knew the real Arthur Jones. When they docked in Liverpool he deserted by simply walking out of the Liverpool docks and assumed life as a Scotsman – in Liverpool.

"What happened to Arthur's body?" asked Mary-Anne.

"Well, before I was rescued by the Brits, I watched the Boers pick him up," he told her. "I was hiding in a warthog's burrow under some Christ-thorn bushes on the slopes of the dam." He added, "They were very close to me, but they never looked far into the Christ-thorn for fear of getting ripped apart by the thorns in the bush." He said he watched them empty Arthur's pockets and they found Joe's ID. Then they actually dug a grave and buried him deep as they always do, so as to stop the *Sangomas* (witch doctors) stealing human bones for their rituals.

Joe continued with his story. "The Boer commandos held a quick Christian service there and then, and even called him by name in prayer, then finished aloud with, '*Vertoue in God en die Mauser.*' (Faith in God and the Mauser). They are a pious lot, these Afrikaners," he said. "I'll say this for them, they gave me a good send-off, then they marked the grave with a wooden cross and put my name on it."

"How on earth would the British army find out about the death?" Mary-Anne asked.

He explained that the Boers always kept good, detailed records of those they killed or wounded, if they knew who they were. They would publish the names and details in the *Statskoerant* (Government Gazette) by the South African war office. "The British war office must have got my name and number from that gazette." A smile cracked on his face, which Mary-Anne found bizarre but the smile was infectious and the red mist faded. She too smiled for the first time in days; she had her wee brother back.

"So, you had Arthur Jones' identification card, but why change to Garland Fraser for goodness' sake? If you want to be inconspicuous, why choose such a conspicuous name?" Mary-Anne asked.

He told her that he felt he just couldn't keep Arthur's name, not with a Scottish accent anyway. He added, "And I couldn't come back and use my real name because the army thought I was dead."

He explained that he wanted to come back to Dundee to tell her the truth about Billy, and also to legally change to a more Scottish-sounding name.

"How can you do that? Is it legal?" she asked.

"I made it legal," he said. "First, I needed to find a name that I could use, that matched my age and accent, so I had to return to Dundee. When I got back, I looked into the reference library first and dug out old newspapers for a birth date of around mine." He went on, "In the *Courier's* birth columns, I found that a George Fraser had been born in 1878 – a year after I was born." Then he said, "I found that he had died as a baby the following year, so I had a name." He added, "I simply went into the Registrar's Office in Commercial Street, paid for a copy of Fraser's birth lines and that's what I used for identification for a few months."

He explained to her that when he came back to Dundee, he simply lodged George Fraser's birth lines with the Registrar General, who legally changed it to Garland Fraser after publishing the change for six weeks."

"How does that work?" she said.

He went on, "I signed an affidavit to say that it was not my intention to deceive or defraud anyone." He told her that his new name was simply recorded on the public register, he paid them one and sixpence, and that was it.

Mary-Anne was still unsure. "But why call yourself Garland, not George?"

Joe continued, "I figured that Garland would be a good code name for you to recognise if you ever heard anything about me, and so now, I feel ready to tell you, so here I am."

Mary-Anne was astonished at the confession but, on balance, knowing what she knew about the shambles at Magersfontein, she accepted his story. "I'll never ask again, Joe, and I see the relevance of the Garland bit to me." She went on, "But you can't call yourself 'Garland' surely?" she said.

"No, I don't, I'm known as Gary Fraser, but I use the Garland bit for the boxing job." Joe explained that on his last visit to Dundee, he had a long talk with Tam Pepper and agreed to work for him in the booths. He wanted to stay out of Dundee as much as possible but there would be times when he would be needed to appear at the Dudhope fairgrounds at the boxing booths when the fair was in town from time to time. Tam Pepper agreed to work with Joe on condition that his stage name would be the only one used. They made the deal and everyone was happy.

When the fair was in Glasgow, Joe shared digs with Tommy in the Gorbals and worked the boxing booths in Glasgow Green. When he was fighting in Portobello, Edinburgh, he shared a doss house in Leith with the other scrappers. When he was fighting in Dundee, however, he thought he could stay with Mary-Anne to help with costs but he never went back to the Crescent to live. He loved the sport in which he earned his living but occasionally it all went too far.

Joe was a sociopath. He knew it; the doctors in the army knew it but kept him in the army because of his devotion to duty – and his ability to turn his aggression into a dependable fighting individual. However, as 'Gary' the boxer he felt free for the first time in his life. The Crescent was a part of his past life and to return to the army would mean death or imprisonment for desertion if nothing else. The boxing booths and the travellers' companions offered the chance to be himself for once – with a different name. It gave him the opportunity to deny that past and the killing of one of the soldiers from the Crescent. He needed to tell Mary-Anne his confession, and that was done; some of the weight had been lifted off his broad shoulders by having the talk with her. She was the only person who knew the truth about that and that was how it had to be. So far so good, he felt, as long as Mary-Anne kept her word and said nothing.

In their conversation, Mary-Anne felt able to tell him everything about her melancholia, or depression as they called it these days, and her fears. Fears for herself, after being stabbed by that 'nutter' Jimmy McKee, fears for her estranged daughter and her mother, but most of all, fears for him. She recognised what he had been through and his state of mind when the red mist came up because she too had been afflicted with the same anger damnation. His plan was to spend all of his time when he was in Dundee, with his sister in Blackness Road, but he changed his mind after their talk and packed a bag the following day.

He took the train to Perth and walked the final mile from Perth Station to Perth Prison. He wore his army uniform and spun them a line to say he was still in the army and he was a relation of the McKees. He spent an hour in the reception then was given the paper with the information he wanted: '346 Garscube Road, top floor door, left, Glasgow' – that's all it said. That was the forwarding address that Jimmy McKee had given to the warden's officers after doing his time the previous year. Before he left Perth Prison, James McKee was obliged to inform them of his intended movements and domiciled address. It was no surprise to the wardens that he was not going back to Dundee on his release. As his cousin, and a regular soldier, according to the story he had given them, Garland Fraser was seen as a 'no risk' relative of the ex-con and was given the information on condition that he did not reveal the source.

Joe had no intention of abiding by that or any other condition and caught the next train to Queen Street Station in Glasgow. He stayed away from his brother Tommy's house in the Gorbals and booked into a doss house, signing to stay on a day-to-day basis. The following day, he wore his civvies, strides, waistcoat, collarless shirt, a scarf and a bunnet, like thousands of other men in Glasgow; he blended in with the rest. Joe walked from his digs in Cowcaddens, the whole length of Garscube Road to Maryhill. On the way he passed the address he knew to be McKee's. It was just an ordinary tenement, but on a busy road he could be seen to enter or leave by anyone passing by or inhabiting the place. He walked up and down Garscube Road twice that day and decided to have a drink in the nearest pub.

Sitting in the corner of the Star and Garter he looked for all intents and purposes like a quiet little man. The local punters soon ignored him and carried on drinking and talking as normal. *Scum*, thought Joe. *Just scum, every one of them.*

At nine o'clock that evening, Jimmy McKee walked in alone. He ordered a pint of heavy and a wee half. He stood by the bar and looked straight ahead, downed the whisky and slowly drank the beer. Only Joe Murphy watched him discreetly and nobody spoke to him. He never ventured a word to anyone other than the barman. He ordered the same again, drank, and when finished said to the barman, "Right Pat, see you tomorrow, same time." He walked out of the bar without anyone batting an eyelid.

Five minutes later, Joe Murphy left the bar and made his way back to his digs in the Cowcaddens, quite happy he'd found his man. The night was a long one in Glasgow and he knew he had to be on his mark very sharpish for what he had to do the following day. In the morning he ate no breakfast at the digs but paid the landlady cash on his way out at nine in the morning. He walked to the station and checked the train times for that day. Then he went into the left luggage department and paid the man the daily rate. He opened a locker with the key provided and placed the bag inside. Joe opened the bag, took the lid off the shaving kit and removed the open razor, slipping it into his inside pocket.

He ate a pie at the Firhill Tavern on Garscube Road and had a pint, feeling impatient but focused. He moved on from the Firhill after half an hour and bided his time by walking along the Glasgow branch of the Forth and Clyde canal. Eventually, it was five to nine and he was excited enough to almost run to the Star and Garter. He slowed down to a walking pace and at ten past nine, bonnet pulled down over the top half of his face he walked into the pub. He looked around, recognised the faces of the same men he saw the night before. McKee was not there. His heartbeat and temper began to rise and the red mist came in. Joe turned to the barman and started to say, "A pint of…" and there, in the mirror behind the barman he saw the face of Jimmy McKee, moving in quick, behind him. He knew instantly that McKee knew he was coming for him and had been waiting for him.

Jimmy McKee was in the process of raising the cosh and instantly, Joe spun round and came face to face with the man he had come to kill.

The cosh came down on Joe's arm as he was reaching into his inside pocket of his jacket. He felt the bone crack in his right arm, but momentum carried him forward and downward so that he head-butted McKee square on the nose. That was enough to stop McKee attacking and he backed off momentarily. Quickly, Joe reached into his jacket with his left hand and withdrew the razor. It swung open awkwardly at the touch of his fingers and, not being his dominant hand, he cut his own fingers on the blade. Regardless, he steadied his grip and swung the razor across the face of Jimmy McKee, cutting clean and deep across his face. Joe knew he had his man beat and brought the blade down from cheek to chin on his target.

McKee fell to his knees. Joe couldn't finish the job as the punters were closing in to stop the action, but felt he had done enough. Calmly, he turned around, the men in the pub parted in front of him and, looking at nobody, he walked out of the boozer. Outside, he closed the razor and wrapped his scarf over his bloodied hand then caught the tram to the railway station in the city.

On the train to Dundee, Joe took his spare shirt from his bag and ripped it into a strip, and bandaged his hand. When he got home to Dundee, he told Mary-Anne he had been attacked in Aberdeen on a trip to visit a friend. She accepted it but knew it was a lie.

Joe Murphy came to Dundee and went off again twice more that year without being recognised but, as ever, Mary-Anne was unhappy with living in a single end in Blackness Road for too long. She decided she could not live next door to a woman who was the reason for her depression coming back. In her mind, she blamed Mattie McGuire for upending her life after getting back with her husband only to end it in misery and poverty again.

CHAPTER 28

Rolled Down the Stair

Mary-Anne eventually moved out of Blackness Road and into another 'room and kitchen single-end' flat in Douglas Street in the Scouringburn area nearer the Crescent. It was closer to her mother's house but, in the knowledge that Annie and Jessie were against her, she couldn't bear to visit them, and they all knew it. Time and again she decided to make the peace with her mother but could not actually bring herself to visit her mother's house in the Crescent without a drink on her.

It took another year or more but eventually, Mary-Anne decided to pay a visit to her mother and settle things with her family once and for all. Her sister, Grace, was by that time in 1907 a sprightly nineteen-year-old and one Monday evening in April, she was helping ten-year-old Jessie with her homework. Annie was cooking Irish stew for the family meal. Jessie was trying her best to do her homework with Grace but was really more interested in the 'piece and dip' from her granny that she had been promised. Suddenly, the door opened and in walked Mary-Anne, steaming again. "Come here, Jessie," she said to her daughter who, seeing the state of her mum, hid behind Grace to avoid the fumes of gin emanating from Mary-Anne and she started to cry. Mary-Anne said, "Come here, I said, you're my bairn and I want ye to come here."

"Leave her alone, Mary-Anne, you're scaring her – and us," said Annie, as calmly as she could.

"Aw, shut yer puss, ye auld bugger, it's all your fault that I've no' got my ain bairn staying with me anymore," and then, suddenly, Mary-Anne slapped her mother across the face, a full blow. She hit her again and again. Jessie was screaming and Grace sprung to her feet.

"Hit my mother, would you?" screamed Grace. "Ye're no' scaring me though, Mary-Anne," and Grace launched herself at her big sister in a furious rage. In between blows, Grace managed a few choice curse words of her own and they grappled and fought each other out of the door. They were locked in furious battle all along the *plettie*, biting and scratching as they rolled down the stairs all the way to the bottom of the *closey*. Exhausted, Mary-Anne finally crawled out from under her younger sister, speechless and defeated, to the sounds of Jessie crying and Grace telling her, "You cannot come in here shouting and swearing and flegging the bairn, and hitting MY mother, I'm no' having it!" Mary-Anne ran out of the *closey* in tears of pain and frustration.

Grace comforted Jessie and Annie after the fight. Annie was distressed to the point of distraction. There was a realisation at her home though, that Mary-Anne had a right of access to Jessie. They just didn't know how to prevent it without incurring costs for a court order.

Bystanders in the Crescent who saw and heard the fight, summoned the police and Mary-Anne was locked up in Bell Street cells for the night again. The following appeared in the *Evening Telegraph* the next day:

ROLLED DOWN THE STAIR

Dundee Domestic Battle

Mary-Anne Murphy or Garland, Douglas Street, a young woman, was brought before Dundee Police Court to-day charged with having conducted herself in a disorderly manner and assaulted her mother and sister in her mother's house on Monday in a state of intoxication. She quarreled with her mother, and cursed and swore at her sister. She struck her mother on the face and seized her by the hair. Grace Murphy, sister of the accused rushed to the rescue, when accused and her sister had a desperate struggle, in the course of which they both rolled down the stair. Baillie Mitchell imposed a fine of 10s and 6d, or seven days in prison.

– *Evening Telegraph, 19th April 1907.*

CHAPTER 29

A New Hat

Johnny and Grace talked about her sister and brother. "What a mess," she said. "My brother Joe won't even look at me and God knows why he is fighting in the ring for a living." Grace went on, "My sister Mary-Anne has completely lost it and gets the jail every five minutes for assaulting her own mother."

Johnny said, "It's not quite as bad as all that, Grace, she only fights people at the weekends." They both laughed again; they did a lot of laughing together these days. Johnny McKee started looking out for wee Grace Murphy in and around the Crescent. He started working for the Scottish and Southern Energy Power Distribution company as a labourer, digging ditches for the new electric cables that had to be laid from street to street. That earned him three pounds a week with overtime.

"I'm working on Saturday and Sunday this week," he said to Grace.

"Why?" Grace asked.

"I intend to buy you a hat," he said.

"I've got a hat," she said.

"Oh, have you? I didn't know that," he said.

"I've been wearing it for six months," she said.

"Well, it's time to get you a new one then. I was going to get you a pair of gloves too but they don't sell them with four and a half fingers."

She clobbered him with her brolly, but not too hard. "Cheeky wee bugger!" she shouted and then they both laughed again. "Come with me to tell my mum about Joe."

"Haven't you told her yet?" said Johnny.

"No, I couldn't, Johnny, it would destroy her," she said.

"Then why tell her now?"

"She believes he is dead. She thinks he was killed in South Africa. I can't let her go on thinking that when we both know he is alive and in Dundee on occasion. She needs to know!" said Grace.

They sat down with Annie early in 1909 and told her that Joe was alive. They never told her exactly what he was doing for a living but they let her think he worked with the high-cheekers in the fairground rides. Annie just could not believe it. "Why have you not said anything about this before? Are you sure it's Joe?"

Grace said, "I only saw him from a distance, Mum, but I did see his tattoo. I called to him but he didn't seem to know me."

Johnny said, "I am sure it is Joe, Mrs. Murphy, I've seen him a couple of times boxing in the booths." He immediately realised he'd let the cat out of the bag.

"Boxing!" she exclaimed. Annie suddenly froze at the thought. Her mind immediately flashed back to the time when her husband John fought in the ring, and nearly died. The thought terrified her.

She turned white and then Annie said hurriedly, "If Tam Pepper says this man was Garland Fraser then he should know, shouldn't he?" she said with pure hope in her eyes.

"Or he could have made a mistake, maybe Joe has lost his memory or something. Let's go up and speak to him – now." Grace and Johnny looked at each other and suddenly realised that it was a possibility.

"OK," said Grace. "We'll go and speak to Mr. Pepper."

They all climbed the Parker Street steps and Annie shuffled along as fast as she could. Breathless and feeling ill, she accepted their help into the Barrack Park and into the beer tent.

Tam Pepper was standing at the bar in the corner of the tent and watched as the trio came in. *Not the usual punters I get in here,* he thought. Then he recognised Johnny. "It's been a while, Johnny, are you people looking for a job? Ha-ha," he kidded them.

"Never mind that, Tam, this is Mrs. Murphy, Joe Murphy's mother. The boxer you call Garland Fraser, he is really Joe Murphy, isn't he?" said Johnny. "We know that, and we told her that. Where is that boxer now?"

Tam Pepper's face drained. He said stoically, "I have not seen him for ages, not since that night you were here, sorry, can't help you."

Grace saw her mother was distressed; she thought she was going to find her son after all these years and this idiot was stopping her. She was about to give Tam a mouthful but was beaten to it by her mother. Annie drew in a deep breath and grabbed Pepper by the balls. "Where is the boxer?" she said. "I'll give you three seconds and then I will rip them off!" She was serious; a look of determination was in her eyes and she said, "Don't mess with me or you'll be sitting down to pee for the rest of your life!"

And with that, he screeched out his answer. "Ohya… He, he stays with his sister in Douglas Street in the Scouringburn. L…Low-door I b-believe. Number… 42, I think," he said, gasping with the pain of it, "when he is in Dundee, but I don't know where he is right now. I mean it – I don't know." Annie gave him another squeeze and, just as swiftly, let him go. Tam Pepper fell on one knee in agony and Grace and Johnny stood back in amazement. For once, Grace was speechless and Johnny made a mental note never to mess with his future mother-in-law. Annie then assumed the poise of a frail old lady once more and shuffled out of the tent, followed by the youngsters.

From the omnibus stop at the gates of Barrack Park they caught the last tram to the Lochee Road and crossed into the Scouringburn, a dense grimy area of tenements mixed with jute mill buildings and of course, boozers on every corner. They reached Douglas Street and found the low-door of number 42. Grace rapped on the door loudly. Slowly, it opened and there was the confirmation they all hoped for, it was Mary-Anne, sober again. However, this time the vision that greeted Annie triggered her worst fears.

A four-year-old shoeless boy hid behind her skirts and Mary-Anne was heavily pregnant, again. "What are you lot doing here?" she demanded. "Where's Jessie? What's happened to her?" The look of alarm was all over her face. That look also came to Annie's face with concern for her own daughter.

Annie looked at her square in the face and said, "Nothing's wrong with Jessie. Wullie and Nellie are playing with her in the Crescent, she's fine."

"What are you doing here then?" she asked. "Chapping at my door at ten o'clock at night, what is it? What's wrong?"

Annie came right out with it. "Is Joe here?"

Mary-Anne said, "Joe? My brother Joe? No, why would he be here? Joe's dead. I live on my own," she said.

"Not with a bairn and another one on the way, you clearly don't," said Annie scathingly.

Grace challenged her. "You're a liar, Mary-Anne, we know he stays here, Tam Pepper told us."

Annie walked right into the house; the others followed. "Where is he?" Annie asked her. "Don't mess me about. I'm not in the mood for you, Mary-Anne." She went on, "And then you can tell us who the father is and where the hell is HE?"

Grace added, "Or they."

"You can't barge in here acting like a gang of bullies! I don't need to tell you anything and I'm not going to tell you anything either!" said Mary-Anne.

Grace and Johnny were checking the living room for signs of her current romantic arrangements. Grace spotted the shaving kit on the jaw box above the sink. The initials GF were engraved on the tin lid. Grace picked it up and showed it to her mother. Annie said, "Who is Garland Fraser?"

That caught Mary-Anne by surprise. "What about him? He… he's a friend," she replied defensively.

"Is he the father of your baby?" said Grace.

"NO!" shouted Mary-Anne. "He is not."

"Is he the father of your boy?"

"NO, he is not!" she shouted again.

"GF, that gies the guff away and at least tells us you know Garland Fraser," Johnny interjected, holding up the shaving kit.

Mary-Anne flashed her teeth at Johnny. "And what the hell has it got to do with you?" She looked daggers at young McKee and then realised that she was looking at the younger brother and version of her lost lover, Billy, and the brother of Jimmy, the man who stabbed her.

Mary-Anne suddenly felt like she'd been hit by a tram, and her resistance crumbled. She slowly started to lower herself onto her armchair and her mother caught her and eased her into the seat. She was in floods of tears with the emotion of it all. "Why did you come here now, before I've had the bairn? Why couldn't you have waited until I was better? Why are you asking about Garland Fraser?" Mary-Anne needed the answers before she could think straight.

Annie sat down beside her and Grace, also crying in sympathy with her big sister, in an emotional moment, knelt down on the floor in front of her, holding her hand. As instructed by Grace, Johnny made tea in the background.

Mary-Anne regained her composure and said, "OK, first things first, John Garland, my man, is the father of my son, wee John, and he is the father of the new baby, which is due next month."

Grace said, "I thought he was in the army again?"

"He is, but he came back and moved in for a while four years ago. And again on leave eight months ago," added Mary-Anne. "He came to see me," she added.

"Obviously," butted in Grace with a look of distain on her face. "And you made up – again?"

"What about Joe, or this other Garland person? What's that all about?" Annie demanded.

"I swore I wouldn't say, Mum. He is never going to forgive me if I tell you," said Mary-Anne.

"Who isn't going to forgive you? Which one? Tell me." Annie looked her in the eyes again. "You are talking about my son here, not yours, now tell me!"

Mary-Anne carried on, "The first time Joe came to see me was one night about four years ago."

Annie slowly curled up with delight to hear that, then shouted, "Four years you've known he's alive, and you haven't thought to tell me?" It was like her heart had been mended and broken again in an instant. "Are you sure, is he all right? Is he well?" she asked with a stern face, not allowing emotion either way to show and her tears ran down.

"He is," was all Mary-Anne said.

"Why hasn't he come to see me? Why hasn't he come home?" Annie asked softly.

Mary-Anne answered truthfully, "He says he can't face anyone in the Crescent anymore."

Annie said, "I don't understand, why can't he face me or any of us?"

Mary-Anne added, "All I can say, is that he has done something wrong in the army that will keep him in hiding and away from the Crescent," Mary-Anne said.

Annie and the two youngsters looked at each other in bewilderment. "What the hell are you talking about, Mary-Anne?"

"I'm saying that Joe is alive and well, and he is hiding from everybody in the Crescent." Finally, she said, "Joe IS Garland Fraser!"

Annie was astonished. "The same person." She said it to herself, aloud. Her son, Joe, WAS Garland Fraser, that's why he stayed with Mary-Anne in Dundee. Annie was full of mixed feelings. To know that her son was alive was like a gift from God, but, at the same time to hear that she was not ever going to see him again because of his own volition was unacceptably cruel. Annie said weakly, "That just doesn't make sense, especially since he is boxing in the booths, working for Tam Pepper."

Mary-Anne relented and told them the whole reason for Joe being in Dundee. "He had to come here with the fair because that's his job. If he knew that he was getting recognised, he says he can never come back again. That's why I haven't told you and, he's doing a job he loves. Nobody knows that it's our Joe – the army, the taxman, or the labour exchange. He feels safe doing it and that's why he uses the stage name Garland Fraser!"

Annie's heart was breaking again, and she had to go, get out of that house; it held only confusion and denial for her. Before she left, Annie asked Mary-Anne, "How are you going to provide for that baby when it comes? Does John Garland even know you are pregnant?"

Mary-Anne said solemnly, "Yes, of course he knows. I told you, he is the father. He is coming back to look after us when he is finished with the Black Watch."

Annie's eyes opened wide in shock, then narrowed. "When does the fair come to Dundee next?" she asked.

"I'll find out and tell you, Mrs. Murphy," said Johnny. Grace and Johnny linked arms on the way home to Littlejohn Street.

CHAPTER 30

Another Home Birth

Mary-Anne had been through childbirth at home twice before. She dreaded it and she never wanted the first two. Now she was about to give birth to another bairn and nothing had changed, she didn't want this one either. This was John Garland's fault again; he had visited her once in three years, and made her pregnant. *Why did I even let him in the house that night?* she thought. She was disgusted with herself and at the same time she had only herself to blame. One consolation was that as soon as he went back into the army she had reported him for deserting her. The army then rearranged his wages and allocated a separation allowance to Mary-Anne. The birth of her son baby John four years ago had meant that she was even given extra child allowance from the army and she managed, with difficulty, to survive from one payday until the next on soldier's wife allowances. Incredibly, this action actually brought them back together again after the first two years of his second stint in the army. On one occasion John Garland stayed with Mary-Anne and his son for a month and they actually found a measure of happiness in that time together.

However, at the end of his leave, Mary-Anne thought he was returning to Barracks in Inverness. He left the family nest all right but unknown to Mary-Anne, took the train to Edinburgh and stayed with 'an old lady friend' for another week before leaving for the Barracks. Nevertheless, true to his word, John Garland appeared a week before Mary-Anne's due date by special permission of the army. He was allowed early release, calling it 'compassionate leave'. The baby girl was delivered at home in the care of the Parish and under strict supervision of the same midwife who delivered Jessie and wee John in Douglas Street on the 22nd June 1908 without complications. The Parish relented fully and cancelled the black mark against Mary-Anne and helped with medical coverage until John Garland returned from the army and started bringing in a labourer's wage from the mills again. Baby Annie was a good baby and not difficult to look after compared to Jessie and wee John. Annie Murphy was reluctantly estranged from her first grandson and from her second granddaughter from the beginning.

CHAPTER 31

Suffragettes

"My sister has been the bane of our lives for years," Grace said to Johnny as they sat on the dyke at the bottom of the Parker Street steps. She added, "I know your brother Jimmy is unstable, but that is no excuse for stabbing her."

Johnny considered her words. "There must be more to it, Grace, and I am trying to find out what made him do it," he said, "but whatever it was, he was on his own and nobody knew he had been holding a grudge against Mary-Anne."

"It's the poverty in the Crescent," she said, "it's just this place, and the drink, it makes you go mad. This country is getting worse!" She added, "It's run by a bunch of silly ruling-class elitist men who couldn't run water from the well."

He said, "You may be right. Look at what's happened – all over Dundee, people have to live here in tenement houses in poverty."

Grace said, "All there is really is the jute mills and they are owned by the jute barons."

He added, "Most of them don't even belong to Dundee."

Grace said, "I don't WANT to work in the jute mills, but I have to – to survive." Grace then announced, "I know, I'll join the suffragettes! Are you with me, Johnny?"

"Why do you want to do that?" he asked.

"To get votes for women, of course, it's the only way we can fix this country. Right now, it's only men that can vote and only if they have property."

"Er, what's wrong with men making the decisions for the whole population?" he said without thinking.

"You sound like that Churchill!" Grace went on. "Because you lot only want to invade other countries and get killed, or you want to keep the millworkers on money that keeps them down among the rats and mice of this society!" she exclaimed, through newfound wisdom.

"Er, I, er, maybe I will join you," said Johnny as he lit a woodbine.

"And then, when all the women get the vote, we'll stop all the drinking and the smoking that goes on," announced Grace.

Johnny rose from the dyke and said meekly, "Aye and what about that quarter ounce of Kendal Brown snuff I see you taking? Are ye going to ban that as well?" he said with a satisfactory grin.

"No, snuff's all right, even my mother takes it!"

Laughing, he said, "I've got to go to work. See ya," and he was gone.

"But, it's Saturday," she said, to nobody because he never heard a thing, on his way to Thompsons bar in Bell Street, thinking, *Phew, that was a close shave.* He ordered a pint and lit another fag.

The following week, the subject of votes for women came up again and they decided it was Churchill and his cronies in Westminster holding the suffragettes back.

"George told me about that Winston Churchill in South Africa," said Johnny. "He was a liar then and he is still a liar now," he explained. "Before the by-election he was full of lies, telling all the mill workers that he represents the working class and now that he is our Member of Parliament, he never comes near the place."

Sneering, Grace added, "When he does come to Dundee, he stays in the best hotel in town and drinks nothing but the best whisky and champagne, yet the papers say he hates the place."

"They found a letter he wrote to Clementine, his missus, in the Queens Hotel the day after he left," Johnny told her. "In it, he says, 'This city will kill me. Halfway through my kipper this morning, an enormous maggot crawled out and flashed his teeth at me.'" They bawled with laughter as the tears ran down their faces with delight. "Then, he says, 'Such are the penalties which great men pay in the service of their country.'"

"Bwahaaha!" Grace roared in total ecstasy at the thought of the fat man getting flashed by a maggot.

When she recovered, she added, "Well, he WAS born in a palace in Oxford and, once a millionaire, always a millionaire, I suppose." Then she asked, "But why on earth is he our Dundee MP then?"

Johnny said, "Because he lost his seat in England and nobody else wanted him." Johnny added, "The by-election in Dundee was the only place he could find to worm his way back into Westminster."

They both laughed at the thought of worms and maggots in the same breath as Churchill. Johnny told her that Churchill's grandfather was the Duke of Marlborough and so, his father was already in the elite circle and ruling class at Westminster when Winston was born.

"So, he never had to work in the mills, did he?"

"No!" she fired back angrily.

Then he said, "He has a country estate called Blenheim Palace that would fit the whole of the Crescent in it twice – and twice the number of people who live here."

"It just makes you sick, doesn't it, Johnny?" she said miserably. "How did he get that big palace in the first place, Johnny?" she asked.

"It came from the royalty – Queen Anne, I think it was – at the time of a battle called Blenheim, hundreds of years ago. The crown has been paying for its upkeep ever since," Johnny told her.

"The crown?" Grace said. "The crown doesn't pay for a thing! You mean us, the people who pay tax. Anyway, how do you know all this, Johnny?" she asked.

"You've got to learn that stuff in approved school – I had five years in Baldovan approved school, so I'm very well informed, for a convict!" he boasted and they laughed again for the umpteenth time in weeks together.

"Right, come on, Johnny," she said as she dragged him into Dundee and in to Draffens store in the High Street. "You're going to buy me that hat," she said, pointing to the hat counter with her half finger. "A green one with purple ribbons, it's the suffragettes' colours! It's in here!" said Grace.

The next weekend, Grace wore her new hat and dragged Johnny off to the Kinnaird Hall in Bank Street, to listen to Emmeline Pankhurst, who was up from London to harass Winston Churchill's public meeting. She was a leading light in the suffragette movement who was drawing the crowds in Dundee whenever Churchill spoke in public. She named Dundee 'Suffrage City' and together with Mary Maloney they urged the ladies of the crowd at the meeting to sign up and take action to disrupt any meeting Churchill addressed.

At the meeting in the Kinnaird Hall, Grace immediately paid her sixpence for full membership of the Women's Social and Political Union (WSPU), which was looking for women of all classes, to bolster their ranks. Grace took the sash of her choice on joining. Hers said 'Deeds not Words' and she took the oath to do all she could to help women get the vote. "It suits me and matches my hat!" she beamed proudly. Grace proudly wore the sash and hat at every opportunity, except at work. There was real animosity there between the women for and against. "It's better not to antagonise them," she told Johnny. "I've already lost one finger and I don't want to lose any more," she joked.

The meeting started in a jovial atmosphere but turned deadly serious when Emmeline Pankhurst told the crowd:

"I know that women, once convinced that they are doing what is right, that their rebellion is just, will go on, no matter what the dangers, so long as there is a woman alive to hold up the flag of rebellion."

When the word 'rebellion' came into it the crowd went wild. "Dundee women like a good fight and no better a fight than this one," Grace shouted into the crowd. She was handed the megaphone from the stage and Grace took up the offer to have a go at the British system of the day. "The plan for women in this city," she said, "is to have women live and die in the mills for the crumbs off the jute baron's table, and we take it because our men canna get work," she fumed. "If you're a man, the only other thing is the army if you're of fighting age. Then they make you fight for the King in London who wants more money for his British Empire." She added, "If you're too old to fight for the king, you'll be a kettle biler just like our faithers before us. Ladies, we must force the government to give the women the vote or we'll be in the mills forever!"

A rousing cheer went up and Grace Murphy was applauded for the tenacity she espoused.

"My father was never a kettle biler," said Johnny.

"Shut up, don't tell them that, you'll spoil it for them," said Grace out of the corner of her mouth. Johnny shut up.

At the meeting, the members of the union made the first WSPU plan, and, it would entail as many violent tactics to campaign for women's suffrage as they could dream up.

The following Saturday, Winston Churchill, MP for Dundee, was visiting Blackness Foundry and addressing a handpicked crowd of Liberals afterwards, at least that was the plan. Johnny and Grace set off to meet the others at the West Port police box at eleven o'clock. When they arrived, the Dundee suffragettes were milling all around the police box. There was already a rammy going on because the women had painted the police box pink with slogans alluding to the cause. Grace handed her new hat to Johnny, saying, "Here, you mind this; I'll be back in a minute."

Johnny stood back in shock then backed further away, guarding the hat, but Grace joined the ranks of the suffragettes in action. Without a moment's hesitation, she plunged into the crowd of ladies and indulged in the pushing and shoving and spitting at the coppers, like all the other women did. Eventually, the crowd of unruly ladies broke away from the half-dozen policemen and started to march up Blackness Road towards the foundry. Grace found Johnny and retrieved her hat. He just looked at her in awe, and then followed in step. They passed a greengrocer shop on the Blackness Road, when she suddenly stopped, turned around and said, "Here, you mind my hat again, I have to get some messages!"

He was bamboozled, thinking to himself, *She is on a protest march and at halfway, she wants to go shopping? What am I letting myself in for?* He scratched his head, still holding the hat.

They caught up with the march further up the road and the

Liberals were starting to assemble around the office door of the Blackness foundry. Winston Churchill appeared from inside the foundry to modest clapping from his followers and boos from the suffragettes. "My good people of Dundee, I would like to say a few words of praise for this city, and…"

Klang, klang, klang.

Mary Maloney had produced a huge school dinner bell and rang it, on and on, drowning out whatever Churchill said. The bell ringing stopped for a few minutes while Mary Maloney repositioned herself on a plinth closer to Churchill and he continued, "The current position in Westminster is that…"

"Winston, hey, Winston!" a female voice from the crowd piped up.

He continued, "Prime Minister Asquith has asked me to…" He stopped again.

"Hey Winston, Winston…" the lady shouted.

He thought he had better play along with the Dundee crowd, and said magnanimously, "Yes, my good woman, speak up, let everyone hear you."

"Awa' an throw shite at yersel'!" she shouted and the crowd roared with laughter, then, as he tried to speak again the bell sounded all over again. *Klang! Klang! Klang!*

He shut up for a moment that allowed Emmeline Pankhurst an opening into his speech. She had the crowd's attention:

"Dear ladies, let me remind you that men make the moral code, and they expect women to accept it. They have decided that it is entirely right and proper for men to fight for their liberties and their rights, but that it is not right for women to fight for theirs," Ms. Pankhurst said.

Another rousing cheer went up and the bell sounded over and

over. Winston, still trying to get a word in edgeways, suddenly was hit on the head with a flying egg! He turned to the suffragettes and another egg came flying at him, catching him on the right shoulder.

Johnny started to laugh and looking around for Grace, saw to his horror, that it was Grace throwing the eggs at Churchill! Another couple of eggs came over like bombs, scattering Churchill's followers and leaving him as a big fat target for Grace to aim at. "Where did you get those?" he cried.

"The grocer's in Blackness Road. I'm just about to start on the tomatoes now!" she said enthusiastically when a couple of brave policemen lifted her off her feet and slung her into the waiting horse-drawn black Maria, a closed police van with separate lockable cubicles. Mary Maloney joined her in the next cubicle without her bell and a few more Dundee women who were also arrested were carted off with her.

Out of the tiny windows they shouted abuse at the coppers and a variety of rebel-rousing slogans. "Courage, ladies, take courage and fight with us."

The crowd continued their harassment of Churchill's intended speech and even the Liberal faithful amongst them enjoyed the spectacle, and chuckled away at the sight of Churchill getting pelted with eggs. One prominent Liberal politician member was heard to say, "I haven't laughed so much, since the hamster pissed in the wife's sherry." Only Churchill and the Foundry managers were embarrassed. In the end, he abandoned it for the comfort of the Queens Hotel and a bottle of Johnny Walker red label.

Grace and Mary were both charged with assault and causing an affray that day and sentenced to thirty days in Perth Prison. "Right, that means thirty days' hunger strike from me," said Mary Maloney.

"And me," said Grace.

That day was the first day that Grace saw the brutality of the prison system. "It's not just Suffragette women, Johnny," she told him after three days on strike. "The turnkeys are pure pigs to everyone," she said on his first visit.

Johnny felt helpless and just wanted to get her out and stop her hurting herself any more. "Grace, just do your time and you'll be out soon. I know what it's like inside. You will not last another week without food, please don't do this," he said through the glass partition and through gritted teeth. He was probably hurting more than her at that point and she knew it. "Don't do it, Grace," he pleaded with her.

Although not yet enshrined in law, by the end of the second week of their hunger strike, the politicians had discussed the implementation of a new draft act that would end the hunger strikers' protest in prison. 'Temporary discharge of political prisoners for ill-health reasons' was the official justification the government saw in force-feeding the hunger strikers.

The act, mockingly called 'The Cat and Mouse Act' in Westminster, was mooted that would allow the wardens to force-feed the women by holding them down in a chair and inserting a rubber feed hose into the stomach by way of the nostrils. Without legal approval, trials were carried out on Grace and her companions. It was a brutal experience she endured every day for the next week in an effort to stop the suffragettes from becoming dangerously ill in prison for their 'cause'. When the women were well again, they were all temporarily released and bound over not to be arrested again as suffragettes, as under the act they would be force-fed again if they embarked on another hunger strike in Perth Prison.

After Grace was released, she recovered sufficiently to return to work in the Verdant mill. She remained an activist for the party in as many ways as she could without getting arrested. She set about raising funds, organising raffles and speaking at meetings but never again was she able to throw eggs, spit at police or chain herself to railings like her suffragette friends for fear of being arrested and the jail again. Johnny never attended her meetings again but was always there, in the background or, outside the halls she spoke in, to watch out for her on the way home and guard her from the non-believers, of which there were a few in Dundee.

CHAPTER 32

The Scouringburn

The fair came back to Dundee for the last time in 1908 and Johnny dutifully organised Grace and her mother to visit the boxing booth to see if Joe was with them. The three walked into the fair in anticipation of a much-desired reunion. They waited patiently outside the booth and eventually, they went through the same routine as the night Joe appeared. This time, however, there was no sign of him. A new boxer was touted as the Scottish middleweight champ. Annie was downhearted but they quickly gained some hope when Johnny suggested they all visit Mary-Anne in Douglas Street in the Scouringburn again. Annie took further comfort that there might even be another baby in Mary-Anne's house that she could at least see for the first time. Of course, when they arrived and knocked on the door, there was no answer. "Nobody's home, Mum," said Grace, peering through the windows.

A gang of small of children, sitting on the pavement out in the street, saw that there were people trying to see into the house. They rushed to Annie enthusiastically to tell them that the family had moved away. Annie felt destroyed. She realised that the son she had lost then found may be lost again, and forever this time. She also was crushed inside at the thought that Mary-Anne had moved away without telling her where they had gone, and she realised that she might never see her grandchildren again – ever.

In her single end in Douglas Street, on the last day of April 1909, Mary-Anne, having given birth to a healthy baby girl, wondered, what the hell was it all for? John Garland had gone out for a pint to 'wet the baby's head' the day before and never came home that night. Baby Annie was brought into the world on a shoestring budget. Without any family to help or support her, Mary-Anne was all alone at home, with two of her three children. Her depression was setting in deeper this time. She hadn't seen Jessie, her first child, for a year. Her mother kept her from seeing her and Jessie had never made any attempt to visit. Now, her husband was failing to provide and be there for them again. Her best friend Catherine was staying away from her for reasons Mary-Anne could not understand.

Still, Mary-Anne insisted on alienating her family in the Crescent for many reasons, not least because of her promise to Joe, her brother in hiding. Her depression was so bad that she never heard the baby crying anymore or saw that John, her son, was starving and cold every night. All she wanted really was to drink – gin, rum, anything that would stop her feeling so sorry for herself and make her life seem worth living. When finally, her husband came back on the third day, she hadn't the strength to argue about his whereabouts, but he brought money and gin, so she forgave him, without knowing where it all came from because she never asked.

Catherine and George McKee planned to marry but they never told Mary-Anne for fear that she would appear at the wedding and cause another rammy. John Garland's working habits became sporadic again – he found any excuse to pack up the mills wherever he had found a labouring job. It was true that the work was drying up in Dundee and the wages were going down.

When he did find a new start in a mill, Mary-Anne was relieved and excited in equal measures. Those feelings were always short lived when he announced that he was paid off or he was too ill to work in 'all that stoor'. When he wasn't working, he looked after the children at home, at least that is what he told his mates in the boozers. Mary-Anne worked when she could but, inevitably, the weekend was the only time they had together as a family. The weekend was also the only time that they had the money to buy alcohol as long as there was one wage coming in. On Mondays, Mary-Anne was depressed and often stayed in bed.

Catherine and George got married and settled into a flat in Littlejohn Street to be close to her mother and, of course his father, old Jim McKee. They had managed to live in relative contentment in the Crescent and, when she heard that, it was something else Mary-Anne couldn't understand. Catherine did visit Mary-Anne on rare occasions but, there was an atmosphere of 'holier than thou' about Catherine, thought Mary-Anne and, although she meant well, Catherine always gave her opinion about the state of Mary-Anne's habits and her concern for her children. She was also John Garland's sister and even if Mary-Anne tried to stop her coming around, John would always say, "Well, I might need a loan of a pound from her so don't upset her." That aside, Catherine was the only one who knew the news about the baby but was sworn to secrecy, not to tell Annie or Grace.

In the first week in July, when she and the baby were strong enough to stand a house flit, John and Mary-Anne Garland took the keys of a two-bedroomed flat in Larch Street, at the far end of the Scouringburn, and the family moved in by means of a 'moonlight flit'.

"At least having the two bedrooms will give us a chance to put the bairns in their own room and lock it to keep them safe," John

Garland said to his wife.

"Lock the door of their room?" Mary-Anne asked. "Why?"

"Well, that will let us get out for a drink from time to time without having to bother about those two," he said as though it was the most natural thing in the world.

"Oh, I get it. All right, we'll try that," she said, smiling to herself and thinking, *This man is not as stupid as he looks.*

Soon, the neighbours started to notice that the Garlands were not looking after their children. John, the little boy, had never worn a pair of shoes, according to the neighbours. Word got to Catherine about wee John and she went to see them at their new place in Larch Street. Catherine felt the poverty as soon as she walked into the living room. Dirty dishes in the sink, stoor on the floor and furniture, what there was of it, and a stink of dirty nappies that no one else seemed to notice. In the conversation, she talked to Mary-Anne about cleaning the place up, and the bairns! – They both looked as if they were refugees from some war or something. Even the baby's clothing was stained and dirty and looked like it had been on for a week.

Mary-Anne was quite aware that the wee lad had never worn a pair of shoes but according to Mary-Anne, that was what all the laddies did in the Scouringburn. "Not true," said Catherine. "It's OK in the summer, I suppose, but it's nearly October and it's getting cold," said Catherine. "He needs a new pair of shoes," she told Mary-Anne.

"Well, YOU buy them for him, go on, you're his auntie, take him for a pair and see how much that'll cost you!" said Mary-Anne bitterly.

The following day, Catherine took him to the Overgate and into Birrells shoe shop to have his feet measured for new shoes. The assistant had to scrub his feet with carbolic soap to get the dirt off the soles and, when they were clean, she saw that his toenails were long and broken. It took Catherine and the shop assistant a full hour to get his wee feet cleaned and toenails trimmed to get him into a pair of leather sandals. Catherine cried when she handed over a ten-shilling note to pay for them but not because of the cost, because of the apparent neglect her nephew was suffering.

Catherine walked back to Larch Street with little John. Inside, she hated the fact that she had to take him back to that house knowing that he would be neglected all over again, shoes or no shoes.

Nevertheless, she left him with his family. All his parents wanted to do, however, was to see him in a pair of shoes and make a fool of him. He felt confused because all he ever wanted was shoes like the other boys but now he had them, his dad and mum were calling him a wee sissy and a girly. As soon as Catherine left his house, wee John took the new shoes off and kicked them under the bed in his room. He made a mental promise to himself that he would never wear them again.

Mary-Anne and John's marriage was in trouble again and the children were the biggest losers. Both children were suffering from neglect but their parents ignored it. The Parish people had been to see them and were so concerned for the children, they reported Mary-Anne and John Garland to the Dundee Council social work department. The social workers visited unannounced one day and in her defence Mary-Anne declared she was ill with the depression. They asked to speak to young John but he was ill in bed with the flu so they did not bother him that day. They asked about his clothing and Mary-Anne showed the man the shoes that wee John kept under the bed. "See?" she said. "That's what he does with new leather shoes. He won't wear them so it's not my fault that his feet are barkit!" Mary-Anne shouted at man from the council.

CHAPTER 33

The Black Watch

Johnny McKee's employer was beginning to reduce the wages for more hours per week and, eventually he told Grace that he had had enough of working for a meagre three pounds seventeen and six a week. He had always wanted to join the Black Watch, ever since hearing from his brothers about their gallant service in South Africa and further afield. "I know you don't want me to go," he said to Grace, "but there is no other work for me here." Johnny explained to her that having been inside and, at the age of twenty-one with no qualifications other than experience of digging roads with a shovel, nobody would employ him. He joined the second Battalion of the Black Watch on the twenty-eighth of May 1909, signing up for ten years.

Grace was inconsolable. He was her other half and she was his and she had only just realised it. How could it be that the country that ruled more than half the world had nothing to offer the young men except to go and fight in other faraway places for the benefit of 'the crown'? It just made no sense.

In December 1909 Grace's younger sister Nellie married Davie Gallagher, a batcher in Camperdown works. She moved out of Annie's house in Littlejohn Street to live with his parents in Stewart Street, Lochee, and gave birth to baby David in March 1910. Young

Wullie Murphy had also joined up with Johnny McKee in the Black Watch and that left just Annie, Grace and Jessie at home in 8 Littlejohn Street in the Crescent.

Annie was unwell and stayed in bed most days. Grace and Jessie had been caring for her for months and she was getting no better, and was suffering from epileptic fits. The doctor confirmed dementia was present.

Grace wrote to Johnny who, was by this time in India with his regiment. "I cannot see how the medicine can help her if she will not take it, the fits can happen at any time and, someone needs to be there to make her take the pills," said Grace in her letter to Johnny. "She is afraid that Joe will come back to her and she will be so sedated that she will not recognise him." Grace knew that family life in the Crescent as she knew it was coming to an end.

"I have to keep on working to pay for the doctor and pay the rent," she wrote. "Jessie is at school all day and I am very worried that something will happen when we are not at home." She bemoaned her life without him and ended the letter with, "However, if you were to leave the army, we could get married and you could move in here with us, so we wouldn't have to move out. If you don't, I will have to put my mother in a home." Knowing that he would rather be with her, she also knew that he would honour his commitment to his beloved Black Watch and never leave before his time was up.

Grace took advice from Father O'Farrell, the priest at St. Andrew's Cathedral. He had some sway with the council authorities and eventually made arrangements for part funds to cover the costs of a care home for Annie. Grace gratefully accepted the offer and, for the first time, the Murphys resolved to move out of the Crescent and into a hospice home at 51 Wilkie's Lane, again in the Scouringburn.

There was an offer of a room in the home for Grace as next of kin but not for Jessie. Annie was devastated at this idea but was by this time so ill, the decision was out of her hands. Grace was understandably distressed at the thought of losing Jessie, who, at fourteen was like a sister to her as they had both grown up in that house. The thought of Jessie being sent back to her parents to live after nine years of separation was, to her, unimaginable. Jessie was very disturbed and unhappy at the idea of living with her mother and father but what else could they do? Jessie had to live somewhere, and, in the end, she went along with it for Annie and Grace's sake.

Soon, she thought, she could leave school, get a job, and with wages to earn, she could soon make her own choice of where she would live. Jessie was pragmatic enough to imagine that living with Mary-Anne and John might even be a good thing, as she would have a place to live and save money from her job. Then, she thought, she could go anywhere at any time. She agreed with the plan. In order for it all to happen, there was a need for Grace to sit down with Catherine and Billy and persuade them to give her Mary-Anne's new address. Despite her objections and honest advice against going to see her, Catherine wrote down the new address in Larch Street where Grace would find Mary-Anne and her family.

Grace and Jessie went to the address one night in July 1910. They found the place but, no one was home. They tried again the next night and the next night but each time, nobody was in. Time was against Grace and to make the move work as planned, Annie had to be the main concern in this dilemma, and that swayed Grace's choice.

At Wilkie's Lane, there was day- and night-time nursing staff to look after Annie for when Grace was at work. Grace thought about it very hard and decided there was nothing else for it. Her mother was suffering in Littlejohn Street so they were moving! It was not Grace's choice, but knowing she had to do something to help her mum, she handed in the keys to the house in Littlejohn Street and supervised the removal of the household possessions to her new accommodation in the Wilkie's Lane home. They got Annie settled into her new room, and Grace stuffed it with all the household effects she could get in, as well as Jessie's things, and left Annie to try Larch Street again.

This time Mary-Anne answered the door. "Oh," she said, coughing at the same time. "What is wrong this time?" Grace and Jessie both stared at the sight of Mary-Anne; drink and bad living had caught up with her. Fag in hand, missing two teeth and dressed like a high-cheeker, she was a sight for sore eyes. Her auburn hair now dull and peppered with strands of silver, matted in places.

"Mum is very ill – she's dying, Mary-Anne, and we've been looking for you and trying to get in here for three days," said Grace.

"Well, there is always somebody in. Ah," she remembered, "the bairns were in, but they must have been in the back room." She laughed and said, "They can't answer it because we keep it locked."

"What?" Grace asked her to say that again.

"Me and John must have been in the Globe in the West Port when you were here. Ye canna be too careful, ye know, we have to make sure the bairns won't go wandering about the streets."

Grace and Jessie looked at each other. They both thought the same thing. "This is not happening, surely," Grace said to Jessie.

"Anyway what do ye want?" said Mary-Anne.

Grace explained what was happening to Annie and that they had moved her out to a hospice in Wilkie's Lane. The conversation continued at the doorstep. Grace told Mary-Anne that Jessie had nowhere to live and they would have to leave her there with her own family. "Leave her with ME? REALLY?" Mary-Anne said. "After all this time?" A smile came to Mary-Anne's face in wonder more than anything else. "Where are you working, Jessie?" asked Mary-Anne.

Jessie spoke for the first time: "I'm still at St. John's School."

"At school? How are you going to pay for yer keep then?"

"Um, I don't know, I'll get a job after school, I suppose," said Jessie.

"Well, in ye come then!" The house stunk of dirty nappies, smoke and drink.

"Where is yer man?" asked Grace.

"Sleeping," said Mary-Anne. "He was on a bender this forenoon and he's sleeping it off."

"It's only half past seven," said Grace in wonder.

Mary-Anne said, "EH, he had a bit o' luck on the cuddies and we had a wee celebration."

"Where are the bairns?"

Grace asked, "Ben the hoose." She shuffled to another door down the small lobby and unlocked it. As the door opened, the smell grew stronger and stronger. She switched the single light on and two-year-old Annie was stirring on the bed. Wee John was playing with marbles under the bed looking out between the bedraggled blankets that were hanging over the side.

"This is where you'll be staying, Jessie, IF, ye're coming back to stay!"

"Come on, Jessie, you're not staying here!" Grace took hold of Jessie's sleeve and started to pull her out of the house.

"NO," Jessie said firmly and drew back and freed her arm. "I'm staying. These bairns need to be helped. They're my brother and sister, aren't they?"

Despite Grace's misgivings, Jessie moved in that night and her father woke up and welcomed her into his home by saying, "That's fine, we have our own babysitter now!"

Grace arranged for Jessie's bed, bedding and a few items to be carted down to Larch Street. She gave Jessie two pounds for her own use, warning Jessie, "If I find you give this to the Garlands, I will not be very happy with you. They'll just drink it by the looks of things."

"I won't, I promise," said Jessie as she started to tidy up the house but by the end of the week, she did give them the money. They conned her out of it by convincing her she needed to pay for her share of gas and electric and food. Jessie knew she was wrong to do it, but wee John and little Annie were looking like they were undernourished only because there was never any money to spare on the right kind of food. Jessie did find a job eventually and duly left school within a month of moving in with her mum and dad. She started work at South Mills as an apprentice machinist earning nearly two pounds a week. She lied to Mary-Anne, saying she only got thirty bob, so that Mary-Anne would not take all her money; she was beginning to learn the ways of the real world.

Grace would look in every day for the first couple of weeks but there was a bad atmosphere between Grace and the Garlands. Knowing it was hard for everybody, she started seeing Jessie in the middle of the week and weekends only. Grace was aware that Jessie had made a difference to the cleanliness of the house and was also looking after her brother and sister, but Grace and Jessie still preferred to go for a walk in the Barrack Park or along the esplanade on the banks of the Tay for some fresh air.

By August of 1910 Annie's epileptic fits were getting worse and with every fit, she was a little bit slower to recover and a little bit dimmer of mind and memory. Grace was grateful for the nursing service they partook of in those sad days, and clearly, Annie was becoming beyond Grace's help and, therefore, beyond hope. All she could do was to sit with her mother at night until they both fell asleep, and Grace's only pastime was prayer when she sat with her mother and writing to Johnny when she was alone in her own room. She wrote mostly at the end of the day and, after three or four days, with nothing else to say, she would take the letter with her for posting on her walks with Jessie.

On the sixth of September Annie had endured a prolonged epileptic fit and died in the room in Wilkie's Lane. Grace was terribly saddened but at the same time, relieved that her mother was not suffering anymore. The funeral was a modest affair with only a handful of loyal friends attending the requiem mass in St. Andrew's Cathedral. Grace never expected Joe to appear but she did expect Mary-Anne and John Garland to be there. The rest of the family was there except Joe and Mary-Anne and her family. On the day of the funeral, however, they never showed up and, that, more than anything else, broke Grace's heart.

Jessie sat close to Grace and held her hand. Grace had organised it and to all intents and purposes, she ensured it seemed to all that Annie was a Catholic. That is what she wanted everyone to see but if they couldn't be bothered to come to their own mother's funeral, *Hell mend them,* she thought. She was unhappy but accepted it.

Grace was given a week to find new accommodation. She knew where she wanted to go but didn't know if she would be able to afford it. The two-bedroomed flat at number 6 Littlejohn Street was empty and the factor promised her access in the time given as long as she could make the rent of seven and sixpence per week. She considered it and knew a way to achieve it. Grace met Jessie as usual on the Wednesday night and they walked a different way from the usual route. Grace had steered them to the Crescent. When they reached the *closey* of number 6 she stopped and just blurted it out. "I'm moving back to the Crescent, Jessie," she said happily. "I'm getting the keys of number 6, two rooms and two stairs up," she said, expecting some good reaction.

"That's good, Grace, can you afford it?"

"Well, I could if I had a flatmate," she smiled.

"Have you got one? Who?"

"YOU," said Grace. "We can move back here over the weekend."

Jessie looked at the window of number 6, then she looked deep into Grace's eyes and after a while she shook her head and quietly said, "No."

"What do you mean, no? Don't you want to get out of Larch Street?" said Grace.

"Yes, of course I do but I can't leave little John and little Annie with my mum and dad," said Jessie. Grace looked dumbfounded, but she understood.

Although Grace tried to persuade her again to join her in the flat in the Crescent, Jessie argued that she felt it her duty to stay with her family for the good of the bairns. Grace knew that no amount of arguing would change her mind and she eventually let it go. She took the house and managed on her own budget in the hope that Johnny would at some stage join her there and, in the meantime, she would ask him for a contribution, if he wanted.

As a consequence of his decision to join the army, Johnny McKee spent a month at the Black Watch (Royal Highlanders) 2nd Battalion HQ at Balhousie Castle in Perth before moving to Aldershot for eight months of training. Thereafter, he enjoyed a week's leave with Grace in the Crescent then he boarded a troop ship with his company from Tilbury, bound for a new Base Station at Sialkot in Umballa in Punjab, India. He trained as a piper and was in great demand as time went on, during stints of garrison duty.

Grace Murphy had to inform him by letter, that his father, old Jim, was being moved out of his house in Littlejohn Street due to the onset of dementia. With no one at home to look after him, Mr. McKee was committed to the Eastern poorhouse at Maryfield, in the Stobswell area of Dundee in November 1911. Johnny was refused leave on compassionate grounds to visit his father and was told that all leave was cancelled for the immediate and long-term future. The battalion saw action in Bareilly and again in Calcutta in 1911. From then on, they were constantly on high alert and in action for the rest of their time in India, until being transshipped to the Western front in 1914 with no home leave applications allowed.

CHAPTER 34

Larch Street

For Mary-Anne and John Garland, life was a challenge. Larch Street was central to the mills at the bottom end of the Lochee Road and there was plenty work once more as the military contracts started coming in to the jute barons on the strength of another war in the near future in Europe. Mary-Anne worked every day that she could when she was able, but John Garland stopped the millwork in favour of shady dealings with the spivs and crooks that ran bookies and drinking dens in the Scouringburn. Due to complaints of child neglect, the Dundee Council social work department had warned her that she could be sent to prison for her continual refusal to keep her children in a clean and healthy condition, and there was already an order from the courts for her to be monitored by the health visitors of the Parish.

In November 1911 the health visitors went to the house in Larch Street and found the front door unlocked. They went in and found an empty home, except for the fact that young John and little Annie were locked in the back bedroom at four o'clock in the afternoon. The Garlands were reported to the police, and, the council authorities assessed the children. Mary-Anne and John Garland appeared before Bailie Forwell at the Children's Court in Dundee:

Industrial school petitions against John Garland (6) and Annie Garland (3), Larch Street, were continued for six and twelve weeks respectively. The Bailie also had to deal with the usual parade of stone-throwers and lamp-extinguishers.

– Evening Telegraph, Friday 17 November 1911.

Mary-Anne did not go home from the Bell Street court appearance that night but found company back in the beer tent with her friends. Jessie was horrified and stayed with the children at home in Larch Street. In their mother's absence, she fed them and looked after them. The following day Mary-Anne staggered home and slept it off for a day. She remained sober for a week and tearfully promised Jessie that she would change her ways, and Jessie promised to help her. Six weeks after the court appearance of Mary-Anne and John Garland, the old habits crept back into the house at Larch Street. The Garlands had disappeared again for another two days with not a word to Jessie of their whereabouts. Suddenly, John Garland appeared at the house, half-cut and unshaven.

"Where have you been, Dad, and where is Mum?" Jessie asked John.

"Never you mind, just you carry on minding the bairns, and you and me will get on fine," he said. Clearly, he and Mary-Anne had fallen out again.

"Have you any money for food for the bairns?" Jessie asked.

"What?" he glowered. "You're the one that's working in this hoose, YOU feed them." He went into the scullery and grabbed the last of the bread and cheese in the press and ate all of it.

"That's the bairns' tea you're eating, I need money for more food," said Jessie. Her father totally ignored her and walked into his bedroom, closed the door, lay down and fell asleep.

Distraught, and on the point of tears, she took the bairns to the Crescent to see Grace. Jessie couldn't even talk, there were tears in her eyes and tears running down her face – she was completely exasperated with the situation. Grace knew that her sister was in trouble for child neglect and, when she saw the state of the kids she, too, felt guilty that her own nephew and niece have had to live like this. Grace quickly made them jam pieces and tea and they wolfed them down. Finally, Jessie regained her composure and explained through gritted teeth, "The kids are starving again and I've no money left. I don't get paid until Friday, and that's two days away."

After they ate, Grace said, "Right, you're all staying here with me. Jessie, can you go to Larch Street and get some clean clothes for these two and I'll make up a bed in the spare room for you all?"

She replied, "I can't, Grace, my dad would never let me leave the bairns here, and anyway, there are no more clothes!" said Jessie.

"OK, let's change the plan then, you stay here with the bairns, and I'll get the clothes," said Grace.

John Garland answered the door when Grace knocked. "Where are the clothes for the bairns?" she demanded.

Garland looked stunned. "Where are the bairns? And that Jessie, where is she?"

Grace said, "Jessie is minding them at my house and they're staying there, with me. I'll ask you again, where are their clothes?" she said.

"What clothes are you talking about? They've got their clothes on," he replied.

"They are wearing flea-ridden, moth-eaten and threadbare rags,

John. You must have other clothes for them here, surely," she said.

"No… I… I don't think so, Grace, but I might be wrong…" said John in reply.

She took him by the collar and made a fist. "If you don't make their clothes appear here in the next two seconds I will break your nose and then, I'll break your legs!" she said.

He scurried off to the scullery and rummaged around the bottom of the press for a minute. Then he appeared with a selection of old unwashed underwear and a shirt, too small for John, but not too big for Annie. After another few minutes scratching around he found some other items of soiled children's clothing. She took all of it and wrapped it up in a boy's dirty shirt and announced, "You get food in for the children and buy new clothes for them by this weekend or, you're for it." Grace went on, "I will be back here on Saturday at two o'clock with Jessie and the bairns and by God, if you haven't got what they need, I will brain you and then I will make sure you will lose those bairns for sure!" She stormed out of the house and ran the length of Larch Street and all the way home to the Crescent, struggling to hold back tears.

The bairns were asleep when she got home but Jessie was still awake and waiting for her. "Right," said Grace, "we'll start with boiling these old clothes and get them clean and ironed for the morning. Then we'll get wee John to school and Annie can go to George and Catherine McKee's for the rest of the day. Your father is going to get food and new clothes for them by Saturday," she told Jessie, who looked at her disbelievingly. "I'm going to give you two pounds for clothes that you can buy at Paddy's market on Saturday morning just in case he doesn't do what he was told."

Jessie looked at Grace with nothing less than hero worship in her eyes. "How do you know he will do it?" she asked Grace.

"Because I think he'd prefer to walk around than get pushed around in a bath chair for the rest of his life," said Grace.

Jessie looked puzzled and then it dawned on her. "You've seen the red mist then." She smiled at Grace.

Grace, Jessie and the bairns appeared at 43 Larch Street at two o'clock precisely and a clean-shaven and presentable John Garland opened the door. They walked in to a roaring coal fire in the fireplace, which was quite unnecessary given the time of year, but it was a show of willingness that Grace recognised. The smell of steak pies on the grate made them hungry again and the table was set for five.

Grace looked around and saw that the house was clean and tidy, although there was no sign of Mary-Anne. Jessie was almost in tears again with joy this time as the kids ran into their room shouting with delight. Two parcels of children's clothes were neatly piled up on the bed they shared. It was the nearest thing they had ever seen to Christmas. There were socks, shoes, shirts, blouses and even trousers and skirts. There was even a pack of handkerchiefs, something that they had never before owned. Grace took him aside and leaned in close. "Where did you get the money for all of this, John? Tell me the truth.

"Catherine and George loaned me ten pounds," he said under his breath.

Jessie held back the tears and even walked over to her father and kissed him on the cheek. "Thank you, Dad, well done!" she said.

"Well," he said, "we have to show your mother that things have changed around here by the time she gets back, right?"

"Right," they all joined in happily.

"Where is she, John?" asked Grace.

Knowing Mary-Anne was in the jail for seven days for being drunk and incapable, "She has had a bit of a fall and is recovering in the DRI," he lied. "No need to visit her, she will be back soon," he said reassuringly.

Grace went back to Littlejohn Street feeling good about the last two days. She couldn't wait to tell John McKee in India about what had just happened. *He won't believe it,* she thought, *but it will be great just to write him something good about Jessie and the kids at last.*

Mary-Anne was released from Bell Street cells at the end of the week. She gratefully and tearfully accepted the welcome the family gave her and she actually felt forgiven. The warnings fell on deaf ears, however, and after another couple of weeks, the Garlands were out in the Westport pubs again. The conversation turned into an argument, and the argument turned into a fight. The pair were thrown out of the Scout bar and they continued to fight verbally and physically all the way home to Larch Street.

Jessie could hear them approaching the house from fifty yards and she quickly got wee John and little Annie into the back bedroom and locked the door from the inside.

"I don't want you going out on your own anymore, Mary-Anne, I canna trust you, you're liable to go away wi' any other man at the drop of a hat!" he shouted at her in the doorway.

"Who do you think you are, John Garland, to tell me what I can and cannae do? After the way you disappear with any bliddy floozie at the first bat of an eyelid!" she spat back at him.

Then, he lost control entirely. "I know you had an affair with Billy McKee when I was away with the Black Watch the first time!" he roared at her.

She stopped arguing and then said, "Nah, you don't know that, you can't know that!"

"I do!" he roared. "He told me," said John.

"What! – When?" she said.

"Just before he died at Magersfontein, he was back here from the Black Watch on leave with his brother, wasn't he?" Garland added, "He told me everything!" He goaded her more. "And I saw him die!" he shouted.

"No, you never!" she spouted.

"I did – and it was deliberate!" he screamed at her.

"What do you mean, deliberate? It was an accident, it was Joe Murphy," she said in a frenzy. "He never meant to kill him, and someone knocked his arm, and it was friendly fire," she said.

"Friendly fire, my arse! Who told you that anyway?" He was laughing. "No, it wasn't friendly fire, it was no accident, and it wasn't Joe – it was me. I shot Billy McKee and I meant to kill him!" he screamed with venom. "And I'll tell you another thing, I shot your brother as well!"

Silence fell on the house. Mary-Anne stood like a statue, looking at the man who had just confessed to the murder of the only man she had ever loved and the attempted murder of her brother Joe.

Jessie had heard every word. She flung the door open and walked into the living room in tears. She was astonished at his admission but not surprised that he, John Garland, was a murderer. Looking at her parents, she solemnly swore that she would never, ever set foot in their house again for as long as they were around. She walked around the house picking up her few possessions while wee John and little Annie tugged at her dress in tears. Finally, she kissed her brother and sister goodbye and left Larch Street for the last time. Jessie moved back in with Grace that night.

The children were used to being left alone every night with nothing to eat until morning. Again, their clothes were in rags and the bairns were filthy from one week to another. John Garland had disappeared again and after some weeks, Mary-Anne began to bring male 'friends' back to stay for the night. From afar, Jessie knew what was happening and couldn't take it anymore and went directly to the police. The council took action. Soon, further council visits and complaints were received from Jessie and concerned neighbours resulting in Mary-Anne being arrested:

Mary-Anne Murphy or Garland, 43 Larch Street, pleaded guilty at Dundee Sheriff Court to-day to having, between 1st April and 2nd May, neglected her two children, John, (6) and Ann (3) by failing to provide them with sufficient clothing and by keeping them in a verminous condition.

Mr. W.D. Williamson stated that everything had been tried with the woman.

Sheriff Neish passed sentence of sixty days imprisonment.

– Evening Telegraph, Monday 13 May 1912

Mary-Anne was jailed for neglecting the children. Grace and Jessie and Catherine had pushed the council for more action. Jessie thought that the world had gone mad. Her sister had been sent to jail and John Garland had moved back into Larch Street. As far as Jessie could determine, the children were completely overlooked by the courts. She was working full-time with little or no time to care for them. Her father was a lazy and dangerous drunkard, and the courts had left him in charge of the bairns. *He will abandon them if he has his own way – or worse,* Jessie thought. She had to stop this madness. Jessie went back to the police in Bell Street and met with the Chief of Police the following day and begged them to help her care for the children. Sadly, the following was published in the local paper:

DUNDEE FATHER'S HEARTLESS CONDUCT
PREFERS TOASTING HIS TOES AT FIRE
To Working For His Children.

The life of children of tender years with parents described as criminal or drunken, is apt to sap their moral fibre, and the plan of authorities is to transfer them from their sordid surroundings to Industrial Schools.

Two such cases engaged the attention of Bailie Don at Dundee Children's Court this afternoon.

Chief Constable Carmichael redirected the attention of the court to the case of John Garland (7) and Ann Garland (3) children of John Garland, Labourer, 43 Larch Street and his wife.

The Chief Constable in his petition craved that they should be sent to an Industrial school, being under the care of criminal or drunken parents at present. He said the mother had been sent to prison for sixty days by the Sheriff for cruelty to her children.

The mother said that if anyone was at fault, it was her.

The father, appealing for another chance, said that his sister had a comfortable home and was quite willing to take the children.

Baillie Don said that he had no hesitation in ordering the boy to be sent to Tranent Industrial School and the girl to Nazareth House, Aberdeen, till they attained the age of sixteen years.

– Evening Telegraph, Friday 14 June 1912

The social workers came to the house in Larch Street the day John appeared at the children's court. Neither John Garland nor Jessie were even there to say goodbye. They broke the lock on the front door and entered the house and found the bairns, locked in the back room.

Hurriedly, John scooped up all the marbles he could find and stuffed them into his pockets. They packed a bag for the boy and another for the girl. Wee Annie had nothing to take to the children's home except her scrapbook but she couldn't find it and left without it. John was taken away by two men to a home for boys just outside Edinburgh and wee Annie was taken away by two ladies to a home for girls in Aberdeen. They had gone to two separate children's homes in two different cities a hundred and fifty miles apart, ostensibly never to see each other again.

Jessie was destroyed. Her heart was broken and her mind was in turmoil. This was worse than anything she ever imagined could happen; she felt she was responsible for pushing the social work and police to prosecute her parents in the first place. It was, therefore, her fault that her little brother and sister were sent away. She went back to the house in Larch Street later that day. The house was a total shambles. The social workers must have left the door open and let the neighbours in when they took the children away. Someone had ransacked what was left of the property. All of the personal effects and items of any value, once owned by the Garlands, had gone.

In all the rubble of empty gin bottles and fag packets there was little that could be considered children's belongings that she could take with her except a small pile of raggedy clothes and a broken, cheap toy or two. She was about to walk out when something made her turn back and go into the bairns' room. She walked slowly around the empty room and, thinking like a child, opened the press in the corner. She saw the empty shelves in front of her and, out of force of habit, raised a foot up to the bottom shelf. With hands on the top shelf, she pulled herself up. Jessie could then see the contents of the shelf, among the worthless things that had been overlooked, in the far-right corner she found a blue scrapbook. Jessie cleared the shelf with a sweep of her arm and stuffing the items into her message bag, she left Larch Street for the last time.

CHAPTER 35

Back to the Beer Tent

Jessie went to Grace's house and tearfully told Grace what she had found. Jessie and Grace both fell apart with guilt and grief. She and Grace cried together, with the items laid out in front of them. Grace wrote to Johnny McKee to explain what had happened to her sister and her children. It was the hardest letter she ever had to write and that he ever had to read. He wrote back in his perfect copperplate handwriting that he would rather have faced the rebellious Indian forces than watch the bairns get split up and put away. He was upset and concerned for Jessie. "What can we do for her?" he asked Grace. "Can you take her to live permanently with you at your place?" Grace had already written that Jessie was actually staying with her in Littlejohn Street, not because she wanted to stay there but because she didn't want to stay with her father and mother anymore. Besides, John Garland had already disappeared, and Jessie had no place else to go.

Jessie was also unfairly subjected to a torrent of abuse at work and in the streets of the Scouringburn, when the news of the cruelty and neglect of the bairns got out. It was not her fault but still, she felt as guilty as her parents were, in the wake of the court decision. Grace told Johnny, "It was better for Jessie that she was back in the Crescent with me around friendlier faces." No one seemed to take account of Jessie's efforts to help little John and wee Annie because nothing was mentioned about her actions in the paper. She understood how people felt but, ironically, she also understood how her father felt. *He was just useless,* she thought to herself; he never had a real family life because he never felt he had a real family. As for her mother, Mary-Anne, she was an alcoholic like him but she was so seriously depressed, she wasn't responsible for her actions. In her father's eyes, only Mary-Anne was responsible for rearing the children and he failed to see it was his problem too. The children were his, but in his mind, he believed the welfare of the bairns was Mary-Anne's job. Grace was relieved therefore when Johnny McKee had suggested that Jessie be offered a room permanently with her. John Garland had already moved out of Larch Street on the same day that they took the bairns away and had discreetly organised himself a flat somewhere up the Hilltown, far away from the Scouringburn and the Crescent.

When Mary-Anne was released from prison in mid-July of 1912, the whole world was against her. She found herself without a home and out of work. New tenants occupied the house at Larch Street and her possessions were gone. Nothing was left for her and she was on her own. She was given a cash handout from the prison service of two shillings and sixpence for food to last her for a week. Shelter was the thing she didn't have. She had no idea where to go and she remembered being in this position before. *What did I do at that time?* She tried hard to clear the fog in her head and to remember. Then it came to her! *The beer tent. Tam will be there.* She wandered through the Scouringburn streets and over the Lochee Road, up Parker Street to the steps. The closer she got to Dudhope Castle the faster she went.

At last, she arrived at the canvas door flap of the boozer and tried to unravel the ties to get in. A voice from the inside shouted, "Wha's that?"

"Mary-Anne Garland," she replied quickly, in anticipation.

After a few minutes of silence, the voice came back to her. "You're barred," it said. "Go away."

"What? I canna be barred out of the beer tent, anyway, it's illegal!" she shouted and swore.

"You are not welcome, go away," the voice said.

Mary-Anne kept the argument up for a full ten minutes until she heard the footsteps of someone coming around the castle towards the tent.

"Tam Pepper," she said with trepidation. "Tam, Tam, they're no' letting me in," she said humbly.

Tam Pepper said, "That's right, I told them you're barred, we know what you did to your bairns."

She looked at him like a beaten puppy. "But Tam, it was all a mistake," she tried to explain. "John Garland was getting me drink all the time and he never gave me money for food or clothes for the bairns," she lamented. "What could I do? I never had any money." She looked pathetic.

"Thank God they are now being looked after in children's homes now, that's all I can say, now away wi' you, Mary-Anne, just leave," he said.

"What aboot a drink then, Tam, to get me on my way?"

"Have ye got the money for drink now?" he asked her. She dug into her skirt pocket and produced a half-crown; it was all the money she had in the world. Tam took the coin. "Right, stay here," he said and ordered the inside man to let him in. She stood back like the social outcast she had become and blended into the shadows in case Tam objected to anyone seeing her there. She felt worthless. He returned with two bottles of Old Tom gin and a sixpence. "There you are, Mary-Anne, and there's a tanner back." Mary-Anne opened one of the bottles and took a straight swig. "Now awa' wi' you and don't come back."

"Just one more thing, Tam," she said.

"Does my brother Joe still work for you at the boxing booth?"

"NO," he said firmly.

Crying, she said, "Well, do you know where he is?"

"NO," was the reply again.

"Tam, I've got to speak to him, it's very important, can you get a message to him?" she begged.

"What message?" Her eyes dried and lit up when he asked that because it told her he knew where Joe was.

"It's about Magersfontein, that's all."

"Where are you staying?"

"Close," she said. "I'll be around here again if you want to get hold of me," she said.

"I'll see what I can do, now beat it." Tam closed the canvas flap to stop letting the light out.

Mary-Anne shuffled out of sight and around the back of the tent; she parted the folds of canvas and hunkered down for the night. *This'll do me till the morning,* she acknowledged to herself. She started to drink and all the worst and darkest thoughts came back to her. She remembered painfully the time when she was happy and in love, with a new home in John Street and their own furniture. Then she remembered the time that she planned to pay privately for the birth of her first child in the hospital.

She then let her mind wander on what could have been. Eventually, as she neared the bottom of the first bottle, she dwelled on the thought of the two bairns she had taken away from her, and she felt the pain again in her heart that only got better with drink. She drank enough out of her two bottles of gin to get to sleep; only by then, was she without thought of little John and wee Annie. In the morning, she awoke to sunshine and a massive hangover. She walked to the pawnbroker in St. Andrew's Street and pawned her sweetheart brooch for ten bob, the last thing of any value she had left in her life.

Garland Fraser, as he was now known in the fairground boxing circuit, was actually still working for Tam Pepper but he never worked in Dundee after being recognised by his little sister Grace. Two days after Mary-Anne came to the beer tent, the message was passed on to him in Glasgow from one of the high-cheekers. Joe cringed at hearing the name of that place in South Africa. A week later he walked into the beer tent and spoke to Tam Pepper. "What's this all about?" he asked.

"Your sister came here last week trying to get in for a drink. I refused." Joe nodded his understanding and Tam told him the rest. "All she said, was that she had to tell you something about Magersfontein and then left. I don't know where you'll find her because she wouldn't tell me where she lives these days." In the beer tent, Joe got all the news about Mary-Anne's jail sentence and the court's decision to send her children away to separate homes. He was in an absolutely foul mood after hearing it all, and he walked out to find her.

He didn't have to look far. As he walked out of the tent and around the castle wall, she stepped out right in front of him. "Mary-Anne, where did you come from?" he asked.

"I've been here watching the tent to see when you were coming out," she replied.

"You mean you saw me going in there?" he asked her.

"Yeah, I did, but they're not letting me in!" she moaned indignantly.

"What the hell has happened to you?" he demanded.

"I've got the depression, Joe, I'm no' well," she said. "John Garland has done all this, Joe; John Garland has ruined me."

"First things first, what's this about Magersfontein?" He winced.

"Joe," she said, "you never shot Billy McKee… John Garland did it."

He looked her in the eyes and said, "What are you talking about?"

She said, "John Garland told me that it was him who bumped your arm and that it was him that shot Billy!"

Joe moved in closer to her and took her by the elbows. "Say that again," he said.

"Joe, YOU never killed Billy McKee, John Garland did it." She said it very deliberately and he could see that even in her sorry state, she was very serious and very sure of what she was saying. "Joe," she said, "and there's something else, it was him who shot you at Magersfontein, on purpose – he tried to kill you as well, Joe!" Joe's jaw dropped open; he was stunned by that news. Mary-Anne looked at her brother. "I know my husband, and I know when he's lying, and I know when he's telling the truth. This time, he is telling the truth."

They moved along the path in front of the castle and came to the Parker Street steps in silence, neither one of them wanting to say another word about it in public.

"Where are you staying?" Joe asked.

"I've been kipping behind the tent since I got out," she said ashamedly.

"Oh, God!" said Joe.

They reached the top of the Parker Street steps and then looked down at the Crescent below them and he said, "What has happened to us, Mary-Anne?" He added, "You are homeless and I am on the run even if, as you say, I don't need to be."

They walked slowly down the steps and into Parker Street. Turning the corner they headed into John Street and strangely, Mary-Anne felt better that she was in old, familiar surroundings. Looking down the street with so many memories, she began to say, "I wish I could start all over again," when Joe saw the sign 'To Rent' above them.

Joe gestured to her. "What about moving back into the Crescent, Mary-Anne?"

She allowed herself a dry smile. "I wish," she said.

"You wait right here, I'm going to see the factors."

She walked up the *closey*, and into the back courtyard and leaned against the wall of the coalbunker, dreaming and hoping it would work.

An hour later he appeared with the keys to number 12 John Street. "How did you manage that, Joe?"

"Garland, my name is Garland, remember," he said with a smile.

They climbed the stairs and Joe turned the key in the lock. They walked into the two-bedroomed flat and switched the lights on, and she knew then, it was happening. She had a home again.

"I've paid the deposit and a week's rent in advance. I'll stay with you for a couple of days but nobody is to know I've been here, understand?" She nodded in agreement, but she didn't understand anything. She just gratefully took the key. "Now, I'm going to the market to get some furniture." He gave her two pounds. "Mary-Anne, this is for food, not drink. I'll be back in a couple of hours, and you get us something to eat in the meantime." She looked at him like he was her saviour. "I trust you, big sister!" he said.

That night, they ate steak pie together, and sat at the kitchen table he had delivered with the rest of the stuff. They had tea and cake to finish but no alcohol. She was beginning to emerge from the depths of depression and it was all through the kindness of her brother. He had his own problems, she knew that, but she also knew that she was unable to help him anymore; she was almost right down and out herself. Now she began to think of getting a new job – the mills were getting busy again – there was another war on the horizon and the jute barons loved it. They were investing in new weaving looms and taking on skilled weavers. She applied for several jobs within the next week but the longer she kept dry the better she felt about going for them. Finally, Baxter Brothers' jute mill in Princes Street gave her a start on probation, but more through desperation than anything else. Up until that point, Joe was in the flat all day and out all night. She never asked why he did that, but she knew he was up to something that she shouldn't ask about. She also knew that he would not be around forever.

At the end of the week, Joe went back to his boxing work in Glasgow, saying he would be back 'sometime'. When she started earning a wage again she began to pay back the kindness he had shown to her. After a month, she had renewed her wardrobe and put some money aside. She took over the paying of rent on the flat and when he returned after another month, she even offered him the two pounds he gave her in the early days. To her surprise, he took it in the knowledge that she was not spending it on gin. "I'm only staying a couple of days, Mary-Anne, but I don't want to lose you again. If you make this place your home, I'll know where you are and how to get in touch with you." Joe stayed away for about three months at a time.

CHAPTER 36

Last Night on the Hilltown

Each time Joe came back he went through the same routine; he stayed a few days in the flat all day, out all night. Mary-Anne never asked him, but she knew what he was doing, she suspected correctly that Joe was looking for John Garland after what she had told him. As the months rolled on, he was more intent on his 'nightwork' when he came to Dundee and less concerned with Mary-Anne's welfare. Mary-Anne was turning her life around again and had been living the quiet life of a single woman in the Crescent, and she had been without a drink for nearly two years. Finally, one night in February 1914, he seemed to go about his night work with a mission. He told Mary-Anne that his 'business' was coming to an end in Dundee and he would have to stop his visits soon. Unhappily, she accepted that.

Later that night, he left the Crescent after dark and made his way along the Overgate, then up the Wellgate and the Wellgate steps. He crossed over the Victoria Road and started walking up the Hilltown, just as he had done, for the weeks and months he had been looking for the man. The Hilltown was a steep uphill road, almost a mile long, leading from the Wellgate steps in the heart of Dundee to the foot of the Law Hill high above the city. His man was known to have moved there after the court case that took his bairns into care. Joe had to find him, but he didn't know where on the Hilltown John Garland was. The whole road up the hill on both sides was festooned with little shops and pubs, shadowy dwelling houses and small theatres that showed the silent pictures to the concentrated population of the area; they all lived there, up the *closeys* in the myriad of tenement homes that lined the pavements on both sides of the hill and through the back yards to yet another hidden labyrinth of tenement homes all served by the same *closey* access from the main road.

From his information, he knew that the Windmill Bar, halfway up the Hilltown, was a pub his man was seen in. It being Friday, the Hilltown was busy with people going up and down and the pubs were mobbed with volunteers in uniform obviously getting into the warring mindset. The Windmill was packed when he walked in; nobody really took any notice of him, the quiet man with the broken nose in the corner of the bar, having a pint.

John Garland walked in with a woman on his arm. They stood at the back of the drinkers who were three deep at the bar, waiting for the barman to serve them. Joe put his beer on the bar, moved in and tapped Garland on the shoulder. John Garland slowly turned around, knowing the tap could have been the lead-up to a head-butt. He stood back from the drinkers and caught the full force of a fist in the gut. He doubled up and the drinkers scattered. Looking up, he recognised Joe. "Joe Murphy, where did you come from? You're supposed to be dead!" he groaned. Joe said nothing.

Before he could throw another punch the punters in the pub jumped on him and stifled the attack. They picked him up and bundled Joe out before anything else could happen. The people in the bar gathered around John Garland and sat him down to revive him from the blow. "Who was that? Why did he thump you? What was it all about?" they all wanted to know.

"I think it was Joe Murphy," he said. "Whether it was him or not, I've no idea why he attacked me, I haven't seen him for years," Garland said. And then added, "He was listed as dead from the Boer War, and that was about a dozen years ago," he told the sympathetic crowd.

John Garland knew he was in danger. He also knew that if anybody knew who he was, they would not be so sympathetic. So he said no more. He decided that there was safety in numbers and the longer he stayed in the pub the better. Gradually, the night wore on and the drinkers left the pub. The crowd changed to new faces who hadn't witnessed the attack and at that point he felt it was safe to move. At half past eight, Garland and his floozie left the Windmill and, watching for his attacker all the time, missed the man in the shadows further up and across the Hilltown, watching him from the darkness deep inside a *closey*. To John Garland, Joe Murphy was nowhere to be seen. In fact, Joe had moved on up the Hilltown in the shadows of the nooks and crannies of the building frontages he had gotten to know well in his mission, because he knew now, where Garland and the woman were heading. John Garland, in drink, began to think he was mistaken, and it could not possibly have been Joe Murphy as he knew Murphy was dead, he'd seen the telegram.

At the top of the hill, however, Joe Murphy took shelter in the dark recess of the fishmonger shop doorway on the corner of Kinghorne Road and Hilltown and waited. Garland and his floozie, now more confident, continued up the Hilltown to the next pub and had another drink. They eventually moved on to the top of the hill and, feeling safe, he decided to have one last pint in the Bow Bridge Bar. Across the road from his vantage point, Joe heard the woman saying she was tired and she wanted to go home. She left him under the Hilltown clock at ten. "See you when you get in," she said. She walked into the close at the top of the hill, across from Kinghorne Street and through to the back land. She never knew she was being followed but she was safe; Joe had no intention of hurting the woman, it was her boyfriend he was stalking, his brother-in-law, John Garland.

This was the man who shot him in the back and tried to kill him. This was the man who also killed Billy McKee deliberately, letting Joe feel the guilt of a mistaken kill. The red mist descended on Joe as he watched Garland disappear into the Bow Bridge Bar. He simmered in anger at the thought that this was the man who had mistreated his sister so badly. Joe couldn't bear to think of the fact that this same man reduced his own wife and children to the point that they felt worthless, to the extent that the bairns were taken from them. This was the same man who single-handedly turned his sister, Mary-Anne, from a solid pillar of the family into a down-and-out alcoholic. All of that was good enough reason to do John Garland in, he thought.

Joe came out of the shop entrance, crossed the road and walked into the same close as the woman had walked in a few minutes earlier. Joe watched from the shadows of the back courtyard as she climbed the three flights of stairs of the hidden tenement. He watched her in silence as she walked along the open *plettie* and unlocked the door at the end and went in.

Joe sat down low on the grass in the darkest shadows and waited. Another hour went by and he began to hear the many drunks from the pubs move along on the Hilltown pavements in the front of the tenements. A few people walked into the close and right past him on their way to their homes in the back land. Joe looked at each of them closely to see if Garland was with them. None of the passers-by noticed him in the dark. At last, he spotted John Garland alone, staggering towards him coming through the *closey* on his way home. At the bottom of the stairs, Garland started to climb but never got to the second step.

Joe sprang on him like a tiger on its prey. He took him from the back with his arm around Garland's neck into the darkness of the grassy back courtyard. No sound could Garland utter as Joe cut off the oxygen to his windpipe with the crook of his arm. With a massive wrench, he heard it snap as he broke John Garland's neck. Garland blacked out, into unconsciousness then death. He dragged the limp body of Garland into the *closey* and forced open the coalbunker door under the stairs. "Get in there, you animal," he muttered as he chucked the body into the dark cellar and closed the door. "That was too quick, and too easy, not like the Boer he killed in South Africa the same way," he said to himself as he straightened his clothing then wiped the sweat from his brow and walked calmly out of the close and back down the Hilltown and into the city.

CHAPTER 37

Australia

Joe Murphy quietly unlocked the door to Mary-Anne's flat and silently packed his bag. He left the key on the kitchen table without a note and silently left the house. He took the train from Dundee station to Queen Street, Glasgow, then he vacated his digs, telling his brother Tommy that he had helped their sister out of a tight spot in Dundee and that he had to go. He stopped at the Clydesdale bank in Buchannan Street and removed all the prize money he had accumulated as Garland Fraser in the last five years from his account and closed it.

Joe then bought a one-way ticket to London Kings Cross Station. He travelled south by train that day and the following morning headed for Tilbury Docks. There, he secured another one-way ticket in the name of Garland Fraser for the next voyage on the SS *Osterly* at the princely sum of forty-five pounds. The passenger steamship was bound for Melbourne. After three days of hanging around the docks, on the 15th of February, he underwent and paid his shilling for a medical examination to verify he had no infectious illnesses and finally he was successfully blood tested for tuberculosis. He presented his birth certificate, British passport and medical passes to the British border control guards for their scrutiny.

The documents were the product of the British Nationality and

Status Aliens Act, 1914. The passport, consisting of a single page, folded into eight and held together with a cardboard cover. It was valid for two years and featured a personal description including the shape of his face: round; complexion: fair; height: 5 feet, 8 inches, and features which read: Nose: large, broken; Eyes: grey; Hair: dark brown and finally; distinguishing marks: Linear two-inch scar above right elbow, gunshot scar through left shoulder front and back, tattoo, right forearm, of Tombstone and adornment.

In the terminal, they wanted to know why he was leaving the United Kingdom, and not waiting for call-up service in the impending conflict in Europe. Garland Fraser explained that he intended joining family in Australia and there, he also told them, he intended to enlist in the Australian military. He waited nervously as his birth lines were verified on the national register. At length, his birth certificate and passport were examined and accepted, as were his medical certificates. The border guards wished him a good trip and good luck; he was on his way to Australia. He boarded the steamship and took his berth settled in for a long voyage along with the 700-odd other steerage, third-class passengers.

CHAPTER 38

The Coalman

In Dundee the coalmen were working their way along Strathmartine Road toward the top of the Hilltown. On a cold day in February, they were much in demand. The woman John Garland had left the night before under the clock at the top of the Hilltown was waiting for them with an empty coal bucket on her arm. "This *closey*, one bag o'churrels, please." She was thoroughly hacked off with John Garland for not coming back to the flat the night before. *Ach, well, never mind,* she thought. He left her the cash for a bag of coal so, *Good riddance to him,* she thought. The coalman pulled a full bag off the cart and heaved it up and on his shoulders.

Leaving his horse-drawn cart outside the close, he made his way through to the back land to the woman standing at the cellar door. "Open the cellar door, will ye missus?" he said. "I've tried but it's stuck."

She replied, "There is something blocking it on the inside and it looks like the lock is broken."

He tried to open it with the key but the door was pushed too far in. He pulled the door and it wouldn't move.

"Come on, coalman, I'm waiting," said the woman. He gave it a kick and that pushed the door further in; it opened about a foot wide and, by the light let in from the *closey*, he saw John Garland's hand on the cellar floor among the coal. "ARGHH!" he screamed. "There's somebody in there!"

"Oh! for fu—"

The woman ran away, through the close and onto the street pavement on the Hilltown, screaming in total fright. The coalman turned and tripped over the bag of coal in his way to get out of the close. "Get the polis, get the polis!" he shouted. "There's been a murder!"

At the top of the Hilltown, the police arrived in minutes after the call. They came into the close and looked into the coal cellar. The cops called for an ambulance from the police box at the junction of Strathmartine Road and Hill Street. Detectives swarmed all over the closes around the top of the Hilltown. They found nothing of significance that bore investigating. There was no sign of a struggle or a fight that they could see so they started to speak to the neighbours.

During the investigations, the neighbours were soon to hear that the dead man was identified as John Garland, the same man that was responsible for neglecting his own children, to the extent that they were split up and sent away to homes over a year before. On hearing that, there was a general reluctance to help the police but the woman he was with told them that John Garland was assaulted by a man in the Windmill bar the night before. She told them that Garland had recognised the attacker and named him as Joe Murphy. The police interviewed everyone they could find who was in the pub that witnessed the assault and it was acknowledged that the name Joe Murphy was mentioned as the attacker. They couldn't work it out. Mary-Anne was traced to John Street and interviewed. She confirmed she was the estranged wife of the murdered man and that Joe

Murphy was her brother who had died, and he died a hero, she told them, in 1900 in the Boer War. Their investigations went on, but no trace could be found of Joe Murphy especially since the army confirmed his death in 1901.

Jessie read about it in the *Courier*. She knew it was her father that had been murdered and, upsetting as it was, she acknowledged it could have been anybody who did it. She remembered the argument he had with her mother in Larch Street on the day Jessie walked out of the house. During that argument he admitted killing a soldier in South Africa and deliberately shooting another. He was also instrumental in her brother and sister being sent to the children's homes more than a year ago. She wondered though, if her mother was involved. That night she decided to visit her mother, Mary-Anne. They had lived just four hundred yards apart in the Crescent for the last two years and never before had either the want or reason to see each other.

Jessie, however, needed to know something. She stood at the door of her mum's house in John Street for a minute to compose herself and firmly knocked on the door. Mary-Anne opened the door a peep and saw her daughter in the gaslit tenement landing. "Yes, it's Jessie," she said and Mary-Anne opened the door fully to her.

"Do you want to come in?" said Mary-Anne.

"No, not really," said Jessie.

"Well, what do you want?" Mary-Anne asked.

Jessie held up a copy of the *Courier*. "It's Dad, isn't it?" she said.

"Yes, it is, the police were here to see me, and they confirmed it's him."

"Do you know who murdered him?" Jessie asked.

"No, I don't know anything about it and I haven't seen John Garland since Larch Street," she said quite honestly.

"Right," said Jessie.

"Was there something else?" Mary-Anne asked.

"Yes," she said. "Have you been to see the bairns in the children's homes?"

"No, I can't, I'm not allowed to, I don't think. I mean, I want to but they won't let me see them."

Jessie said, "How do you know that? Have you asked?"

"No, I'm feared," again, she answered honestly.

"Of what? You're their mother, surely you have the right to see them."

Slowly, she held her head up and admitted to Jessie that the children may not want to see her.

Jessie said, "OK, I'll come in."

The house was clean and bright, there were curtains to match the rugs and the wind-up Berliner gramophone had a record spinning on it in silence. Clearly, Mary-Anne had been sober for long enough to buy these things and Jessie felt a tinge of happiness for her mother but sad at the same time because she could see how different it all could have been. They had a cup of tea together and spoke only briefly about the murder but mostly about the bairns. In the end, Jessie convinced her mother that she should make the trips to Edinburgh and Aberdeen to see John and Annie as soon as she could.

After fifteen minutes in the house, "Time to go," said Jessie as she stood up and thanked her mother for speaking to her. They made no effort at physical contact but, as Jessie walked to the door, she turned around to face her mother one last time and held out an arm. "If you ever see wee Annie again, give her this please." Jessie held up the blue scrapbook that Mary-Anne knew well. "It is Annie's but I can't give it to her because they won't let me visit her in Nazareth House, because of what you did."

CHAPTER 39

Churchill's War

At the outbreak of the Great War in 1914, Winston Churchill, English aristocrat and MP for Dundee, mysteriously attained the position of the First Lord of the Admiralty. He was directly responsible for the disastrous planning and executing of the failed, naval only, attempt in April 1915, to attack and control the Turks in Constantinople. This, Churchill decided, was to be achieved by sailing the fleet of battleships up a 38-mile-long channel, fully exposed to Turkish artillery into the Dardanelle straights. In the event, after the loss of six ships, Churchill had the fleet withdraw in favour of sending in troop ships at Gallipoli laden with British, Australian and New Zealand troops to take the capital of the Ottoman Empire. This was to lead to another disaster with the loss of some 220,000 casualties altogether.

Not surprisingly, Churchill was consequentially demoted, and he resigned from Government, but not from his seat as an MP for Dundee. He then rejoined the army and, being an ex-officer in the Hussars, was inexplicably given the rank of Lieutenant Colonel of the 6th Battalion, The Royal Scots, an army unit that had suffered horrendous casualties alongside Dundee's own Black Watch, at the Battle of Loos on the Western Front. It is mooted that he was not popular with the men of his unit and it was no wonder. When preparing the battalion for front-line service, he drilled them constantly, and, was so confused that he forgot he was no longer in a cavalry unit and had the men "fix bayonets and trot to the right in threes", apparently. He took the opportunity to resign the army and indulge himself again in politics in 1916.

CHAPTER 40

Dundee's Own, The Black Watch

The 2nd Battalion The Black Watch became part of the 7th (Meerut) Division and left India for the Western Front in France at the beginning of the Great War. Johnny McKee landed with the Battalion in Marseille on October 12th, 1914, and was immediately in action with his comrades. Johnny fought in the action on the Western Front within the first few weeks of arrival in France at the battles of La Bassee, the 1st Battle of Messines, Armentieres and the Battle of Givenchy. He survived with most of his comrades as the battalion took part in the Battles of Neuve Chappelle in March and Festurbert in May 1915. There, trained and hardened soldiers from the heat of the Punjab, found that the weather alone necessitated a difference in attitude and tactics to those required at the onset of winter in Europe. The efforts of the forced march under fire at the frontline in France were a challenge for mobility of the men of the battalion on arrival in France after years in India. There, the Black Watch came under disciplined sniper fire and constant shelling which determined the difference in warfare tactics.

The whole Highland Division was up against a well-trained and well-equipped enemy, which forced the British army into serious trench warfare. This was something that was new to his battalion of the Black Watch, who were more used to the dry rocky landscape of

India. Private John E. McKee, however, was a consummate soldier and knew how to mark time under fire and under orders. As a rifleman in the unit, Johnny McKee had become highly regarded as a reliable man, and a good all-rounder. He excelled under pressure many times and became a stretcher-bearer for the battalion, as and when the need was called for. Because of the weapons shortage, his battalion had been ordered to make their own bombs, something the men were never properly trained to do. This was a disastrous instruction, as many were killed or injured trying to carry out this order and suddenly they knew they were fighting a very different war from that of India. The issue of ammunition was short and the army clothing issued to the division coming from India was inadequate; great coats in particular, were not available for months.

It was on 26th September 1915, when Johnny's 2nd battalion merged with the 1/4th (City of Dundee) Battalion, the Black Watch, after heavy casualties. Johnny was about to see the most devastating action ever at the Battle of Loos, which, by any standard was massive. The German frontline defences had been greatly reinforced and supplied with machine-gun redoubts and barbed wire defensive belts. The second and third lines of defence were almost as strong. To get to the German front lines, the Black Watch had to cross the expanse of no-man's land, a bombed-out shell-hole-ridden stretch of muddy land strewn with corpses of both sides, who fought and died for the privilege, and just lay there – evidence of a battlefield of hate. The fifteen-yard distance between the first and second German lines, were saturated with a new type of barbed wire that could not be easily cut with British army wire cutters. That was where they were going when the order was given, and he also knew there was little chance of surviving the hail of German machine gun fire or their heavy gun barrage if they were hung up on the wire.

The British opened up with their own heavy field artillery against the German dug-in troops. Germany's use of weaponised gas was widely condemned by the British and the western world in general and the Black Watch donned their gas masks in anticipation of incoming gas. After the British artillery bombardment, it was the British that made use of chlorine gas against the enemy for the very first time ever. By 1915, all frontline British soldiers carried a small box gas filter and if Johnny hadn't worn his, he would have died there and then, like the pals he saw falling and drowning in their own sputum because they thought it was a waste of time to put it on.

Johnny watched, and fired his weapon at the enemy, who without gas masks, had urinated on their spare socks and stuffed them inside their tin hats to cover their faces in a bizarre ritual they had been advised to do in such a situation. He witnessed the devastation it caused to friend and foe alike, as over six hundred German soldiers died on the field in front of him with the effects of poison gas. Then, as the gas drifted back in the swirling wind, into his own lines toward him and his fellow soldiers, he watched it kill several dozen of his own comrades.

The army of the British Expeditionary Force was standing by in their own frontline trenches in the rain behind no-man's land, under enemy shellfire when, on September 26th at 05:50 a huge subterranean mine went off right in front of the Black Watch and directly underneath the German lines. Clearly, the tunnellers had been busy as hundreds more German soldiers were blown up and thrown up a hundred yards into the air in that single explosion, along with the ground they sheltered in. The British heavy shelling increased and hit the German front lines for the duration of a full forty minutes. Two minutes after the British barrage finished, the order to advance was given and the Highland Division went over the top. German machine guns and rifle fire sprayed across the lines of the oncoming Black Watch as they returned fire and drove into the German trenches.

They watched as the infantrymen of 1st Battalion, the Gloucesters on the right flank of the British first army, pushed through the old enemy, razor-sharp barbed wire. That wire prevented any kind of unified infantry charge as it was used in defence of the static German trench system. As the Scots dug in again, no backup heavy gun barrage was forthcoming that could have helped them in their next charge and, for that reason alone, a successful German counterattack was made to retake the trenches at the end of the first day. The Scottish divisions were held back by the relentless German machine gunners opposite them.

The ensuing days were hard, fighting between the opposing front lines and over no-man's land. Moving forward, and into the enemy lines again, the battalion was threatened by the vicious counter-bombardment that fell across the newly captured trenches. Naturally, the German guns had the range measured to within an inch.

On the second day, as dusk was falling, then came the most devastating shelling ever, showering the Scottish soldiers with white-hot jagged scraps of metal that burned as they tore into the flesh. Johnny realised at that point that shelling was the biggest killer of this war. He would never forget the hell that was inflicted on those young lads of all nations on that battlefield. Johnny understood instinctively there and then what they meant when they said that there were no atheists in the trenches.

On the third day, Johnny's battalion moved forward through no-man's land and captured the first line of German trenches again, but they were still pinned down by enemy sniper fire and shelling. There, he learned that the battlefield atmosphere of Loos was unrelenting warfare, unlike any other he experienced. As part of the Black Watch Brigade, Johnny took part in the largest British army offensive ever, up to that date, involving six divisions comprising thirty-six Scottish battalions of some 30,000 Scots going 'over the top together' towards the defending German trenches in a coordinated attack.

On their first night in the German frontline trenches, in captured German ground, the platoon sergeant asked them, "Have you been able to get a shot at the Germans?"

Benny Black awkwardly answered. "Well, there was an old gentleman with a bald heid and a white handlebar moustache. He pokes his head up every now and again but, I never shot him, he's never done me any harm," he said thoughtfully.

"He's the bliddy enemy ye eejit and he'll shoot YOU if he gets the chance," shouted the sergeant.

The following day, Johnny shot him in the face; they never saw him pop up again. By the end of the second day in the German trenches, the battalion advanced again. Johnny and Benny – a big man and a fellow piper – made it to the German second line and took cover.

Whenever a British barrage did start, Johnny and Benny could see that about 30% of the British shells were duds and then they surmised that the artillery must have ran out of ammunition. It was either a shortage of ammo or the top brass had decided to stop the action with thousands of highlanders lying in enemy trenches or in shell holes, in the middle of no-man's land. It didn't matter, he was under orders to kill or be killed.

"We can't stay here much longer; we'll get blown to bits, Benny," Johnny said.

"Yes, you're right, and anyway, I'm starving. I'm out of rations and I canna eat bullets." They both laughed amid the pounding of shells exploding all around them, near and far.

By the third night in the German trenches, Johnny and Benny decided to join a raiding party to 'look for food'. When darkness fell, they climbed up and over the top and into other trenches along the line, full of Black Watch soldiers, also starving.

They were approaching the third line of German trenches but, *Needs must,* they thought and pressed on. On the 2nd October, by the light of the occasional flare sent up by the British, they chose the time to get up and out of the muddy water they had been sitting in for two days and nights. Into another foxhole and down into a larger crater they went and into more mud.

"So far so good, eh Benny?" said Johnny.

"Eh, come on, Johnny, I'm stervin'!"

They carried on in the darkness, ducking every time another flare went up and, hearing the German bullets whizzing past their ears, they hit the mud again face down. It didn't matter, they were driven by hunger.

Finally, they reached the same trench that he shot the old man in, and they each lobbed a couple of grenades into the darkness, all along the trench. With bayonets fixed, they slithered over the lip and down into the trench floor. They moved along the trench until Johnny stumbled over the first body. "Shite!!" he exclaimed.

"Shhh, John, for God's sake. Shhh, someone will hear you," Benny said.

Another flare went up and they instinctively ducked down beside the dead Germans. The smell of decaying corpses hit them.

"They canna hear anything, they're all dead, every one," Johnny was relieved to say.

"Right, let's see if they have anything to eat on them," said Johnny. They rifled through the pockets of the soldiers lying in bits before them. "Nothing here, nothing here either. Christ, they must have been as hungry as us in this place," said Johnny. "How many deed sojers are here, Benny?" Johnny asked his pal.

"God knows, John, but I think there are more heads than legs and arms, that's all I can tell you."

They started to laugh quietly, and then another flare went up. At that moment Benny gestured to one dead German and said, "Look! That's the old man you shot!" Johnny came right back at him. "What, is he still deid?" he joked. Benny looked worried but Johnny thrust a hand into the trouser pocket of the dead man and found something.

"Benny, Benny, look," he whispered. "Biscuits," he said with glee, and, with the light of the dying flare, "with jam on," he said as the flare died out.

"Jammy biscuits. Oh, ya lucky wee bastard, oh yes!" roared Benny.

They emptied the pocket of a considerable hoard of hardtack biscuits and scrambled back through no-man's land into their 'own' foxhole. They felt good; they found food and achieved what they had set out to do. The idea was to dominate no-man's land, to say to the enemy, "It's not no-man's land, it's ours." There, they ate the biscuits and waited quite happily until dawn.

As the sun rose in the early winter sky, Johnny saw that the crumbs of the German biscuits were darkly coloured and wondered what kind of jam it might be. On picking up a few more crumbs and wetting them with spit, he realised, it wasn't jam, it was blood.

The following day, the German counterattack came upon their position and the artillery shells devastated their trench. Johnny and Benny were blown out of the trench fifty yards apart. They landed like a pair of rag dolls out of a pram, flattening the barbed wire and sinking into the mud. They were among another twenty Black Watch soldiers that would take no more part in the Battle of Loos. Johnny was presumed dead with a huge hole in his side. Benny was decapitated.

Three battalions of Dundee's own Black Watch took part in the battle including Johnny McKee's 2nd Battalion, at devastating cost: 19 of Dundee's 20 officers and 230 of the 423 Dundee men were killed. Over 700 more Dundee men were wounded during that battle.

CHAPTER 41

Adelaide

Garland Fraser disembarked in Melbourne on April 1st 1914. On arrival, all the Australian border guards wanted to know was when he was reporting to the military for service. "Three months' time," he said and, as Australia was a British colony, they checked his birth lines against his 'passport', medical papers and he cleared immigration easily. With that, he made for the nearest pub. There, he found like-minded punters who had left Britain to get away from "the shit in Europe" as they put it, and they welcomed him to Australia.

He was running out of money and wondered where he was going to live. Talking to a local at the bar he noticed the familiar scars of a fighter and the conversation got around to boxing. Bert Miller introduced himself and in reply Joe said, "Garland Fraser, just call me Gary, just off the boat from the UK, pleased to meet ye."

Miller, a Cornishman, explained that the "best money to be made is in the bare-knuckle set-up" and that he could help Garland with this and gave him an address in Adelaide where he could find him. "Anytime you're in Adelaide, Gary, look me up."

After too many beers to remember, Bert put him on the train from Port Melbourne Station to Flinders Street Station in downtown Melbourne. Gary felt drowsy on the train and put his head down on the knapsack that held all the important stuff – money, birth lines, passport and references from Tam Pepper that he might need. As the hot sun warmed the compartment, the humid air mixed with the beer and he drifted off to sleep. He awoke with a start at the termination of the line to find that his suitcases were missing from the overhead parcel rack above. Gary looked around in a haze at the empty carriage. The realisation that he had been robbed, made him laugh. *Christ*, he thought. *I've been shot in battle, fought hundreds of fighters in the ring, killed more men than I can say and the minute I get to Australia, I get frigging robbed when I'm sleeping.*

He left the train station and wandered around Flinders Street with the crowds milling all around, trying to figure out what to do next when he searched his pockets. To his great relief, he saw his purse was still intact in his vest pocket. In the 'Southern Cross' pub he had a beer and ate a steak then paid in Scottish notes which were accepted by the barman, another Scot. The barman listened to him and told him he'd heard his story a hundred times. "People just forget that this is not the UK," he said. "It is a country full of ex-cons and they still think like ex-cons fifty years after they get out." He advised Gary to forget it and move on. "The cops won't help a Jock here, mate, they'll bang you up as quick as look at you. And," he said, "even the cops will rob you blind here if you don't keep your eyes open."

Gary Fraser realised what the barman was saying and that was OK by him. He left the bar and put a new plan into action. As darkness fell, he picked his mark: Patrick Partridge, a middle-aged, suited, booted, collar-and-tie man who looked like a shopkeeper in a dark street on his way home. He ambushed the complete stranger with a thump on the nose that made the man give up completely. Garland Fraser took the silver watch and chain from the man's waistcoat pocket and relieved him of his wallet as well. It wasn't much, but the twenty-two Australian pounds made him feel better and he felt he had gotten his own back on this country that tried to rob and demoralise him before he even had time to unpack a case. Then, he remembered, he had no case to unpack. *God,* he thought. *Now I know how Mary-Anne felt when she was homeless back in Dundee.*

Gary slept that night in a downtown hotel and, the following morning purchased a new suit of clothes and accessories from Coles Store, on Smith Street in Collingwood. He packed them all into a small valise he picked up cheaply from a stall on the pavement and off he went quite happily. He returned to Flinders Street Station to make his way out of Melbourne. Keeping a low profile, he decided to take Bert Miller's advice and head for Adelaide. He boarded the train to Sandbridge Station then, after a wait of ten hours, boarded another one, the Adelaide Express sleeper, bound for the Middle Brighton Station in Adelaide. Fifteen hours later he arrived in Adelaide, ready for the day.

The Scottish barman's words were on his mind and that gave him an idea. It was in another pub in North Street he got information on where he could find bar work that included a place to stay. He pitched up at the Black Bull Hotel on Hindley Street at six o'clock, new suitcase in hand. The owner, Mary Kelly, a big Irish woman of about sixty, with wild dyed black hair and the reddest lips he had ever seen, opened up the bar and let him in.

"Whut the feck is a single Scotchman doing in a shithole like Adelaide anyway?" she asked. "Whut are ye running from?"

"Nothing," said Gary. "I just wanted a change. I've already been in a war and I don't want to get into another one," he said.

"Whut war?" she demanded.

"The Boer War," he answered.

"Whut regiment?"

"The Black Watch," he lied.

"By the fecking looks of ye, ye have been in a few fecking wars. Whut's yer name?" she asked.

"Garland Fraser, but you can call me Gary," he said.

"I'm Mary Kelly, they call me Hairy Mary but you can call me Mrs. Kelly. Ye'll maybe do for me, Garland Fraser," she laughed, "if that's yer real name. Tehehehe. Four pound ten a week, cash in hand and yer keep, but you leave the girls alone and keep yer nose clean," she said. "Also, never, ever rob the punters that come in here, understand?"

"I do, but why did you say that?" said Gary.

"Because half of the cops in Adelaide ARE the punters," she said flatly.

"Got ye," said Gary. "What's the job by the way?" he asked.

"Well, this is a working hotel," she said with a glint of mischief in her eyes, "if ye follow me?" She flicked her eyes at the sign above the bar. His eyes followed hers, and he read it:

'The Bull is tame so fear him not,

So long as you can pay your shot,

When money's gone and credit's bad,

That's what makes the bull go mad!'

"We get all kinds in here, and by ten o'clock every night it's usually full of Ahem… hoors and comic singers, if ye follow me."

She went on, "That's what brings in the punters, Gary. Sometimes, nah, most times after the punters have had their err, straw hats and trumpets, if ye follow me, they try to forget they have to pay for the... err, services, if ye follow me. And when they do, I want someone to persuade them to pay up... if ye follow me," she said. "That's the job, Gary, do ye follow me?" she asked him.

"Oh yes, Missus Kelly, I do and I'll have it!" Gary said. "With pleasure," he smiled and said. "That's the job for me, Missus Kelly," he said.

"Mary, please, oh, and Gary, grow a beard," she said.

"Why grow a beard?" he asked her.

"Because no one in Adelaide goes around looking like a big bare-faced Jessie, that's why!"

"Right." And with that he thought of Jessie, Mary-Anne's oldest girl in Dundee, then he thought of Mary-Anne, and he said to himself, "She would like it here right enough."

Gary Fraser settled into a small room in the Black Bull Hotel. Mary Kelly gave him a tour of the place and showed him which rooms were 'respectable' and which were used by the 'working girls'. The stables at the back were a special area he had to keep an eye out for customers running out of, as were the balconies of the rooms all around the building.

Taking it all in, he asked, "How many girls work here?"

"It depends on the success in the gold mines on the day, it could be ten a night or it could be twenty," said Mary.

"How many bouncers have you got working here?" Gary asked.

"Just one, you," she said.

"What happened to the last one?"

"He got hung," she said.

"When do I start?"

Mary said, "Tonight."

The place was buzzing every night in the first week and the need for a bouncer was very real. Hairy Mary watched Gary as he extracted cash from drunken men who thought he was an easy mark. Gary had free reign to bash, clobber and belt defaulting punters at will, as the Australians put it. He had little or no interest in the working girls and seemed to get his satisfaction out of sorting out the punters. At the beginning, he couldn't tell which punters were cops so he just bashed anyone who crossed the line. No one objected. Hairy Mary was happy with all of that, but there was something troubling her: Gary never made friends; he was a loner and he appeared to like it that way. She liked him but she just wondered if she could really ever trust him. She was gossiping with the girls for their take on him and they unanimously agreed, he was a strange one. "Gary never relaxes or mixes with the others," said Mary. "I've got to say, what has he got to hide, if ye follow me?" she said.

Bert Miller walked into the Black Bull one Saturday night in August of 1914 and made enquiries at the bar. Mary Kelly recognised him as trouble from long ago, but was wary of giving anyone that impression. Bert cordially greeted her and said he was looking for Gary Fraser, an old friend, he said. She told him that she would make it known that Gary Fraser was a wanted man. She laughed with Bert. Mary passed on the message that Bert was looking for him and asked, "Is everything all right? This guy is trouble, I know it, if ye know what I mean."

"Yes, Mrs. Kelly, he is an old friend," Gary said. "I wrote to him to say I was working here." Relieved, she gave Gary the night off to relax with 'his buddy'.

Gary and Bert went off in a cab to the 'Edinburgh Castle' pub in Currie Street. There, they met up with Jimmy Sharman who ran a boxing tent in and around South Australia. Bert explained that Jimmy was a bit of a legend in Adelaide who had a 'troop of young, mostly aboriginal fighters in his stable'. "All pretty handy in the bare-knuckle rings." Jimmy went on to tell him that he was interested in finding a *'Whitefella'* to take on the *'Blackfellas'*. "That's what'll bring in the punters," he said, "and listen to this," said Jimmy. "A round or two for a pound or two," Jimmy said proudly, with a grin. "That's my slogan. Have you ever heard anything like it?"

Gary smiled for the first time since the meeting started. "As a matter of fact I have," said Gary. "Tam Pepper has a slogan very close to it," he said. "A pound around," said Gary and showed him the reference from Tam Pepper with these very words in the letterhead.

Gary watched Jimmy and started to laugh, under his breath at first and then out loud and uncontrollably. "What's so funny, Gary, have I said something?" asked Jimmy.

"It's you and Tam Pepper, ye're at opposite ends of the world and yet ye're like twa cheeks o' the same erse," he said aloud in his Dundee accent. They all burst out laughing and went on to close the deal.

"I've heard of Tam," he said, "and he is well respected in the business." He went on, "If you want to come and try to win good money, Gary, I'll be happy to have you in my tent," Jimmy told him. They drank like old friends and they laughed like old friends and clearly they were three of a kind. "So I can expect you at the tent next Saturday night then?" asked Jimmy.

"I'll try, Jimmy, I need to get Hairy Mary to let me off again, but I'll try."

The following Saturday, Hairy Mary refused to let him off for the night. "It's our busiest night, Gary, I need you here."

The lure was too much. "I'm jacking it then, Mary, I've found another job," he told her that morning.

Hairy Mary was incensed. "If you go it'll be all the worse for you, if ye know what I mean," she said.

"No, I don't know what you mean." And he gave her a look to scare her out of her wits. Gary picked up his wages, packed his grip and left the Black Bull for the last time.

He made his way to the boxing tent in North Adelaide and checked in with Jimmy and Bert. "Good to see ya, Gary boy," said Jimmy. "Mary let ya off all right then?" Jimmy asked.

"No, she wouldn't let me go so I jacked it in," said Gary.

"Holy shit, that's not a good idea in this town, mate," he said.

Gary shrugged his shoulders. "I was getting twitchy in that place anyway, this is more my line of work," Gary told him.

"No worries, mate, get something to eat then I'll show you around."

Late in the afternoon Gary was sparring with one of the locals and warming up for his debut. A face he recognised appeared at the tent. "Hey, you," said the face. "Are you Gary Fraser?"

"Who wants to know?" said Gary.

"I'm the cutman," he said.

"Yes, OK, that's me," said Gary.

The cutman left the tent as quickly as he had come in. Gary shrugged again.

The crowd gathered around just as it used to, in the Dudhope fairground in Dundee. Jimmy was adorned in similar attire to that of

Tam Pepper in the old days. "A pound or two for a round or two," Jimmy roared into his megaphone, over, and over.

"And introducing, at middleweight, Garland 'the gnasher' Fraser," he added. "All the way from Scotland," he shouted at the crowd. "Against our own Abbo Champ, Tommy Rose," he said, extending a hand in both directions of the ring. The crowd applauded in anticipation and paid their money to see the new white man take on South Australia's best. They started eyeing up the newcomer and the betting started. The crowd began to drink more and more beer, and the bets got bigger. "Love it, Gary, I just love it," Jimmy said, watching the betting cash bucket fill up. "This could be a nice little earner for us, my boy, just try to last the pace with the abbo," said Jimmy. "A new whitefella against the blackfella, come and see how good he is."

The rules were exactly the same as Tam Pepper's, and the money was just as good. Gary checked out his opponent and thought very little of him. Strong upper half, weak back and skinny legs. He was bigger than Gary, at least a light-heavyweight and over twelve and a half stones. Gary being a middleweight at eleven stone six, would be faster and harder. "Let's get on with it," he said to Jimmy. "By the way where is my cutman?"

"Cutman?" said Jimmy. "Bert is your cutman," he said.

"What about the other cutman? The guy who was in here an hour ago."

"No idea what you're frigging talking about, Gary, we don't use two cutmen at this weight this early in the proceedings."

The bell went for the first round and Tommy Rose ran out of his corner and started windmilling his arms and fists at Gary's head. Gary caught him with two killer blows to the ribs and Tommy stopped, stood back and caught his breath. They met in the centre of the ring and Gary threw a jab to the head and a right cross to the jaw, and Tommy dropped to his knees. The crowd started to get into Gary's style and the betting increased. "He's never been down in the first before!" someone shouted from the ringside.

The second round was much the same with Gary winning well on points. "Take it easy, Gary," said Bert. "They've just started to get the big bets in the bucket."

"You've got all night, ya know," said Jimmy.

Gary never listened; he was enjoying himself too much. In the third round, Tommy Rose started to fight like a girl to Gary's mind and that was enough. Gary brought a thunderous right up from the floor to Rose's solar plexus followed by another thunderous left hook, knocking Tommy Rose out cold. The crowd went mad, and so did Jimmy. "That's no good, you Scotch idiot!" he shouted in the heat of the moment. "You've lost us a fortune," he said, clamping a hand on his forehead and turning away.

The mysterious 'Cutman' appeared at Jimmy's back. "Garland Fraser, I'm arresting you for running an illegal gambling racket, you're nicked," said Detective Inspector Jake Brown, Adelaide Fraud Squad. No one else was lifted in the melee, just Gary, as he was being huckled out of the tent.

He realised who the 'cutman' was; he was the first punter he had beaten up on the first night working for Hairy Mary in the Black Bull. *That bitch has grassed me up,* he thought. He figured she must have told the cops he was going to fight in the boxing tent and there would be gambling there. Bare-knuckle boxing was not against the law, Gary knew that, but he never knew that gambling would be taking place, or that it was illegal. It made no difference whether he knew the law in South Australia or not, he was getting banged up. That was something Gary never wanted; he had to stay clear of the cops for the rest of his life or they could find out who he really was.

Gary was detained for the night in Angas Street Police Station while their investigations were ongoing. He was strip-searched and his clothes were taken away. All his clothing was from Coles and that seemed to be suspicious to the cops. Everything else they had searched in his possessions led to nothing, then they looked at his silver watch in the interview room. To Gary's surprise, Brown pushed a secret button and the back flipped open. He pushed it again and another silver casing sprung open revealing the workings of the Half Hunter. Gary couldn't see what the cops were looking at, but he asked Gary how he had come by the watch. Gary told him he bought it in Coles. "Really?" said Brown. Inside the silver inner casing were the initials P. P. "Coles don't sell silver watches." Then, "Who is P. P?" asked Jake Brown.

Gary looked confused. "I don't know," he said. "Why?"

"Garland Fraser, you are charged with unlawful possession of a silver Half Hunter watch and chain."

Gary was questioned but could tell them nothing more other than his story as he 'saw it'. He realised the game was up and he said nothing more to the cops. Before he appeared before the magistrate in Port Augusta, near Adelaide, the police had his immigration details on file and interrogated him about his intentions in Australia. "You told us when you entered Australia, that you were going to join the army, Mr. Fraser, why haven't you?" said Brown.

"I have been looking for the army base," he said sheepishly.

"Well, it's not hiding from you," Brown replied. "When you get out, we are going to take you to the Australian army base in Adelaide and make sure you find it. Then you can join up like all the other eligible men in Australia," said the inspector.

"OK," said Gary.

He appeared in court the next day and was given a two-month sentence. It was recorded in the Australian Police Gazette:

Garland Fraser, labourer, native of Scotland, 38 years of age, 5ft. 7 1/2in. high, dark-brown hair, grey eyes, fair complexion, large nose, mark near adornment representation of tomb-stone tattooed on right forearm. Tried at Port Augusta on August 24th *1914, unlawful possession; two months.*

Gary served his time in Adelaide Prison on top of the three months he got for illegal gambling and on release he was escorted to Hampstead Barracks, the Australian army base in the Adelaide suburb of Greenacres just north of Adelaide central. He was able to stay out of the army for another six months on account of his criminal record and carried on boxing at Jimmy's for his living. On the 9th September 1915, he was called up and enlisted as a rifleman in 'B' company, 2nd Depot Battalion as a new recruit. On enlisting, his next of kin was detailed as Mary-Anne Garland, Sister, John Street Dundee, Scotland.

Nobody knew that he had already been in the British army and acquitted himself well in battle many times in the Boer War. He served as a soldier in the base as a permanent staff instructor specialising in weapons training. Gary never had to go back to war because he was seen as too valuable an instructor at the army base in Adelaide. He became unwell and ironically, Private Garland Fraser, 39 years old, died on 15th May 1916 of tuberculosis of lungs, at Micham Camp, Adelaide.

CHAPTER 42

The Royal Victoria Hospital, Belfast

Johnny McKee woke up after surgery in the recovery ward of the Royal Victoria Hospital in Belfast. Stretcher-bearers had recovered the wounded soldiers 24 hours after being blown out of the German trench. He had lost so much blood that the field first aider left him for dead initially but because of the amount of blood he lay in, they knew he was still alive. He was given a debridement and a blood transfusion in the dressing station and his heart and blood pressure stabilised. He received emergency treatment on the Lens-Basse road in an ambulance and slipped into a coma. That state persisted until he regained consciousness in the troop carrier and then set sail from Le Havre, on the 6th October 1915, for Belfast.

In the Royal Victoria Hospital, doctors cleaned the wound of all dirt and foreign matter that was too damaged to heal. That included the removal of three ribs and a piece of lung and kidney tissue. The surgeons performed antiseptic surgery using only phenol, iodine and alcohol and ironically chlorine, the stuff that nearly killed him at the start of the Battle of Loos. It took two weeks in intensive care to close the battlefield wounds and another three weeks to heal sufficiently to release Johnny.

His brother George received a telegram informing him of the wounds Johnny McKee received in action. George, in turn, passed the news on to Grace Murphy in number 6 Littlejohn Street. George and his wife Catherine discussed her options with Grace. She could go to see him in hospital or she could stay where she was and wait to see what developed. If she went to Belfast she would need a loan for the train fare and boat fare, plus she would need to stay in accommodation that was available at a reduced cost for relatives of the wounded. She was not a relative, she reminded George. "But I could be," she said, "and I will be." She wrote to the hospital and with the help of George and Catherine, she explained that Johnny and Grace were to be married.

Five days later, a letter arrived at her door carefully advising that Johnny was recovering slowly, but well from wounds, however, his memory appeared to be affected. "He does recall you very well but has no recollection of proposing marriage. That," the letter said, "is something that you and Private McKee will perhaps need to work on when he is released from hospital next week."

Grace was ecstatic and at the same time nervous. She knew she did not have to spend money she didn't have on a trip to Belfast and, he knew what was on her mind by all accounts. She went to see his father in the poorhouse but his illness had taken a grip and Mr. McKee had no recollection of her, or Johnny. Instead, she made a pact with George and Catherine; if Johnny agreed to marry her, she would look after him on his return to the Crescent and take care of his wounds like his nurse.

Oh dear, thought George. *That's what I was afraid of. She'll kill him with kindness.* Then he said, "Yes, of course I agree, but you need to be sure he wants to marry you first!"

"Of course he does," said Grace. "You'll see!"

Johnny was released from hospital on the 5th of November and escorted by a nurse to the ship at Belfast Royal Naval Docks. On the transport vessel, the ship's medics tended to him. He took a walk on the deck to get the night air. The Belfast skyline sparkled with firecrackers and playful explosives to commemorate Guy Fawkes' Night in the distance. It took him back, reluctantly, to the horrors of the battlefield. The medic with him offered a sedative but Johnny refused it. The explosions and destructions he saw for real in France came back to terrify him once more. "I've got to keep my strength up for tomorrow when I meet my lass, Grace," Johnny said.

"Why, what's she going to do?" asked the medic. "She's going to marry me. I just hope I'm strong enough for her, but don't tell Grace Murphy I said that."

They docked at Greenock and the medic guided him onto the train bound for Dundee.

Two days and nights after leaving Belfast, he eventually arrived at Dundee East train station. As the train pulled to a stop at the platform, the steam swirled all around the slam door of the carriage. He opened it and stepped gingerly down, onto the concrete platform. The steam cleared like a cloud blown away, and there, in the front of a small crowd of familiar faces was Grace with a huge smile on her face and bottle of Johnny Walker red label in her hand. "Well, if it's good enough for Churchill, it's good enough for you," she said.

Johnny thought first then said, "They say perfection doesn't exist, but that's not quite true, it's right here in front of me." Grace was unsure if he was talking about her or the whisky; she thought it best not to ask.

Johnny was so happy to see her that he nearly proposed to her there and then. They embraced, kissed and he opened the whisky. "Gie's that," he said. "I've no' had a drink in three months."

"You'll need it," she said.

"Why?" he said, knowing what was coming.

"I've got something to ask you," said Grace. "Will you marry me, Johnny McKee?"

He thought about it for a minute. "Only if I can move in with you tonight," he replied.

"OK. But it's the spare room for you until the weekend," she said.

"Why the weekend?" said Johnny.

"Because I've booked the cathedral for ten o'clock on Saturday morning and Father O'Farrell is expecting us."

They were married on the 15th November 1915 in St. Andrew's Cathedral as planned. No time or effort was spent on a honeymoon; it was more important to them to get Johnny better. Jessie moved out of the flat and into Catherine and George's place to give them the privacy that a newly wedded couple needed. In the honeymoon period, they spent no time talking about the future. They knew there would be a time when he had to go back to his unit as the war in Europe was growing into a world conflict. That told them there was no end to war in sight. They just needed the time together, loving each other, and they were happy just to do that. Grace and Johnny spent the next two weeks in the flat in the Crescent together and at the end of it, Johnny felt a lot better, but Grace felt very, very tired and literally worn out getting him "better".

The first two weeks in December were spent rehabilitating Johnny. The army made it his duty to keep them informed on his progress. Grace knew Johnny had to go back when he was fit enough and, as it happened, he was a quick healer. Likewise, he knew she had to go back to work soon as with the jute mills, 'no work, no pay' was the rule.

CHAPTER 43

Mesopotamia

In late December 1915, Johnny said goodbye to Grace and rejoined his Battalion in Le Havre. The 2nd Battalion Black Watch, was on the move to Mesopotamia (Iraq), landing at Basra on 31st of December 1915. The battalion resumed warring activities against the forces of the Ottoman Empire immediately. The British forces at Kut, where the Battalion was headed, were under siege by the Turks. The 7th Division, of which the Black Watch was part, in its efforts to relieve Kut subsequently suffered more losses at the battle of Shaik Sa'ad on 7th January, and again at the battle of Wadi on 13th January. Johnny was again in the thick of it and, despite overwhelming odds, the battalion attacked the Turks again and again in the knowledge that their fellow comrades were enduring hell inside the town of Kut.

The battalion continued to suffer further losses to warfare and sickness and began to resemble a shadow of itself by 20th January. Johnny found himself back fighting for enemy frontline trenches again, and this time, only a mere 200 yards separated the opposing forces.

After an effective artillery barrage by the British guns, the much-reduced battalion of Black Watch surged forward and took the Turks' front trenches in hand-to-hand combat. Then, they found themselves let down on each flank to the left and right, by the Buffs and the Dogas, as their regiments failed in their attempts to equal the Black

Watch success.

Johnny's battalion was surrounded in the captured enemy trenches by the sheer weight of Turkish numbers all around them. They held out against overwhelming odds but at a great cost of killed and wounded Dundonians in battle. After some desperate hours of trench warfare including more hand-to-hand fighting, the British 9th Brigade finally relieved the Black Watch. The following day, the battalion reported strength was 5 officers and 164 other ranks. This was all that was left out of the original strength of 29 officers and 900 men who had arrived in Basra just three weeks before. Johnny McKee did not expect to be granted leave anytime in 1916 and the 2nd Black Watch joined with the 1st Seaforths, strengthening their position in Mesopotamia permanently.

His days there were spent on rotation in and out of the front line in a circular fashion. This consisted of a spell of 70 days in the front line, 30 days in the support lines, then time in reserve at rest as and when conditions allowed.

Grace carried on in Dundee oblivious to Johnny's day-to-day danger and continued to keep him informed every week by letter. Her letters arrived telling him what the latest talk was in the Crescent. She told him she had visited his father and that they all understood why his leave was cancelled. She mentioned that the murder of her brother-in-law up the Hilltown, had never been solved, and that her sister Mary-Anne had moved back into the Crescent. Then she let him know by writing simply, "Oh, and by the way, I'm having a baby."

Johnny was thrilled by that news. Regardless of his own situation, he went about his days in the hope that for THIS reason, at least, he would get some home leave at some stage. Grace was due to have the baby by the end of September 1916, and that, was something Johnny looked forward to.

September came along and, owing to heavy losses, the battalion could not afford to grant him home leave. His son, John, was born on time at home in Littlejohn Street with no complications. Catherine and Jessie were in attendance, but Johnny was not there for the birth.

All was well with Grace and she and Jessie looked after the baby alternately, allowing them both to work full-time in the Jute mills. Grace and John had to live with the fact that he missed baby John's birth but they looked forward to a grand family reunion when Johnny came back from the war.

One day in April of 1917, the baby was sitting up on the rug with his mum playing with his toys. At nine months, he was on to solid food and making good progress. Grace let him have a bit of chocolate with nuts in, and then, another piece.

He was fine and then suddenly he started coughing and spluttering trying to swallow the sweet. She picked him up and turned him upside down and patted him on the back to clear his throat. It wouldn't clear, and she tried reaching with her fingers into his mouth to clear any solids that way.

That didn't work. She could see the baby was not getting in enough breath. After five more minutes, he still couldn't breathe and she was panicking. "Get a cab, Jessie, be quick, please, we need to get him to the DRI."

The cab stopped at the corner of Littlejohn Street and they all got in. "Go, DRI, quick," said Jessie. Still baby John couldn't breathe. They arrived at the Accident and Emergency door and rushed him in, Grace still blowing air into his mouth as the baby turned blue.

"He's choking!" Grace screamed. "He's choking."

The hospital staff took over and although there was huge concern for John, they managed to get some air into his lungs and he breathed somewhat. There were signs of serious trauma to the windpipe, however, and he was put into an intensive care ward and kept in hospital.

Grace told the doctors through her tears that she had been feeding him chocolate that may have had a nut in it, but she wasn't sure if he swallowed it. As if her grief were not enough, they told her, "A nine-month-old baby is too young to feed nuts to." She felt completely scolded and responsible for something she had caused.

The following day, he was showing increasingly worrying signs of infection in the trauma area and they continued to treat him, assuming lung complications. The surgeons performed a tracheotomy on baby John but no foreign body was found. Much pus came out of the throat, however, indicating an infection.

That night she wrote to Johnny with a full explanation of what had happened. Sadly, she had to tell him in detail what she had done and how it happened that he was in intensive care in the DRI. Johnny, in turn, felt her pain and thought about it all night when he got her letter. He wrote back to tell her that it wasn't her fault and that any loving mother would do the same. He reassured her that the baby would be all right and she should have faith in the doctors at the hospital. It was important to him that she never blamed herself for this but he assured her they would soon be together and all would be well. Johnny didn't even bother to ask for leave this time as he knew full well that it would be denied – again.

After four weeks in the DRI, Baby John seemed to be doing OK but then things changed for the worse. He died unexpectedly on the 1st June. Grace had just walked in to the ward on her daily visit to see him and was shocked to be asked to "come into the ward anteroom" by the nurses.

"What's wrong, where's my baby?" she asked.

The doctor and nurse told her that he "had just passed away".

Everyone in the ward was in shock. "How could he die? Had something stuck in his throat?" she said weakly, stunned by the doctor's words.

"We don't really know why, Grace, but we will try to find out."

After a few days they did an autopsy but it was inconclusive. The report detailed that the wee boy had pneumonia; possibly as a result of the tracheotomy they performed when he was admitted. It was also possible, they said, that he inhaled a piece of shell from the nut or a piece of paper from the bag the nuts were in. This could have lodged in his lungs and caused the infection. It was also possible that he could have had pneumonia that caused his lungs to fill with pus and that may have caused him to gasp for breath, looking like he was choking. In any case, Baby John was dead. He died in the care of the health system but in her eyes, a care system wasn't exactly accurate. She tried to say it in her own words in a letter to Johnny but they never came. Grace was grieving deeply when she wrote to her husband and, in the end, "He died, Johnny," she simply wrote, "and it was all my fault."

Johnny McKee saw the words and listened to the regimental padre's words of consolation. It was quite surreal to have lost a son he never knew and still feel the pain. For the remainder of the Great War, owing to heavy casualties of his battalion again, Johnny never did get back to see his wife.

In May 1917, his father Jim McKee died in the Dundee Eastern Poorhouse, of complications due to dementia. Johnny missed that funeral too. In January 1918, the 2nd Battalion, the Black Watch, moved to Palestine, arriving at Suez on 13th January 1918. By the end of that year, Johnny, like Grace, understood very well, that the pain doesn't fade away with time. The only difference is the ability to bear the pain. Johnny McKee had served his ten years and was released from the army at the end of the war. He returned home to his wife Grace for the first time since they married in 1915, three years before.

CHAPTER 44

The Crescent

Johnny and Grace McKee walked to the grave at the Eastern Cemetery and said a prayer. "This is all we can do, Johnny," she wept at baby John's graveside. "I'm sorry," she said, "but I can't show you a photograph because we never had one taken. I can tell you though, how much you would have loved his wee face and his wee mannerisms but that's all, because he's gone now and it's too hard to say these things."

They were both deeply saddened by the death of their young son but life went on, at least that's what they told each other. Both of them, however, felt the loss was not the end of the world and that, in the fullness of time, their family life together could start again. In June 1919, Grace walked into the living room and told Johnny she was pregnant. Their daughter, Annie Divine McKee, was born on the 9th of February 1920.

After the war, there was an economic slump in Scotland and Dundee was hardest hit again. Sadly, over four thousand two hundred men never returned to Dundee from the war and that left those who did come back, competing for their old jobs. Jute was no longer in such demand, though, and those men who could get a job in the mills had to settle for less money than they earned before the war. The jute industry collapsed and thousands of people lost their jobs. Dundee was again full of 'kettle bilers' as more soldiers returned from the 'Great War'.

Ireland was a growing trouble spot to the British government who promised the Irish favourable terms of independence in exchange for Irish combatants in the war. When it was denied, the IRA began to harass the politicians and the people who supported the union. Churchill recognised a need to bring the Irish back into line with the rest of the UK and saw how to do it with a military might that was looking for a fight. Churchill set up the Royal Irish Constabulary (RIC), better known as the Black and Tans and recruited solely from ex-war veterans, in particular, Scottish veterans were his choice. Dundee, however, being strongly populated by the Irish since the famine some sixty years earlier and sympathetic to the Irish cause was a melting pot of tension between loyal soldiers of the king and the Irish cause.

Mary-Anne seldom received letters and never before, a parcel. One day in 1920, however, she received both. Both were postmarked Australia and both were from the Australian Imperial Force. She was bewildered to see her name on the items and dream-like, she opened the large envelope first. She took out the scroll and stared at the ornate Royal Coat of Arms and elaborate copperplate writing below it:

He whom this scroll commemorates was numbered among those who, at the call of King and Country, left all that was dear to them, endured hardness, faced danger and finally passed out of sight of men by the path of duty and self-sacrifice, giving up their own lives that others might live in freedom. Let those who come after see to it that his name not be forgotten.

And below it the name, in red, **Garland Fraser.**

*

She was beginning to feel the effects of shock; her dry mouth tried to utter the name, but nothing came out as she mouthed her brother's name. She opened the parcel to find a round, solid bronze memorial plaque, four and a half inches in diameter, showing Britannia and a lion on the front. It bore the inscription, *"He died for freedom and honour"*, and on the right-hand side of the plaque, the name 'Garland Fraser, 1462' was engraved. No information regarding rank, unit or decoration did all Australian casualties make shown, befitting the equality of the sacrifice. (Source – *Dead Man's Penny: a biography of the First World War bronze memorial plaque*.)

Mary-Anne put the plaque and the scroll back in their respective packages and placed them neatly in the shelf in the press, beside the blue scrapbook.

Johnny, unemployed since returning from the war, was tempted to join the Black and Tans for money. Sitting in Thompson's bar in Bell Street with his ex-Black Watch comrades one night, Two RIC recruiting sergeants came into the pub. They recognised the ex-soldiers easily by their demeanours and approached the men. "Good money in Dublin and Cork if ye want it," the sergeants said and impressed on them the riches to be made just to keep 'the paddys' in line.

Johnny thought about it for about a minute then said, "No, not me."

"Why the hell not? Don't you want to feed your family?" a sergeant said, holding a hand full of cash up for them all to see.

Johnny took a swipe at the hand and scattered the cash all over the pub. "Keep yer blood money, ye shower of stupid buggers, get out of here," and with that the fist fight started and ended with the recruiting sergeants limping out of the pub never to return.

Johnny McKee settled down again at his home in the Crescent with his wife Grace and their new family. He started work as a navvie, digging and laying some of the many new roads in Dundee since the Great War. One of the biggest projects he was involved in was the construction of the road from the bottom to the war memorial at the top of the Law Hill. He was in the crowd on 16th May 1925 when the new 520-foot memorial was unveiled, to those Dundee men who died in the Great War. Inscription reads: "In memory of the Battle of Loos, in which many members of the local Black Watch regiment lost their lives."

Johnny was not congratulated or mentioned for his part in the war effort but at least he had a job.

EPILOGUE

Winston Churchill had taken his seat in Dundee in 1908 as the Member of Parliament after he crossed the floor from Conservative to Liberal in Westminster. He represented the poor in Dundee under false pretensions and was voted in by the legions of Irish jute workers living on the breadline. What they never knew initially, was that he lived the lavish life of an extravagant ruling-class elite in London.

Dundee was in fact a 'seat of convenience' to him and the only place that he could successfully win a by-election because of his previous involvement with the cotton weavers in Oldham, the seat he held and he lost.

Churchill, however, turned his back on the plight of the mill workers and the poverty in Dundee in general, in favour of national and international affairs. He was appointed Home Secretary in 1910 and as a cabinet minister, he made Dundee wait for every issue that demanded his attention in favour of the bigger stage of Government control.

During his tenure as MP for Dundee, he became the Government protagonist for the coal pit owners, which was the cause of the Tonypandy riots in 1910 and 1911. Striking miners from the valuable coal mines in the Rhonda Valley, were starving and asking for more wages than the pittance they earned. The strikers were actually attacked by police and troops because Churchill ordered it. He decided that troops be deployed wearing policemen's helmets, clearly to fool the protestors into thinking the army was not used.

Churchill's wish to send in the British army against its own people in Wales to reinforce the police, led to several violent confrontations. He later took the decision to send in a company of Lancashire Fusiliers and a squadron of the 18th Hussars to physically engage with the rioters. In the event, sixty policemen and five hundred rioters were injured, and one fatality, caused by 'blunt instruments'.

The voters of his constituency in Dundee read the news as the Tonypandy riots played out and again, watched Churchill's actions nearer to home in Glasgow's 'Battle of George Square'. In January 1919, the Liberal government of which Churchill was part was under pressure from trade unions to change working conditions in the heavy engineering industry. Engineering workers in Glasgow were legally striking to reduce the working hours from fifty-seven to forty per week. By this time Churchill was Secretary of State for War.

He recommended arresting the strike leaders under the 1914 'Defence of the Realm Act', contributing at cabinet level for the mobilisation of ten thousand British troops of Scottish and English regiments to Glasgow on standby to "assist" police in the enforcement of their duty in the face of the strikers. Six tanks and one hundred trucks backed up the army regiments, presumably for the transporting of strikers.

The voters of Dundee saw all of these "nationalistic" actions as a betrayal of the working class. The Dundee Catholic Herald touted him a 'dangerous, double-dealing, oily-tongued adventurer' in 1921. The final confirmation that Churchill was an impostor in the city came when voters realised that his ill-conceived brainchild of recruiting ex-British forces into the Black and Tans (Royal Irish

Constabulary) were sent into Ireland in March 1920. The IRA was actively seeking Ireland's independence as promised by the British government after the First World War.

In reprisal to numerous home-rule guerrilla tactics, the Black and Tans carried out several extrajudicial killings, savage brutal beatings and the destruction of property by burning, started by incendiary bombs. These properties included public buildings and residential homes in Cork. The fire brigades began to fight the fires in view of the British forces but were prevented from saving the properties because the Black and Tans would cut the fire hoses and even pour petrol on the fires to ensure the spread of damage.

All of this was Churchill's fault in the eyes of the Irish Dundonian jute mill workers who used the only power they had to remove him in the General Election of 1922. He had rarely visited the city in the 14 years he represented it and when he did, he was never hesitant to criticise and even condemn it. Churchill did say to the press, however: 'The trouble with the Irish is they don't want to be English.' On the wall of his office in Westminster, he had a plaque saying proudly:

"Success is the ability to go from one failure to another with no loss of enthusiasm."

– Winston Churchill

THE END

ABOUT THE AUTHOR

Ian Campbell was born in Dundee in the twilight Churchilian years and, like many of his generation, served his apprenticeship in the boom of post-war Britain. In his case it was the shipyards like his father and grandfather before him. Old Dundee as described herein was part of his youth and was the backdrop to his life before they tore old Dundee down. His familiarity and local knowledge is therefore first hand or has been passed down from his family before him and is reflected in the book.

He has travelled extensively throughout the world for work commitments and lived in a variety of far lands. Ultimately, he returned to Dundee and by coincidence, attended Dudhope Castle when it was Dundee Business School to complete a master's degree in Business Administration. Dudhope Castle is central to the book and rightly so, as it stood proudly overlooking the population of 'The Crescent' for decades. This is the author's first book.